That beautiful, desirable woman wanted him.

But she was inside, and Cash was sitting out here in his car. And why? Because he was afraid that he'd finally met the one woman he couldn't walk away from. And he'd already had a taste of what passed for love in a woman's mind. It had destroyed his life.

But Tippy wasn't just any woman. She had a past of her own to live with. She understood him. She aroused a rage of passion in his body, in his mind...in his heart.

He tried to convince himself that he should drive away, but he got out of the car and rang the doorbell. There was an answering buzz as the door unlocked. He went up the stairs, his heart pounding madly. He wouldn't think about tomorrow.

She was waiting for him upstairs. As she slowly moved towards the bedroom, he followed. "We're both insane," he choked.

She nodded slowly, her lips parted. "Turn out the light. Please."

It was the last thing she said.

DIANA PALMER

One Night in New York

First published in Great Britain 2006
by Harlequin Mills & Boon Limited, Eton House,
18-24 Paradise Road,
Richmond, Surrey TW9 1SR

© Diana Palmer 2004
(Orginal titled *Renegade*)

ISBN 0 263 85035 8

135-0406

Printed and bound in Spain
by Litografia Rosés S.A., Barcelona

International bestselling author **Diana Palmer** got her start in writing as a newspaper reporter and columnist, where she acquired many of her writing skills during her 16-year tenure. Once she wrote her first novel for Silhouette Books in 1982, however, she never looked back. Diana has a gift for telling the most sensual tales with charm and humour. With over 40 million copies of her books in print, she is one of the world's most beloved authors and considered one of the top ten romance writers in America. Diana's hobbies include gardening, archaeology, anthropology, iguanas, astronomy and music. She has been married to James Kyle since 1972, and they have one son, Blayne Edward.

One Night in New York

CHAPTER ONE

CHAPTER ONE

IT WAS A LAZY MONDAY MORNING. Not much was going on at the Jacobsville, Texas, Police Department. Three patrol officers were fixing coffee at the small refreshment table in the main lobby. A sheriff's deputy had stopped by to drop off a warrant. A local citizen was writing out a statement against a perpetrator who'd just been brought in by one of the patrol officers. The secretary who usually sat at reception was missing.

"That's it. That is it! I don't have to work here. There are jobs going right now at the Save-A-Lot grocery store, and I am going right over to put in my application!"

Heads turned at the unfamiliar sound of the police chief's secretary yelling at the top of her lungs. There was a quick muffled reply, and then the sound of something metallic hitting the floor. Hard.

A furious, spiky-haired teenaged girl in a short skirt and deep-cut blouse sprinkled with glitter came stalking down the hall, eyes flashing fire, long earrings jangling like alarms. Men in uniforms moved quickly aside. She went to her desk, picked up her overstuffed purse, and started for the front door.

A tall, darkly handsome man in the chief's uniform came down the hall just as she reached the door. His hair and clothes were liberally covered with coffee grounds, pieces of discarded tape, and two sticky Post-it notes, while a tissue was stuck to the top of a big, highly polished black shoe. There was another Post-it clinging to the long black ponytail at his nape.

"Was it something I said?" Cash Grier wondered aloud.

The teenager, whose lipstick was black, like her fingernail polish, groaned under her breath and stalked out the glass door, shutting it furiously behind her.

The uniformed officers tried valiantly not to laugh. Many sounded as if they'd just developed bad coughs. The man filling out the statement almost choked with mirth.

Cash glared at them. "Go ahead. Laugh. I can get another secretary anytime I want one!"

Judd Dunn, his assistant chief, was lounging

against the counter, his black eyes twinkling. "That was the second one since you were appointed chief."

"She worked in a grocery store before she came here," Cash muttered, removing sticky things and coffee grounds from his immaculate uniform. "She only got this job because her uncle, Ben Brady, is the acting mayor and he said I'd never get funding for those new bulletproof vests I need if she didn't get hired." He sighed angrily. "He's shady, that man. He wouldn't be the acting mayor if Jack Herman hadn't had a heart attack and stepped down. I have to put up with Brady until next May when we get a special election to choose Herman's successor."

Judd listened without comment as a scowling Cash continued ranting. "The city election won't come too soon to suit me," Cash snapped. "Brady's giving me fits about making drug cases, and he won't listen to any ideas about improvements in our department. They say Eddie Cane's going to run for mayor against him."

"He was the best mayor we ever had and I think he'll win," Judd said.

"More's the pity we have to wait until May to vote Brady out." Cash winced as he pulled the sticky note from his ponytail. "If he suggests a new secretary to replace that last one, I'm resigning."

"You'll have to find somebody to replace her, and quick, before he finds you a new candidate,"

Judd ventured. "If you can get anybody sane to work for you."

"I'll put an ad in the paper, and women will trample us applying for the opportunity just to be in the same room with me!" Cash said.

"Maybe you should just take some time off and calm down," Judd recommended. "The Christmas holidays are coming up." He stared at Cash intently. "You could take a trip."

Cash lifted an eyebrow. "I took one last month, with you, to that premiere in New York."

"Tippy said you could come back whenever you liked," Judd pointed out with a wicked grin, referring to the model-turned-actress Tippy Moore, the "Georgia Firefly" of modeling fame. "Her young brother liked you. He'll probably be home from military school on holiday."

Cash was reluctant to take the trip. The model had really gotten to him once he realized that she wasn't the vain, vampy woman he'd first thought. Her vulnerabilities appealed to him in ways her blatant flirting hadn't.

"I guess I could phone and ask her if she meant the invitation," he said.

"Good man," Judd said, clapping him on the shoulder. "You can get on the next flight out, and I can sit at your desk and be acting chief!"

Cash was getting suspicious. "This wouldn't have

anything to do with that squad car that you keep trying to talk me into? There's a city council meeting
next week…"

"They'll postpone it for the holidays," Judd assured him. "I would never try to talk the city council into a squad car you don't really want. Honest."

Cash didn't trust that gleaming smile. Judd was
like him. He rarely smiled unless he was up to something or in a temper.

"Much less hire a secretary before you get back,"
Judd added, not meeting Cash's eyes.

"Oh, that's it," Cash said at once. "That's it.
You've got somebody in mind. You're going to
stick me with some retired woman colonel from the
army or another conspiracy theorist like the secretary we had when my cousin Chet Blake was
chief?"

"I don't know any out-of-work mercenaries," Judd
said innocently.

"Or any ex-colonels?"

He shrugged. "Maybe one or two. Eb Scott has a
cousin…"

"No!"

"You haven't met her…"

"I'm not going to meet her! I'm the chief. See
this?" He pointed at his badge. "I fight crime. I do
not fight old women!"

"She's not old. Exactly."

"If you hire anybody before I get back, I will fire her the minute the plane lands! In fact, I won't leave town!" Cash threatened.

Judd shrugged. "Suit yourself." He studied his clean fingernails. "I hear the sister of the planning commissioner wants a crack at you. She may ask the acting mayor for a recommendation."

Cash felt hunted. The planning commissioner, a delightful and gentle man, had a favorite sister who also had a crush on Cash. She was thirty-six, twice divorced, wore see-through blouses and was a hundred pounds overweight. The planning commissioner doted on her. He was also the best dentist anywhere around. Even an ex-black ops specialist like Cash couldn't handle this kind of heat in a small town.

"When would the colonel like to start?" Cash asked through tight lips.

Judd burst out laughing. "I don't know any colonels who want to work for you, but I'll keep my eyes open…!" He moved just in time to avoid a roundhouse kick. "Hey, I'm a police officer! If you hit me, it's a felony!"

"It is not," Cash muttered, turning back toward his office. "It's self-defense."

"My lawyers will be in touch with you," Judd called after him.

Cash threw him an insulting gesture over his head.

BUT ONCE HE WAS SAFELY back in his office, with the trash can refilled and repositioned, and the floor swept, he thought about what Judd had said. Maybe he was a little touchy lately. A few days off might make him less…irritable. Judd and Crissy's two babies reminded him painfully of the life he'd lost.

Besides, Tippy Moore had a nine-year-old brother named Rory who idolized Cash. It had been a long time since anyone had looked up to him. He was used to curiosity, awe, even fear. Especially fear. The boy didn't have a man in his life, except for his friends at military school. What would it hurt to spend a little time with him? After all, he didn't have to tell them the story of his life. He winced, thinking of the only time he'd ever come clean about his past.

He sat down behind his desk and pulled a small address book from his pocket. In it was a New York telephone number. He picked up his cell phone and dialed it.

It rang two times. Three times. Four times. He felt bitter disappointment. He started to put the receiver down. Suddenly, a sultry, soft voice came on the line. "This is the Moore residence," it purred. "Sorry I'm not here. Please leave a brief message and a number. I'll get back to you." There was a beep.

"It's Cash Grier," he said.

He started to give his number when a breathless voice came on the line. "Cash!"

He laughed softly to himself. It showed that she'd dived for the phone before he could hang up. He was flattered.

"Yes, it's me. Hello, Tippy."

"How are you?" she asked. "Are you still in Jacobsville?"

"Still here. Except I'm chief of police now. Judd left the Texas Rangers and he's working with me as assistant chief," he added reluctantly. Tippy had been smitten with Judd, just as he himself had once been smitten with Judd's wife, Christabel.

"So many changes." She sighed. "And how is Christabel?"

"Very happy," he replied. "She and Judd had twins."

"Yes, I heard from them at Thanksgiving," she confessed. "A girl and a boy, right?"

"Jared and Jessamina," he said, smiling. The twins had captured their godfather's heart the second he laid eyes on them in the hospital. Of course, Jessamina was Cash's favorite and he made no bones about it. "Jessamina's such a little doll. A head full of jet-black hair and her eyes are dark blue. They'll change, of course."

"How about Jared?" she probed, amused at his fascination with the little girl.

"Looks like his dad," he replied. "Jared belongs to them, but Jessamina is mine. I told them so. Repeatedly." He sighed. "It does no good, of course, they won't give her to me."

She laughed. It was like the sound of silver bells on a summer night. Her voice was one of her greatest assets.

"How are you?"

"Working on a new film," she told him. "We've just stopped shooting so that we can all have Christmas at home. I'm glad. It's got a lot of physical stuff in it, and I'm out of shape. I'll have to work out more if I'm going to have to be athletic."

"What sort of physical stuff?" he wanted to know.

"Tucks and rolls, bouncing off trampolines, falls from high places, martial arts, that sort of thing," she said, sounding tired. "I'm bruised all over. Rory's going to pass out when he sees me. He says I've got no business doing rough stuff like this at my age."

"At your age?" he asked, because he knew she was only twenty-six.

"I'm old," she said. "Didn't you know? From his perspective, I should be walking with a cane!"

"That puts me in my place," he chuckled, mentally noting that he was twelve years her senior. "Is he coming home for Christmas?"

"Sure. He comes home every holiday. I have a nice little place here, near Fifth Street in the lower East

Village, near a bookstore and a coffee shop. It's very pleasant, for a big city."

"I like a little more room."

"You would." She hesitated. "Are you in trouble or anything?"

He felt odd. "What do you mean?"

"Do you need me to do something for you?" she persisted.

He'd never had anyone offer. He didn't know how to handle such a statement.

"I'm fine," he bit off.

"Then why did you call…?"

"Not because I want anything," he said, more harshly than he meant to. "You don't think I might have called just because I wanted to know how you were?"

"Not really," she confessed. "I didn't make a great impression on people around Jacobsville while we were filming down there. Especially on you."

"That was before Christabel got shot," he reminded her. "You changed my mind in a split second when you stripped off that expensive sweater you were wearing without a second thought and used it to put pressure on her gunshot wound. You made a lot of friends that day."

"Thanks," she said, sounding shy.

"Listen, I thought I might come up to New York for a few days before Christmas," he said. "Did you mean what you said, about the rain check? I could take you and Rory out on the town."

He could hear the excitement in her voice. "Wow. That would make Rory's day."

"Is he there?"

"No. I have to take the train down to Maryland and pick him up at the academy. They won't release him unless I sign him out. We had to arrange it that way to keep my mother from taking him to extort money from me." She sounded bitter. "She knows how much money I'm making and she wants some. She and her boyfriend would do anything to get their hands on money for drugs."

"Suppose I pick him up and bring him to New York for you?"

She hesitated. "You'd…do that?"

"Sure. I'll photocopy my ID and fax it to the school. You can call them and verify who I am. Rory will recognize me."

"It would be the thrill of his life," she confessed. "He's talked about nothing except you since you met at the premiere of my film last month."

"I liked him, too. He's honest."

"I taught him that honesty was the most important part of character," she said. "I've been lied to so much in my life that I value nothing more," she added quietly.

"I know how you feel. Well, I'd planned to leave here on the nineteenth. Tell me how to get to the military academy," he added, "and the address of your apartment and what time you want us there. And I'll do the rest!"

JUDD WAS HIGHLY AMUSED at Cash's animation and changed mood after the older man spoke with Tippy.

"You don't smile much these days," Judd said. "Nice to see that you remembered how."

"Tippy's brother's at military school," Cash said. "I'm going to pick him up on the way and drive him there."

"Will your truck make it all the way to New York?" Judd chided, recalling the big black pickup that Cash drove around town. It was a nice one—but inexpensive—and it had some wear on it.

Cash looked oddly hesitant. "I have a car," he said. "It's garaged in Houston. I don't drive it a lot, but I maintain it. It was for emergencies."

"Now you've got me curious," Judd said. "What sort of car?"

"It's just a car," Cash said, shrugging, too embarrassed to tell Judd what sort of car it really was. He never talked about his finances. "Nothing fancy. Listen, are you sure you can handle the work here while I'm gone?"

"I was a Texas Ranger."

Cash grinned. "Yeah, but this is a *hard* job…!"

He moved out of the way just in time to avoid retribution.

"You wait," Judd threatened with dancing eyes. "I'll hire you the ugliest secretary east of the Brazos River!"

"You would," Cash sighed. "Well, at least get me somebody who isn't so skittish, would you?"

"Why exactly did she quit?"

Cash sighed. "The punk rocker was upset about not being allowed into my filing cabinet. I didn't want to tell her about my baby python being in there temporarily, so I told her I kept top secret flying-saucer material in there."

"That's when she upended the trash can over your head," Judd guessed.

Cash shook his head. "No, that was afterward. I told her the filing cabinet was locked for a purpose, and that she'd better stay out of it. I went out to talk to one of the patrol officers. While I was gone, she got a nail file and forced the lock. Mikey, the python, had squeezed out of the cage and was sitting up on top of the file folders when she pulled out the drawer. She screamed like a banshee and when I went running back to see what was the matter, she threw a pair of handcuffs at me! She accused me of booby-trapping the cabinet to upset her."

"That explains the scream I heard," Judd agreed. "I told you it wasn't a good idea to keep Mikey's cage in the filing cabinet."

"It was just for today. Bill Harris only gave him to me this morning and I didn't have time to take him home. I put him in there until I got off work, so he wouldn't frighten anybody who came into the office and saw him. I'm certainly taking him home this afternoon," he said indignantly, "to make sure he doesn't get traumatized any more than he already is!"

"The acting mayor's niece is afraid of snakes. Imagine that," Judd mused.

"It does strain the imagination," Cash had to agree.

"You didn't give her a reason to sue us, I hope?" his friend persisted.

Cash shook his head. "I just mentioned that I had Mikey's dad in the other filing cabinet and asked if she'd like to meet him. That's when she quit." He smiled pleasantly.

"If you fire people, the city has to pay them unemployment. If they quit voluntarily, you don't. So I helped her quit voluntarily," he added with a grin.

"You villain," Judd said, trying not to laugh.

"It's not my fault. She had a king-sized crush on me. She thought if her uncle got her this job, she could hike up her skirt and throw out her chest and seduce me," he said irritably. He frowned. "Maybe I should have filed a sexual harassment suit."

"Oh, that would go over well with Ben Brady," Judd said tongue in cheek.

"I'm tired of being chased around my desk by secretaries."

"They're called administrative assistants," Judd said helpfully. "Not secretaries."

"Give me a break!"

"That's why I want you to go to New York."

"I've got a pet to take care of," Cash protested.

"You can take Mikey back over to Bill Harris before you leave town. He won't mind taking care of your baby while you're gone. You need a break. Honest."

Cash sighed and slid his big hands into his pockets. "For once, I agree with you." He hesitated. "If her uncle calls and asks why she left…"

"I won't say a word about the snake. I'll just tell him that you were having mental problems from being followed around by aliens all day," Judd said complacently.

Cash gave him a dirty look and went back to work.

LATE THE NEXT DAY, Cash presented himself in the commandant's office at the Cannae Military Academy in Annapolis, Maryland. The name of the school was amusing to him, denoting as it did the monstrous defeat of mighty Rome at the hands of the Carthaginian guerilla, Hannibal.

The commandant, Gareth Marist, was known to him. He'd served with the man years before during Operation Desert Storm in Iraq.

They shook hands like brothers, which they were, under the skin. Few men had ever had to endure what these two had when they'd gone in behind enemy lines. Marist had escaped. Cash had not.

"Rory told me all about you," Gareth said, "before I realized who you were. Sit down, sit down! It's good to see you again. You're working in law enforcement now, I believe?"

Cash nodded, dropping gracefully into a chair across the desk from the uniformed man, who was about his age, but taller and with a receding hairline. "I'm police chief of a small town in Texas."

"It's hard to give up the military life," Gareth told him. "I couldn't. So I got this appointment, which was great for me. I love helping mold the soldiers of the future. Young Rory has a lot of potential, by the way," he added. "He's very intelligent, and not rattled by boys twice his size. Even the bullies leave him alone," he chuckled.

Cash grinned. "He's not afraid to speak his mind, that's for sure."

"And his sister," Gareth said, with a long whistle. "If I weren't a happily married man with two delightful children, I'd be crawling on my knees after Tippy Moore. She really is beautiful, and she loves that kid," he volunteered. "When she first brought him here, she was scared to death. There had been some trouble with her mother, but she downplayed it. She showed me papers that gave her full custody of the boy, and she made sure we knew that we were never to let his mother get her hands on him. Or his so-called father." He studied the other man closely. "I don't guess you'd know why?"

"I might," Cash replied, "but I don't share secrets."

"I remember," Gareth replied, and with a grim smile. "You never broke under torture. I only knew one other guy who managed that, and he was SAS—the British Special Air Services."

"He was in there with me," Cash told him. "A hell of a guy. He went right back to his unit after we escaped, like nothing had ever happened."

"So did you."

Cash didn't like talking about it. He changed the subject. "How's Rory doing academically?"

"Very well. Top ten percent of his class," he said. "He's an officer, too." He smiled. "You can always tell the ones who have leadership ability. It shows up early."

"Indeed it does." He cocked his head. "No financial problems keeping him here?" he fished.

The commandant sighed. "Not at the moment," he said. "Although Tippy's income is sporadic, you understand. There have been times when we've stretched due dates…"

"If there are ever other times, could you let me know, without telling Tippy?" He slipped a business card out of his wallet and slid it across the sleek wood of the desk to the commandant. "Think of me as part of Rory's family."

Gareth was hesitant. "Grier, this is a hell of an expensive place," he began. "On a policeman's salary…"

"Look in the parking lot at what I'm driving."

"There are lots of cars out there," the other man began, rising to go to the window.

"You'll notice it."

There was a pause and a whistle when he saw the beautiful, red custom-made Jaguar. He turned to Cash. "That's yours?"

Cash nodded. "I paid cash for it," he added deliberately.

The other man let out a sigh. "Lucky devil. I drive an SUV." He turned back to his desk. "I gather that special ops pays well."

"No, it doesn't," Cash disagreed. "But I was heavily into other work before I did special ops," he added. "And I don't talk about it. Ever."

"Sorry."

"No harm done. It was a long time ago, but I invested wisely, as you see." He smiled. "Now. How about calling Rory in?"

The commandant knew when an interview was over. He smiled back. "Okay."

RORY CAME INTO THE commandant's office breathless, flushed with excitement. Two boys had come down the long hall with him, but they stopped outside the office, and stood watching from across the hall.

"Mr. Grier," Rory greeted, breaking into a wide smile. "Gosh, it's nice of you to come pick me up! Sis and I usually take the train!"

"We're driving," Cash said, smiling with a little reserve. "I hate trains."

"Oh, I like them, especially the dining car," Rory proclaimed. "I'm always hungry."

"We'll stop and eat before we start up to New York," he promised the boy. "Ready to go?"

"Yes, sir, I've got my kit right out here in the hall! Sis is beside herself," he added gleefully. "She's cleaned the apartment three times and polished all the furniture. She even cleaned out the guest room, so you'd have a place to stay!"

"Thanks, but I like my own space," Cash said easily. "I've booked a hotel room near her apartment."

The commandant chuckled when he heard that. The Cash he'd known had always been a stickler for protocol. He wouldn't spend a night in a single woman's apartment, no matter how many people thought it was acceptable.

"My sister said that you probably wouldn't stay in the apartment," Rory said surprisingly. "But she wanted you to think she's a good housekeeper. She's practiced cooking beef Stroganoff, too. Judd Dunn told her you like that."

"It's my favorite," Cash confessed, impressed.

Rory grinned. "Mine, too, but I'm glad you like it."

"Do I have to sign him out?" Cash asked Gareth.

"You do. Come on out and we'll take care of the formalities. Danbury, have a good holiday," he told Rory.

Cash was shocked to hear the boy's last name. He'd assumed the child's last name was Moore, like Tippy's.

Rory saw the surprise and laughed. "Tippy's real last name is Danbury, too. Moore was our grandmother's last name. Tippy used it when she started modeling."

That was curious. Cash wondered why, but he wasn't going to start asking probing questions right now. He signed Rory out, took time to shake hands with Rory's fascinated friends, and escorted the boy out to his car.

Rory stopped dead when he saw Cash push a button and the trunk of a flashy red Jaguar popped open.

"That's your *car?*" Rory exclaimed.

"That's my car," Cash told him, smiling. He tossed the boy's bag into the boot and closed it. "Climb aboard, youngster, and let's be off."

"Yes, sir!" Rory replied, waving frantically to the two spellbound boys at the front door of the office. Their noses were actually flattened against the glass when Cash roared out of the parking lot and onto the street.

CHAPTER TWO

CHAPTER TWO

CASH STOPPED BY HIS HOTEL to check in before he drove Rory to Tippy's apartment in Manhattan, in the lower East Village.

Tippy was waiting at her door after she buzzed Cash and Rory up to her flat on the second floor. She looked like a stranger, in jeans and a pullover yellow sweater, with her long red-gold hair flowing down her back. With the casual attire and minus any makeup, she didn't look like the elegant, beautiful woman Cash remembered from the premiere of her movie, the month before.

She fidgeted nervously as she opened the door, smiling. "Come in," she said quickly. "I hope you're both hungry. I made beef Stroganoff."

Cash's dark eyebrows rose. "My favorite. How did you know?" he added with wicked dark eyes.

She cleared her throat.

"It's my favorite, too," Rory laughed, coming to her rescue. "She always makes it for me on the night I come home."

Cash chuckled. "That puts me in my place."

She was looking around behind him. "No suitcase?" she asked. "I cleaned the spare bedroom."

"Thanks, but I booked a room at the Hilton, downtown," he said with a warm smile. "I like my own space."

"Oh. Right." She laughed self-consciously, before she awkwardly turned away and hugged Rory. "It's great to have you home for the holidays!" she said. "You made good grades, I hear, too."

"I did," he assured her.

"And got detention for fighting," she added deliberately.

He cleared his throat. "An older boy called me a name I didn't like."

"Yes?" She folded her arms across her chest and kept staring at him, unblinking.

Rory's eyes flashed. "He called me a bastard."

Her own green eyes flashed as well. "I hope you knocked him down."

He grinned. "I did. He's my buddy now." He glanced at Cash, who was watching the byplay with interest. "Nobody else ever stood up to him. He had the makings of a real bully, but I saved him from that awful fate."

Cash burst out laughing. "Good for you."

Tippy pushed back her hair. "Let's eat. I haven't had lunch," she added, leading the way into a small but cozy kitchen. The table was set with an embroidered tablecloth, on which rested colorful plates, cups, saucers and elegant silverware. She pulled a jug of milk out of the refrigerator and poured two crystal goblets full of it.

"Got another glass?" Cash asked as he paused by a chair. "I like milk."

She gave him a startled look. "I was going to offer you a whiskey…"

His face tightened. "I don't drink hard liquor. Ever."

She was taken aback. "Oh." She turned away with real embarrassment. She hadn't said one thing right since he'd walked in the door. She felt like an idiot. She got out another crystal goblet and filled it to the brim with milk. He was such a puzzling man.

He waited until she had the food on the table, and she sat down before he took his own seat. His graciousness made her feel at ease.

"See that?" she told Rory. "There's nothing wrong with good manners. Your mother must have been a charming woman," she added to Cash.

Cash took a sip of milk before he answered. "Yes. She was." He didn't enlarge on the brief admission.

Tippy swallowed hard. This was going to be an ordeal if he was this tight-lipped all night. She recalled what Christabel Gaines had told her once about Cash, that his parents' marriage was broken up by a model. Apparently the memories were still painful.

"Rory, say grace," she murmured quickly, adding another shock to Cash's growing collection of them.

They all bowed their heads. She lifted hers a minute later and gave Cash a mischievous glance. "Tradition is important. We didn't have any to start with so Rory and I decided on a few of our own. This was one."

He picked up the serving bowl at her nod and helped himself to Stroganoff. "And the others?"

She smiled at him shyly. It made her look younger. She wasn't wearing makeup, except for a light lipstick, and her hair looked fresh and clean swinging loose around her shoulders. "We add a new ornament to the Christmas tree every year and we hang a pickle in the tree."

His fork poised in midair. "A what?"

"A pickle, Cash," Rory replied. "It's a German custom, for good luck. Our grandfather on our mother's side was German." He finished a bite of meat and washed it down with milk. "What were your people, Cash?"

"Martians, I believe," Cash replied seriously.

Tippy's eyebrows lifted.

"Right." Rory chuckled.

Cash grinned at him. "My mother's mother was from Andalusia, in Spain," he said with a smile. "My father's people were Cherokee and Swiss."

"Quite a combination," Tippy remarked, studying him.

He stared at her curiously. "Your ancestors must have been Irish or Scottish," he said, noting her hair color.

"That's what I think," she agreed, but she didn't meet his eyes.

"Our mother's a redhead," Rory interjected. "Tippy's is natural, too, but lots of people think she dyes it."

Tippy took a long sip of milk and said nothing.

"I thought about dyeing mine purple, but my cousin, who was our former chief, said it might offend people." Cash sighed. "That was about the same time he made me take off my earring," he added disgustedly.

Tippy almost choked on her milk.

"You wore an earring?" Rory exclaimed, delighted.

"Just a simple gold one," Cash admitted. "I was working for the government at the time and my boss was so politically correct that he wore a sign apologizing for stepping on bacteria and killing it." He nodded emphatically. "That's a true story."

Tippy was wiping her eyes. She laughed so hard that she was almost crying. It had been years since she'd felt so lighthearted with anyone. From their rocky beginning to laughter was a big step.

"She never laughs," Rory commented with a grin. "Especially on location shoots. She hates photographers on account of one made her sit on a rock in a bikini and she got bitten by a tern."

"The stupid bird dive-bombed me five times," Tippy had to admit. "On its final assault, it took part of my scalp away!"

"You should tell him about what the pigeons did to you on that shoot in Italy," Rory prompted.

She shivered delicately. "I'm still trying to forget it. I used to like pigeons."

"I love pigeons," Cash said, grinning. "You haven't lived until you've had them delicately wrapped in puff pastry and fried in olive oil…"

"You barbarian!" Tippy exclaimed.

"It's okay, I eat snakes and lizards, too, I'm not strictly a pigeon man."

Rory was all but rolling on the floor. "Gosh, Cash, this is going to be the best Christmas we've ever had!"

Tippy was inclined to agree. The man across from her bore very little resemblance to the antagonistic, hostile law enforcement officer she'd met while filming in Jacobsville, Texas. Everybody said Cash Grier was mysterious and dangerous. Nobody said he had a howling sense of humor.

Seeing her confusion, Cash leaned toward Rory and spoke in a loud whisper. "She's confused. Back in Texas, they told her I kept military secrets about flying saucers in a locked file."

"I heard it was aliens," Tippy murmured without cracking a smile.

"I do not keep aliens in my filing cabinet," he said indignantly. A minute later, his dark eyes started to twinkle. "I keep *those* in a closet in my house."

Rory chuckled. Tippy was laughing, too.

"And I thought *actors* were nuts," Tippy remarked on a sigh.

AFTER LUNCH, CASH announced that he was taking them to the park. Tippy changed into an emerald-green pantsuit and put her hair in a braid, adding just a touch of makeup to her oval face.

Her apartment was on a quiet, tree-lined street. It was a transitional neighborhood that had gone from fairly dangerous to middle class. The renovations were noticeable, especially in Tippy's apartment, which had black wrought-iron banisters that led up the stone steps to her two-story apartment.

In her heyday as a model, she'd had money to burn, and briefly she'd lived off Park Avenue. But after her year's absence from the profession, when modeling jobs became thin on the ground, she had to budget. That was when she'd moved here, just before she started shooting the movie in Jacobsville that had unexpectedly restarted her career. She could probably have afforded something better now, but she'd become attached to her neighbors and the peaceful street where she lived. There was a bookstore just down at the corner and a food market past it. There was also a small mom-and-pop café which served the best coffee around. It was lovely in the spring. Now, with winter here, the trees were bare and the city looked cold and gray.

Cash's red Jaguar was parked just outside the steps that led into her apartment building. She did a double take when she saw it, but she didn't comment. Rory climbed into the back seat, leaving Tippy to sit up front with Cash.

"I thought Central Park was dangerous," Rory remarked as they strolled along the sidewalk after the short drive, glancing at the pretty carriages hitched to horses that were waiting for customers. "And should you leave your car parked there?" he added, looking over his shoulder at the beautiful car.

Cash shrugged. "Central Park is much safer now. And anybody who can get past my pet rattlesnake is welcome to drive my car."

"Your what…?" Tippy burst out, looking around at her ankles.

He grinned. "My alarm system. That's what I call it. I've got an electronic monitoring system installed somewhere in the engine—if anybody tries to hot-wire the car, or steals it, it will take about ten minutes for the police to find it. Even in New York City," he added smugly.

"No wonder you look so confident," Rory said. "It sure is a beaut of a car, Cash," he added wistfully.

"It is that," Tippy remarked. "I can drive, but it's impractical to have a car in this city," she said, indicating the abundance of taxis buzzing up and down the streets. "Usually, when I went on modeling jobs, I didn't have time to waste looking for parking spots. There are never enough. Cabs and subways are quicker when you're in a rush."

"They are," he agreed. He glanced down at her, fascinated by her fresh beauty that was only accentuated by the lack of makeup.

"Where are you shooting the movie?" he asked.

"Here in the city, mostly," she said. "It's a comedy with touches of a spy drama mixed in. I have to wrestle with a foreign agent in one scene, and outrun a gunman in another." She grimaced. "We only just started filming before we broke for the holidays, and I've got bruises everywhere already from the fight coordinator's choreography. I actually have to learn aikido for the film."

"A useful martial art," Cash remarked. "It was one of the first forms I learned."

"How many do you know?" Rory asked at once.

Cash shrugged. "Karate, tae kwon do, hapkido, kung fu, and a few disciplines that aren't in the book. You never know when you'll need to fall back on that training. It comes in handy in police work, now that I'm not stuck behind a desk all the time."

"Judd said you worked in Houston with the D.A.'s office," Tippy said.

He nodded. "I was a cybercrime expert. It wasn't challenging enough to suit me. I like something a little less routine and structured."

"What do you do in Jacobsville?" Rory wanted to know.

Cash chuckled. "I run from my secretaries," he said sheepishly. "Just before I phoned your sister about coming up for the holidays, the new one quit and dumped a trash can over my head." He made a face and touched his dark hair. "I'm still picking coffee grounds out of my hair."

Tippy's green eyes widened. She stopped and looked up at Cash. She couldn't believe he was telling the truth. She remembered how efficiently he'd stopped the assistant director on her first film from touching her when she'd objected to his familiarity.

Rory was laughing. "Really?"

"She wasn't really cut out for police work," he said. "She couldn't talk on the phone and type at the same time, so she didn't do much typing."

"Why…?" Tippy fished.

"…did she empty a trash can on me?" he finished for her. "Damned if I know! I told her not to force the lock on my filing cabinet, but she wouldn't listen. Is it *my* fault my baby python, Mikey, jumped out of the drawer at her? She scared him. He has a nervous condition."

They'd both stopped now and were staring at him.

He sighed. "Isn't it strange how snakes make some people nervous?" he asked philosophically.

"You have a snake named Mikey?" Tippy exclaimed.

"Cag Hart had an albino python that he gave to a breeder after he got married. The python's mate had a litter of the cute little things, and I asked for one. The day he gave me Mikey, I didn't have time to take him home so I put him in the filing cabinet, temporarily, in a little plastic aquarium with water and a limb to climb. It was working very nicely until my secretary jimmied the lock. Sadly, Mikey had escaped and was sitting on top of the files in the filing cabinet drawer."

"What did she do?" Rory asked.

He scowled. "She scared the poor little thing half to death," he muttered. "I'm sure he's going to have psychological problems for the rest of his…"

"Afterward!" Rory interrupted.

His dark eyebrows rose. "After she screamed bloody murder and threw my spare handcuffs at me, you mean?"

Tippy just stared at him, her green eyes twinkling.

"That was when she dumped my trash can over my head. It was almost worth it. She had a spike haircut and black lipstick and nail polish, and body piercings with little silver rings all over visible space. Mikey's slowly getting over the trauma. He's living in my house now."

Tippy was laughing too hard to talk at all.

Rory shook his head. "I almost had a snake once."

"What happened to it?" Cash asked.

"She wouldn't let me out of the pet shop with it," Rory sighed, pointing at his sister.

"Doesn't like snakes, hmm?" he drawled with a wicked glance at Tippy.

"It wasn't because I was afraid of it, it was because he couldn't take it to school with him and I'm not home long enough to take care of a pet. But if you really need a secretary, as soon as I finish this movie, I'll have my nose pierced and my hair spiked, first thing," she said, tongue in cheek.

Cash's perfect white teeth flashed at her. "I don't know. Can you type and chew gum at the same time?"

"She can't type a word. And she *is* scared of snakes..." Rory began enthusiastically.

"Stop right there," Tippy murmured with a quick

look at her brother. "And don't you let him corrupt you," she cautioned. "Unless you want me to tell him *your* fatal weakness!"

Rory held up both hands. "I'm sorry. I'm *really* sorry. Honest."

She pursed her full lips. "Okay."

"Look! There's the guy with the bagpipes! Give me a twenty, sis, would you?" Rory exclaimed, nodding toward a man in a kilt standing just outside a hotel near the park with a set of bagpipes. He was playing "Amazing Grace."

Tippy pulled a large bill from her fanny pack and handed it to Rory. "Here you go. We'll wait here for you," she said with an indulgent smile.

Cash watched him go, his eyes sliding to the bagpiper. "He plays well," Cash said.

"Rory wants a set of bagpipes, but I doubt the commandant would be inclined to let him practice in his dorm."

"I agree." Cash smiled wistfully as he listened to the haunting melody. "Is he here often?" he asked her.

"We see him all around the neighborhood," Tippy replied lazily. "He's one of the nicer street people. Homeless, of course. I slip him some money whenever I have a little extra, so he'll be able to buy a blanket or a hot cup of coffee. A lot of us around here indulge him. He has a gift, don't you think?"

"He does. Know anything about him?" he added, impressed by her concern for a stranger.

"Not much. They say his whole family died, but not how or when…or even why. He doesn't talk to people much," she murmured, watching Rory hand him the bill and receive a faint smile for it as the piper halted for a moment. "New York is full of street people. Most of them have some talent or other, some way to make a little cash. You can see them sleeping in cardboard boxes, going through Dumpsters for odds and ends." She shook her head. "And we're supposed to be the richest country on earth."

"You'd be amazed at how people live in third world countries," he remarked.

She looked up at him. "I had a photo shoot in Jamaica, near Montego Bay," she recalled. "There was a five-star hotel on a hill, with parrots in cages and a huge swimming pool and every convenience known to man. Just down the hill, a few hundred feet away, was a small village of corrugated tin houses sitting in mud, where people actually lived."

His dark eyes narrowed. He nodded slowly. "I've been to the Middle East. Many people there live in adobe houses with no electricity, no running water, no indoor facilities. They make their own clothing, and they travel in pony carts pulled by donkeys. Our standard of living would shock them speechless."

Her breath drew in sharply. "I had no idea."

He looked around the city. "Everywhere I went, I was made welcome. The poorest families were eager to share the little they had with me. They're mostly good people. Kind people." He glanced at her. "But they make bad enemies."

Tippy was looking at the scars on his lean, strong face. "Rory's commandant said that they tortured you," she recalled softly.

He nodded and his dark eyes searched her light ones. "I don't talk about it. I still have nightmares, after all these years."

She studied him curiously. "I have nightmares, too," she said absently.

His eyes probed hers, seeking answers to the puzzle she represented. "You lived for a long time with an older actor who was known publicly as the most licentious man in Hollywood," he said bluntly.

She glanced toward Rory, who was sitting on a bench, listening as the bagpiper started playing again. She wrapped her arms close around her chest and wouldn't look up.

Cash moved in front of her, very close. Strangely, it didn't frighten her. She met his searching gaze. It almost winded her with its intensity.

"Tell me," he said softly.

That softness was irresistible. She took a deep breath and plowed ahead. "I ran away from home when I was twelve. They were going to put me in foster care, and I was terrified that my mother might be able to get me out again—for revenge because I called the police on her and her boyfriend after he…" She hesitated.

"Come on," he prompted.

"After he raped me repeatedly," she bit off, and couldn't look at him then. "I wouldn't have gone back to her, not if it meant starving. So I went on the streets in Atlanta, because I had no way to earn money for food." Her face clenched as she remembered it. Cash's expression was like stone. He'd suspected something like that, from the bits and pieces of her life that he'd ferreted out.

She continued quietly, "The first man who came up to me was handsome and dashing. He wanted to take me home." Her eyes closed. "I was hungry and cold and scared to death. I didn't want to go with him. But he had the kindest eyes…" She swallowed the lump in her throat.

"He took me to his hotel. He had an enormous suite, luxury fit for a king. When we got inside, he laughed because I was nervous and promised he wouldn't hurt me, that he just wanted to help me. I was so scared, I spilled a glass of water down the front of my shirt." She smiled. "I'll never forget the shock on his face as long as I live. I had short hair and I was never voluptuous, even back then, but the wet shirt…" She looked up at Cash, who was listening intently. "But of course, he wasn't interested in me in that way…"

Cash's lips parted on a soft explosion of breath. "Cullen Cannon, the great international lover, was gay?" he asked, astonished.

She nodded. "He was. But he hid it with the help of women friends. He was a sweet and gentle man," she recalled wistfully. "I offered to leave, and he wouldn't hear of it. He said that he was lonely. His family had disowned him. He had nobody. So I stayed. He bought me clothes, put me back in school, shielded me from my own past so that my mother wouldn't be able to find me."

Her eyes misted as she continued her story. "I loved him," she whispered. "I would have given him anything. But all he wanted was to take care of me." She laughed. "Perhaps later, when he'd put me in modeling classes in New York, he liked the image it gave him to have a pretty young woman living with him. I don't know. But I stayed there until he died."

"The media said it was a heart attack."

She shook her head. "He died of AIDS. At the last, his biological children came to see him, and they buried the past. They resented me at first, suspected me of trying to play up to him for money. But I guess they finally realized that I was crazy about him." She smiled. "They tried to make me take his apartment over, when he died, tried to give me a trust account out of their inheritance. I refused it. You see, I nursed him the last year he lived."

"That's why you didn't model for a year, just before you were offered your first film contract. They said you were in an accident and had to heal," Cash recalled.

She was flattered that he remembered that much when he'd literally hated her in Jacobsville. "That's right," she said. "He didn't want anybody to know about him. Not even then."

"Poor guy."

"He was the best man I ever knew," she said sadly. "I still put flowers on his grave. He saved me."

"What about the man who raped you?" he asked bluntly.

She looked at Rory, who was talking to the bagpiper. Her expression was tormented. "My mother said he was Rory's father," she managed.

Now his intake of breath was really audible. "And you love Rory."

She turned to him. "With all my heart," she agreed. "My mother's still with Rory's father, Sam Stanton, on and off. They are both drug addicts. Sam and my mother have fights and he beats her up and she calls the police. He always comes back."

"How did you end up with Rory?" he asked.

"The police officer who saved me the last night I was at home—when Sam raped me—called me when Rory was just four years old. I was still living with Cullen and he was powerful and rich. Cullen went with me to see Rory in the hospital after he was severely beaten by his father. My mother was quite taken with Cullen," she recalled coldly. "So after Rory was released she brought him to the hotel where we were staying. Fishing, for money. Cullen offered to buy the child. And she sold him to us," she added icily. "For fifty thousand dollars."

"My God," he bit off. "And I thought I'd seen it all."

"Rory's been with me ever since," she told him. "He's like my own child."

"You never got pregnant…?"

She shook her head. "I was a late bloomer. I didn't even have my first period until I was fifteen. Pretty lucky, huh?" She pushed back wisps of red hair. "Real lucky."

"But your mother wants Rory back now."

"The money ran out years ago. She's having to get her drug money by working in a convenience store, and she doesn't like it. Sam works when he feels like it, and I don't think he does anything legal, either. My attorney paid my mother off last year when she threatened to go to the tabloids about the brutal way I was treating her," she scoffed. "Rich movie star allows poor mother to live in poverty while she rides in stretch limousines." She smiled cynically. "Get the picture?"

"In Technicolor," he agreed coldly.

"So now she's decided she wants Rory back. She sent Rory's father up to the military school and he tried to get him out. Rory told the commandant what his father had done to him—and to me—and the commandant called the police. The rat ran for his life before they got there."

"Good for the commandant."

"But that doesn't rule out kidnapping. I'd pay anything to get Rory back, and they know it. I don't sleep very well these days," she added. "Rory's father has a cousin who lives near here, in a really bad part of town. They're close, and the cousin has his dirty fingers in a lot of illegal pies."

Cash was doing mental gymnastics. "Does Rory care for his father or his mother?"

"He hates our mother," she replied. "And he doesn't know that Sam Stanton is his real father."

"You haven't told him?" he probed.

"I haven't had the heart to," she explained. "He took a real beating from Sam. The psychologist says he'll have mental scars for the rest of his life from that ordeal."

"How about you?"

"I've lived through enough to make me strong, with occasional lapses. But mostly, I'm tough," she murmured.

"Not tough enough, just yet," he commented. "But you will be, if you hang around with me long enough."

She glanced at him with a teasing smile. "Am I going to?"

He shrugged. "It's up to you. I have a few quirks."

"So do I. And a few hang-ups," she added.

He put his hands in his pockets while he stared down at her, to the music of New York traffic. "I don't like ties very much. I'm making no promises. I want to see you while I'm here. Period."

"You don't pull any punches."

He nodded.

She searched his dark eyes. "I don't find you repulsive," she said bluntly. "That's new. But I've got some terrible scars of my own. I can put on a good act as a vamp when I'm around men. But it's all a ruse. I haven't ever had consensual sex."

He whistled. "That's a heavy load to put on a man."

She nodded.

He smiled slowly. "So, it's back to Dating 101."

She laughed. "I hadn't thought of it like that."

"We'll go slow," he said, noting Rory's sudden reappearance. "That took a while," he commented when the boy came back laughing.

"He wanted to know about military school. Guess what? He was a soldier in Vietnam." Rory grimaced. "Sad, huh, that he'd end up like that."

Cash's eyes were haunted as he studied the man, who lifted a hand and waved before he went back to his bagpiping. Cash waved back. "Too many veterans wind up like that," he commented quietly.

"Not you," Rory said proudly.

Cash smiled at him and ruffled his hair. "No. Not me. How about going to the Statue of Liberty? It's closed, so we can't go up in it, but we can see it. Are you game?"

"Lead me to it!" Rory laughed.

Cash took Tippy's slender hand and locked her fingers into his, noting their coldness and faint trembling. It was like electricity sparking between them. Tippy caught her breath audibly. She looked up with wide, fascinated eyes, feeling as if the ground had rocked under her feet. It was magic!

He searched her eyes. "Lesson One, Page One, Hand-holding," he whispered as Rory paused to look in a store window.

She laughed breathlessly. It sounded like silver bells.

CHAPTER THREE

CHAPTER THREE

THE DAY SPENT SIGHTSEEING with Cash was, Tippy thought later, one of the best days of her entire life. He seemed to know New York like the back of his hand, and he enjoyed sharing little-known bits of history with Tippy and Rory.

"How do you know so much about this place?" Rory wanted to know when they were back in Tippy's apartment that evening.

"My best friend in basic training was from New York City," he confided. "He was a gold mine of information!"

Tippy laughed. "I have a friend who's like that about Nassau," she said. "She's on a modeling trip now, to Russia, of all places."

"What is she modeling?"

Tippy gave him a mischievous look. "Swimsuits."

"You're kidding!"

"I'm not! The powers that be thought it would be sexy to have her pose with the Kremlin in the background, wearing fur boots and a fur coat."

"She'll be pickled if she does that here, won't she?" he asked.

"It's fake fur," she pointed out, laughing. "But it's very expensive fake fur, and it looks real."

"How about a sandwich, Cash?" Rory called from the kitchen.

"Not for me, thanks, Rory. I'm going back to my hotel to unwind," he added with a smile. "I had a great time today."

"So did I, Cash," Rory said sincerely. "Are you coming back tomorrow?"

"Are you?" Tippy echoed.

He glanced from Rory's curious expression to Tippy's radiant one. "Why not?" he mused, smiling. "I can stand a tour of the museums if you can."

"I love museums!" Rory enthused.

"As long as I don't have to pose in one." Tippy sighed. "I have terrible emotional scars from posing with one leg up, leaning back, in front of a Rodin sculpture for four hours."

"I wonder if it's the one I'm thinking of?" Cash drawled, chuckling when her cheeks went pink.

"I'm sure it was one that contained totally clothed people," she lied.

He shook his head. "You wish," he said. "What time do you people get up on a holiday week?"

"Eight," Rory said.

Tippy nodded. "We're not big on late nights around here. One of us is used to military routine, which begins at daylight, and the other one has to get up before daylight to work on films," she said, tongue in cheek.

"Eight it is, then. I know where there's a bakery," he told them. "They have homemade cinnamon buns, bear claws, filled doughnuts..."

"I can't have sweets," Rory replied sadly. He pointed at Tippy. "She has no willpower. If something sweet comes in the door, it will never leave."

Tippy laughed delightedly. "He's right. I've spent most of my life fighting excess pounds. We have bacon and eggs for breakfast. Pure protein. No bread."

"Shades of basic training." He sighed. "Okay. Can we have breakfast here? But you'd better make coffee," he added sternly. "I am not having breakfast without coffee, even if that means bringing it in a sippy cup."

"A sippy cup?" Tippy teased.

"I look sexy holding a sippy cup," he replied, and the smile on his lips was a genuine one. It had been a long time since he'd smiled at a woman and meant it. Well, except for Christabel Gaines. But she was married to his best friend now.

"Well, I'm having a sandwich before I go to bed," Rory called. "Good night, Cash! See you tomorrow!"

"That's a deal," Cash called back.

He caught Tippy's soft hand in his and tugged her to the door with him. "I'll check and see if there's anything good at the opera or the ballet, if you'd like…"

"I love either one," she exclaimed.

"Symphony orchestras?" he asked, testing.

She nodded enthusiastically.

"I guess it won't kill me to wear a suit," he sighed.

"You took Christabel Gaines to a ballet in Houston, I recall," she said, with just a hint of jealousy that she couldn't disguise.

It surprised him. His dark eyes probed her light ones until she moved restlessly under the intensity of the gaze. "Christabel Dunn, these days. And, yes, I did. She'd never been to one in her life."

"I thought she was a spoiled little princess," Tippy commented. "I was wrong all the way down the line. She's a very special woman. Judd's lucky."

"Yes, he is," he had to agree. Christabel was still a sore spot with him. "They dote on the twins."

"Babies are nice," she said. "Rory was precious even at the age of four." She smiled wistfully. "Every day's an adventure with a child."

"I wouldn't know."

She looked up, surprised by the expression on his lean, hard face.

He averted his eyes. "I've got to go. I'll see you in the morning."

He let go of her hand and left her standing. She divined that something in his past had wounded him deeply, something to do with children. Judd had told her that he thought Cash had been married once, but no more than that. He was a puzzle. But he appealed to her in ways no other man ever had.

CASH ARRIVED AT EIGHT SHARP the next morning, carrying a silvertone coffee holder in one hand and a paper sack in the other.

"I made coffee," she said quickly.

He lifted the holder. "Vanilla cappuccino," he said, waving it under her nose. "My only real weakness. Well, except for these," he waved the sack.

"What's in there?" Tippy asked, following him to the breakfast table she'd already set, where Rory was waiting to start eating.

"Cheese Danishes," he said. "Sorry. I can't give up sugar. I think it's one of the four major food groups, along with chocolate and ice cream and pizza."

Rory burst out laughing. So did Tippy.

"Amazing," she said, giving his powerful body a

lingering scrutiny. "You don't look as if you've ever tasted fat or sugar in your life."

"I work out every day," he confided. "I have to. Those uniforms are sewn on us, you know," he added deadpan, "to emphasize what nice muscles we have."

Her eyes glanced off his biceps, very noticeable in the knit shirt he was wearing with dark slacks, as he swung his black leather jacket onto an easy chair on his way to the kitchen.

"No comment?" he taunted.

She sighed. "I was just noticing the muscles," she murmured dryly.

Rory had excused himself to go to the bathroom. Cash caught Tippy's long skirt and pulled her close to his chair. "If you play your cards right, I just might take my shirt off for you one day," he purred.

She didn't know whether to laugh or protest. He was so unpredictable.

"Not right away, of course," he added. "I'm not that kind of man!"

Now she did laugh. Her eyes lit up, sparkling like emeralds. He grinned, too. "Here. Have a cheese Danish. I brought enough for all of us."

She reached down into the bag, very aware of his dark eyes on her face.

"Your skin is beautiful, even without makeup," he noted deeply. "It looks like silk."

Her head turned. She met his eyes evenly and her heart jumped. He was very sexy.

"What are you thinking?" he murmured.

"I'll bet you know everything there is to know about women," she confessed huskily.

His eyes narrowed. "And you know next to nothing about men."

Her eyes misted. "I haven't wanted to," she said softly. Her gaze fell to his wide, chiseled mouth.

"Careful," he said quietly. "I've kept to myself for a long time."

"You wouldn't hurt me," she whispered daringly, meeting his searching gaze. "I wish…oh, I wish!"

"You wish…what?" he prompted, his jaw clutching as the fragrance of her body drifted down into his nostrils. She was so close that he could see her heart beating at the neck of her blouse. He wanted to jerk her down into his arms and kiss her until her beautiful mouth began to swell.

She was feeling the same hunger. She looked at his mouth and wondered how it would feel to kiss it intensely, the way she'd stage-kissed her fellow actor in the movie they'd made at the Dunn ranch. She could almost taste Cash's hard mouth. Her body felt swollen, achy. It was like a thirst that no water would ever be able to quench.

Her breath caught noisily in her throat as her full lips parted. "I wish…"

The sound of the toilet flushing broke them apart. She stood up, forgetting the Danish, and went to the sink to wash her hands because she needed something to still them.

Rory came back, totally oblivious to what he'd interrupted, and helped himself to a Danish. After a minute, Tippy poured coffee for herself and orange juice for Rory, and sat down at the table as if nothing at all had happened.

THEY WENT TO THE AMERICAN Museum of Natural History first, to see the renovated dinosaur exhibit on the fourth floor. There was a long line because of the special exhibits, one that included a film and a shop concerned only with Albert Einstein. They stood in line for over an hour before they were able to get their tickets.

Rory went from one of the fossils to another, eagerly climbing a flight of stairs above the tallest skeleton so that he could look down on the massive shoulder blades and hip joints.

"He loves dinosaurs," Tippy remarked, sauntering along beside Cash in her long green velvet skirt with boots and a white silk blouse under her black leather coat. Her hair was around her shoulders, and she was drawing attention from men as well as women, despite the very light touch of cosmetics she'd used.

Beside her Cash felt a surge of pride in her company. She really was beautiful, he thought, and it had so little to do with surface appearance. She was pure gold inside, where it counted.

"I like dinosaurs myself," he commented. "I was here several years ago, but I missed the dinosaurs because this exhibit was being reworked. They're impressive."

She leaned closer to a sign to read it.

"You aren't wearing your glasses," he remarked.

She laughed self-consciously. "I'm a walking disaster when I have them on," she said dryly. "I clean them with whatever's handy. The lenses stay scratched, and I've already had them replaced twice."

"They have new lenses that don't scratch easily," he pointed out.

"Yes, that's the kind I got. Sadly, they aren't foolproof." She lifted a beautiful shoulder. "I wish I could wear contacts, but my eyes don't like them. I get infections."

He reached out a big, lean hand and caught a strand of her hair in it, testing its softness and bringing her close up against him in the process. "Your hair is alive," he said quietly. "I've never seen this color look so natural."

"It is natural," she replied, feeling her knees go shaky at the unexpected proximity. He smelled of cologne and soap—clean, attractive smells. Her hands rested on his shirt, feeling the warm muscle and the faint cushiony sensation of hair under her hands. She wanted to pull the shirt up and touch him there with a fervor that made her breath catch. She'd never felt desire so torrid in her life.

"And nothing about you is artificial?" he probed.

"Nothing physical," she agreed.

His dark eyes searched her green ones for longer than he meant to. His face seemed to clench. She knew he could probably feel her heart racing. She couldn't help it. He was a particularly masculine man. Everything feminine inside her reacted to his touch. "I don't trust women."

"You were married," she recalled.

He nodded. His fingers curled around the strand of hair he was holding. His eyes were haunted. "I loved her. I thought she loved me." He laughed coldly. "She certainly loved what I could buy her."

She felt cold chills run down her spine. "There's so much in your past that you don't talk about," she said softly. "You're very mysterious, in your way."

"Trust comes hard to me," he told her. "If people can get close to you, they can wound you."

"And the answer is to keep everyone at arm's length?" she replied.

"Don't you?" he shot back. "Except for Rory, and briefly Judd Dunn, I don't recall ever seeing you keeping company with anyone. Especially a man."

She swallowed hard. "I have horrible memories of

men. Except for Cullen, and there was no physical contact there. He liked women as friends, but found them physically repulsive."

"Did you love him?"

"In my way, I did," she said, surprising him. "He was one of two people in my entire life who were good to me without expecting anything in return." Her smile was cynical. "You can't imagine how many times you get propositioned in my line of work. It took years to perfect a line that worked."

"You can't blame men for trying, Tippy," he said curtly. "You look like every man's dream of perfection."

Her heart jumped. "Even yours?" she asked in a teasing tone. Except she wasn't teasing. She wanted him to want her. She'd never wanted anything so much.

He let go of her hair. "I gave up women years ago."

"Aren't you lonely?" she wanted to know.

"Are you?" he retorted.

She sighed, studying his strong features with a vague hunger. "I've got cold feet," she said huskily. "Once or twice over the years I took a chance on someone who seemed nice. But nobody wanted to talk to me, to get to know me. They only wanted me in bed."

His eyes narrowed. "Can you…?"

Her gaze fell to his chest, where the muscles were outlined by the close fit of his knit shirt. "I don't know," she replied honestly. "I haven't…tried."

"Do you want to?"

She bit her lower lip and frowned, staring at the dinosaur without really seeing it. "I'm twenty-six years old. I don't risk my heart, and I'm happy enough. I have Rory and a career. I suppose I've got all I need."

"It's a half life."

"So is yours," she accused, looking up at him.

"I have an even better reason than yours," he said coldly.

"But you won't share it," she guessed. "You don't trust me enough."

He rammed his hands into his slacks pockets and glared down at her. "I was married once, years ago. I was in love for the first time in my life and crazy to share everything with my wife. She'd just told me she was pregnant. I was over the moon. I wanted to tell her all about my life before I married her." His eyes grew cold. "So I did. She sat and listened. She was very calm. She didn't say a word. She just listened, as if she understood. She was a little pale, but that wasn't surprising. I did horrible things in my line of work. Really terrible." He turned away from her. "I had to go out of town on business for a few days. She saw me off very naturally, no fuss. I came back with little presents for her and something for the baby, even though she was only a few weeks along. She met me at the door with her suitcases."

He leaned forward against the banister. He didn't look at her while he spoke. "She told me that she'd gone to a clinic while I was away. She'd seen a lawyer, too. Just before she walked out the door, she told me that she wasn't bringing the child of a cold-blooded killer into the world."

Tippy had thought there was something traumatic in his past, besides his work. Now she understood what it was. The hunger he displayed for Judd and Christabel's twins made sense now. She could almost feel his pain, as if it were her own. She was deeply flattered that he trusted her with something so intimate.

"No comment?" he drawled poisonously, without looking down at her.

"Was she very young?" she asked softly.

"She was my age."

She lowered her eyes to his hands on the steel rail. He wasn't showing any emotion at all, but his knuckles were white from the pressure he was exerting on the bar.

"I won't step on an insect if I can avoid it," she said quietly. "I would never be able to sleep with a man without using protection unless I loved him. I think a child is part of that."

His head turned slowly and he looked down at her curiously. "She was right. I was a cold-blooded killer," he said flatly.

She searched his hard face and her eyes were soft and tender. "I don't believe that."

He scowled. "I beg your pardon?"

"Rory's commandant told him that you were part of a crack military unit in special ops," she said. "You were sent in when negotiations failed, when lives were at stake. So don't try to convince me that you were a hit man for the mob, or that you killed for money. You aren't that sort of person."

He didn't seem to be breathing. "You know nothing about me," he said abruptly.

"My grandmother was Irish. She had the second sight. It's a gift. All the women in my family have it, except for my mother," she added. Her eyes softened on his face. "I know things that I shouldn't know. I feel things before they happen. I've been very worried about Rory lately, because I sense something dangerous connected to him."

"I don't believe in clairvoyance," he said stiffly. "It's a myth."

"Maybe it is to you. It isn't to me." She glanced around the room, looking for her little brother and picking him out of a crowd looking up at a stuffed coelacanth suspended from the high ceiling of the room.

Cash felt violated. He felt as if he'd become transparent with this woman, and he didn't like it. He kept to himself, he kept secrets. He didn't want Tippy walking around inside his brain.

"Now I've made you angry. I'm sorry," she said gently, without looking at him. "I'm going to the Einstein shop. Rory wants a T-shirt. I'll meet you both in the lobby in an hour or so."

He caught her hand and tugged her back to him. "No, you won't. We'll go together." He tipped her chin up so that he could see her eyes. "I told Rory once that I value honesty."

"No, you don't, not if it concerns having anyone else guess about your private life."

"I told you about my private life," he replied. He took a slow breath. "I've never told anyone else about my child."

"I have that kind of face," she said with a tender smile.

"Yes, you do." He touched her cheek lightly. "I've got more emotional scars than you have, and that's saying something. We're both damaged people. That being the case, it would be insane of us to get involved with one another. So that's not going to happen."

Her eyes became shy, curious. "You would… you've thought about…getting involved with me?" She asked the question as if she didn't believe what she'd heard.

That it flattered her was obvious. He was surprised. He hadn't thought she felt attracted to him. It would be difficult for her, with her past.

"With your past…" he murmured aloud.

She moved a step closer to him. It made her breathless. "You're forgetting something. You're a cop."

"And that's why you're not afraid of me?" he murmured. He was feeling a little breathless himself at her proximity. She smelled like flowers.

One perfect shoulder lifted nervously. "Judd Dunn was a Texas Ranger. I felt safe with him."

"Are you making a point?"

She nibbled her lower lip and her high cheekbones flushed a little. "I don't feel…safe…with you, exactly. You stir me up inside. I feel…shaky. I feel swollen all over. I think about touching you, all the time. I keep wondering," she whispered while they were briefly isolated from the other visitors, "how it would feel if you kissed me."

He couldn't believe she'd said that. But her eyes were saying it, too. She seemed almost dazed.

His lean hands contracted a little roughly, pulling her up closer to the long, heated, muscular length of his fit body. He felt her breath catch. His dark eyes dropped to her full lips. "I think about touching you, too, Tippy," he said deep in his throat. His thumbs edged out under her arms, tracing just at the curve of her full breasts. His mouth hovered inches from hers. His breath was warm, minty. "I think about the silky feel of your skin against my chest. I think about breaking your mouth open under mine and tasting you, inside, with my tongue."

Tippy gasped. Her body trembling. She leaned her forehead against his chest while she tried to breathe normally. Her nails bit into his chest. "Cash," she groaned.

His thumbs became insistent. Desire coursed through him like a great flood. He felt himself going rigid, losing control. He thought about stepping back, but her hips moved just faintly and he shuddered at the lash of pleasure he felt.

She looked up, surprised by the immediate response of his body. She knew why men's bodies grew hard like that, but it had always been repugnant to her before. Now, it was fascinating, glorious. Her lips parted as she searched his stormy eyes. He wanted her!

She started to move again, desperate to please him, but his hands suddenly dropped to her slender hips and grasped them roughly.

"If you do that again," he said through his teeth, "there's going to be a whole new definition of public exhibition, and we're both going to figure in it prominently."

"Oh. Oh!" She swallowed hard, looking around with embarrassing color. Fortunately, nobody seemed to be watching.

He put her completely away and straightened, reciting multiplication tables in his head to divert his thoughts. It had been a long dry spell, but even so, his reaction to Tippy was unsettling.

She was feeling something similar. She'd gone from frigid apprehension to passionate anticipation in the space of seconds. Suddenly, all she could think about was a bed, with Cash in the middle of it. She could almost picture that powerful body without clothes…

She made a faint sound and couldn't have looked at Cash to save her life.

He couldn't help the soft chuckle that escaped his tight throat. She was an open book. It was flattering to know that he could arouse her with such innocent love play. She stirred him up, too, but he didn't trust her. Or did he? He'd never told another living soul about his wife.

As if seeking comfort, her beautifully manicured hands went to his shirt and pressed there, unsteadily. She kept a discreet distance between her body and his. She didn't dare look up at him. She'd never felt so insecure, so shy. She'd never felt so happy or so…stimulated.

His big hands caught her tiny waist and pressed there. Around them, people were moving, talking, laughing. But they were alone in the world. It was a sensation Cash could never remember feeling in his life.

"I could hurt you," he bit off. "And I don't mean physically. I'm a bad risk. I'm too used to my own space. I don't share. I don't…feel much emotion anymore."

He sounded vulnerable. She was fascinated. Her soft green eyes looked up into his turbulent dark ones and it was like lightning striking. She actually caught her breath, and it was audible. "I'm feeling things I never dreamed I could."

His hands jerked on her waist. His teeth clenched. "It would be suicide!" he said roughly.

She remembered a line from a book, and her eyes were brilliant as she whispered, with faint amusement, "Well, do you want to live forever?"

It broke the tension. He laughed.

Her face was radiant. "I didn't know if I could be with a man, even a few days ago," she confessed huskily. "But I'm almost sure I could be with you. I know I could!"

Now he looked fascinated, too. He studied her in a rapt silence. "To what end, Tippy?" he asked after a minute.

Her mind wasn't working. Her body felt bruised with need. "End?" she said blankly.

His chest rose and fell. "I do not want to get married again," he said flatly. "Period."

Her eyes widened and she realized what she'd been insinuating. She had just enough wit left to spare herself any more embarrassment. "Now, just you wait a minute, buster," she said, "that was not a proposal of marriage. I hardly know you. Can you cook and clean house? Do you know how to keep a checkbook? Can you darn a sock? And what about shopping in the mall? I absolutely could never think seriously about a man who didn't like to shop!"

He blinked twice, deliberately, and twisted his ear. "Could you say that again?" he asked politely. "I think my brain took a brief recess…"

"Besides all that, I have high standards for a prospective husband, and you aren't even in the running yet," she continued, unabashed. "Stop rushing your fences, Grier. You're only on probation here."

His dark eyes twinkled. "Ooookay," he drawled.

She pulled away from him with a toss of her head. "Don't get a swelled head just because I agreed to go out with you. And remember that we have a chaperone, so don't get any ideas."

He began to smile. "Okay."

She frowned. "Do you know any two-syllable words?"

He grinned wickedly and started to speak.

"Don't you dare say it!"

His eyebrows arched.

"I know you don't believe I can read minds, but I just read yours, and if I were your mother, I'd wash your mouth out with soap!"

The reference to his mother wiped the smile off his face and made him introspective.

She grimaced. "Sorry. I'm really sorry. I shouldn't have said that."

He frowned. "Why?"

She avoided his eyes and moved toward a skeleton in a case. "I know about your mother. Crissy told me."

He was utterly silent. "When?"

"After you made me cry," she confessed, not liking the memory. "She told me it wasn't personal, that you just didn't like models. And she told me why."

He rammed his hands deep into the pockets of his slacks. Terrible memories were eating at him.

She turned and looked up at him. "You can't forget it, can you, after all those years? Hatred is an acid, Cash. It eats you up inside. And the only person it hurts is you."

"You'd know," he said curtly.

"Yes, I would," she said, not taking offense. "I know how to hate. I had the living hell beaten out of me, so that I was in such pain that I couldn't even fight back. I was bruised and bleeding, and afterward I was raped over and over again, screaming for help that never came, while my own mother…" She swallowed hard and averted her eyes.

He was sick to his stomach, looking at her, feeling her pain. "Somebody should have killed him," he said in a flat, emotionless tone.

"Our next-door neighbor was a cop," she said huskily. "I've always thought he might be my real father, because he was always looking out for me. He heard the screams and came running—fortunately, it was his night off. He arrested Stanton and my mother and had them both carried off to jail. He took me to juvenile hall himself. He was so kind to me." She swallowed hard. "Everyone was kind. But my mother could talk her way out of murder, and so could Stanton when he really tried. I knew they'd find a way to get me back, and I'd have preferred death. So I sneaked out past a sleeping guard and took off."

"Did they look for you?" he asked.

"Apparently, but Cullen covered my tracks and he had enough money to keep me safe. I was made legally his ward when I was fourteen, and my mother wasn't stupid enough to try to take me away from him. He knew certain people in dangerous professions," she added—with a wry smile at him—because he certainly fitted the category. "He had a friend who used to be big in mob circles, Marcus Carrera. He's legitimate now. He has casinos down in the Bahamas and elsewhere, and he and Cullen were partners in a venture of some sort. He's really reformed in recent years, although his reputation is enough to keep most people from making trouble for him."

"Carrera's not gay. I know him myself," Cash mused. "He's a decent sort, for a former gangster."

"Anyway, Cullen told my mother that if she made any attempt to regain custody of me, he'd have a talk with Marcus. She knew about his reputation. She never tried to get custody of Rory, after that."

"Do you see her?"

She folded her arms across her chest. "No. I don't see her or talk to her, except through my attorney. But the last I heard she was down to her last dime and talking about the tabloids again." She looked up at him. "I'm just starting in a new career. I can't afford to have my name splattered all over in such a way that it would adversely affect my ability to work. Mud sticks. I could lose everything, including Rory, if she started talking about my past. She has nothing to lose."

CHAPTER FOUR

CHAPTER FOUR

"YOU DON'T KNOW ME YET," Cash told her quietly. "But I hope you know that I'd do anything I could for you and Rory. All you have to do is call and ask."

She studied him worriedly. "It wouldn't be fair to involve you," she began.

"I have no family," he said flatly. "Nobody, in all the world."

"But you do," she protested. "I mean, you told me that you have brothers and that your father's still alive…"

His face hardened. "Except for Garon, my oldest brother, I haven't seen my other brothers or my father in years," he replied. "My father and I don't speak."

"And you and your brothers?" she pressed.

His eyes were dark and troubled. "Only Garon," he repeated. "He came to see me a few weeks ago. He did say that the others wanted to bury the hatchet."

"So you're on speaking terms, at least."

"You could call it that."

Her thin brows came together. "You don't forgive people, do you?"

He wouldn't look at her. He wouldn't answer her, either. He turned his attention to the skeleton they were standing in front of.

"She must have been a very special person, your mother," she ventured.

"She was quiet and gentle, shy with strangers. She loved to quilt, crochet and knit." He sounded as if the words were being torn from him. "She wasn't beautiful, or exciting. My father met the junior league model at a cattle show, where they were filming a fashion revue at the same time. He went crazy for her. My mother couldn't compete. He was cruel to her, because she was in his way. She found out that she had cancer, and she didn't tell anybody. She just gave up." His eyes closed. "I stayed with her in the hospital. I wouldn't even go to school, and my father stopped trying to make me. I was holding her hand when she died. I was nine years old."

She didn't even think about other people around them. She turned and put her arms around him, pressing close. "Go ahead," she whispered at his throat. "Tell me."

He hated this weakness. He hated it! But his arms closed around her slender body. The offer of comfort was irresistible. He'd held it inside for so long…

He sighed at her ear, his breath harsh and warm. "He had his mistress at the funeral, at my mother's funeral," he said coldly. "She hated me, and I hated her. She'd conned two of my three brothers, and they were crazy about her and furious with me because I wouldn't let her near me. I saw right through her. I knew she was only after Dad's property and his wealth. So to get even, she threw out all my mother's things and told my father that I'd called her terrible names and that I'd make my father get rid of her."

He drew in a long breath. "The result was predictable, I guess, but I never saw it coming. He sent me away to military school and refused to even let me come home at the holidays until I apologized for being rude to her." He laughed coldly, his arms hurting around her slender body, but she never protested. "Before I left, I told him that I'd hate him until my dying day. And that I'd never set foot in his house again."

"He must have seen through her eventually," she prompted.

His arms loosened, just a little. "When I was twelve," he replied, "he caught her in bed with one of his friends and kicked her out. She sued him for everything he had. That was when she told him that she'd lied about me, to get me out of the way. She laughed about it. She lost the lawsuit, but she'd cost him his oldest son. She rubbed it in, to get even."

"How did you know?"

"He wrote me a letter. I refused to answer his phone calls. He said he was sorry, that he wanted me to come home. That he missed me."

"But you wouldn't go," she guessed, almost to herself.

"No. I wouldn't. I told him I'd never forgive him for what he did to my mother and not to contact me again. I told him if he wouldn't pay to let me stay in the school, I'd work for my keep, but I wasn't going back to live with him." He closed his eyes, remembering the pain and grief and fury he'd felt that day. "So I stayed in military school, made good grades, got promotions. When I graduated, they said he was in the audience, but I never saw him.

"I went right into the army afterward, from one special ops assignment to another. Occasionally I did jobs in concert with other governments. When I got out of the army, I went freelance. I had nothing to live for and nothing to lose, and I got rich." He stiffened. "I didn't need anybody in the old days. I was hard as nails. Funny, nobody tells you that there are things you can't live with, until you've already done them."

Her soft hand reached up to his lean, scarred cheek, and traced it tenderly. "You're still there," she said quietly, and her eyes had an eerie paleness as they met his reluctant ones. "You're trapped in your own past. You can't get out, because you can't let go of the pain and the hatred and the bitterness."

"Can you?" he shot right back. "Can you forgive your attacker?"

She let out a soft breath. "Not yet," she confessed. "But I've tried. And at least I've learned to put it in the back of my mind. For a long time, I hated the whole world and then Rory came to live with me. And I realized that I had to put him first and stop dwelling on the past. I can't let go of it completely, but it's not as much a burden as it was when I was younger."

He traced her eyebrows with a lean forefinger. "I've never spoken of this to anyone. Ever."

"I'm a clam," she replied gently. "At work, I'm everyone's confidant."

"Same here," he confessed with a light smile. "I tell them that governments would topple if I told what I know. Maybe they would, too."

"My secrets aren't that important. Feel better?" she asked, smiling up at him.

He sighed. "In fact, I do," he said, surprised. He chuckled. "Maybe you're a witch," he mused, "putting spells on me."

"I had an uncle who said our family came from Druids in ancient Ireland. Of course, he also said we had relatives who were priests and one who was a horse thief." She laughed. "He hated my mother and tried to get custody of me when I was ten. He died of a heart attack that same year."

"Tough break."

"My life has been one long tough break," she replied. "Sort of like yours. We've both been through the wars and survived."

"You don't have my memories," he said quietly.

"You might think of bad memories like boils," she commented, not totally facetiously. "They get worse until you lance them."

"Not mine, honey."

Her eyebrows lifted. She was fascinated by the endearment, uttered in that soft, deep tone. She colored a little. Odd, because she hated that word when it was tossed around by a parade of would-be lovers who used it like a weapon against her femininity.

He lifted a single eyebrow and looked roguish. "You like that, do you?" he drawled. "And you know that I don't use endearments as a rule, too, don't you?"

She nodded. "I know a lot of things about you that I shouldn't."

His chin lifted and he looked down his long,

straight nose at her. "I only *thought* you were dangerous in Jacobsville. Now I know you are."

She grinned. "Glad you noticed."

He laughed and let her go. "Come on. We're going to qualify as an exhibit if we stand here much longer." He held out his hand.

She cocked her head. "Is that the only body part you're offering me?" she asked; and then colored wildly when she realized what she'd just said.

He burst out laughing, linking her fingers with his. "Don't be pushy," he chided. "We haven't even had a torrid petting session yet."

She cleared her throat. "Don't get your hopes up. I have a prudish nature."

"It won't last long around me."

"I call that conceit."

"You won't when you see me in action," he teased, and his fingers contracted. His voice dropped as he leaned closer. "I know twelve really good positions, and I'm as slow as the blues in bed. If I weren't so modest, I could even give you references. I am a sensual experience that you'd never forget."

"And so modest," she teased.

"A man with my skills can do without modesty," he murmured wickedly.

She wouldn't admit it, but the prospect made her utterly breathless. He saw that in her face. The smile grew broader.

THEY HAD LUNCH in a Japanese restaurant, where Tippy and Rory were fascinated to hear Cash converse fluently with the waiter. He was competent with chopsticks, too.

"I didn't know you spoke Japanese," Tippy exclaimed. "Have you been to Japan?"

"Several times," he replied, lifting a piece of chicken to his mouth with the chopsticks. "I love it there."

"Do you speak any other languages, Cash?" Rory wanted to know.

"About six, I think," he replied lazily. He smiled at the boy's fascination. "If you ever want to get into intelligence work, languages will get you further than a law degree."

"No, you don't," Tippy told Rory when he started to open his mouth. "You're going to get a nice job as a computer technician and get married and have a family."

Rory glared at her. "I'll get married when you do."

Cash chuckled.

"Better yet," Rory added, "I'll get married when *he* does," and he pointed to Cash.

"I wouldn't take that bet," Cash advised Tippy.

"Neither would I," she had to admit.

He glanced at her curiously, but he didn't smile. In fact, he was feeling sensations he'd never experienced in his life, and getting a vicious case of cold feet. This woman made him want things, need things, that he feared more than bullets. He ached to take her to bed, and it was becoming obvious that she would let him. It was a prospect that made his head swim. He could almost picture having that perfect body under his on crisp sheets, feeling her long legs curling around him, her full lips clinging to his mouth. She knew nothing about consensual sex, she'd said, but he could teach her. He had plenty of experience, plenty of skill, and he could introduce her to a veritable feast of physical pleasure. In fact, he was dying to do just that. Could she see it? Did she know?

Her eyes were full of delight in his company. She might be second cousin to a virgin, but she certainly had the intelligence to see desire in a man's face, as well as in his body. Of course she knew. He felt trapped.

He forced himself not to look at her while he tried to decide what to do next. Coming to New York, he told himself angrily, had been a bad idea. He needed to get out, while there was still time.

HIS CHANGE OF ATTITUDE was all too evident to Tippy, who was suddenly very sensitive to nuances of expression in his hard, lean face.

She withdrew as well. She was polite and cheerful, but the same distance that was in Cash now was also in her.

They went back up to her apartment, where a boy

about Rory's age was standing at the door, ringing the bell impatiently. He turned at the approach of the others.

"Hey, Rory! Mom says she'll take us to see that new fantasy flick, and you can spend the night!" He glanced at Tippy and Cash and grimaced. "I guess you won't want to, though, since you've got company…"

"Oh, Cash isn't company, Don, he's family," Rory said without hesitation, completely unaware of the expression on Cash's face. "I'd love to go! Can I, sis?"

Don Hartley and his family lived next door, and they knew about Tippy's troubles with her mother. They'd never let Rory out of their sight.

She hesitated. "Well…" she began.

"I'll bet Cash is dying to take you out somewhere fancy, just the two of you," Rory prompted. "And you won't even have to bribe me!"

Cash burst out laughing. "We could go to the ballet," he said. "I, uh, have tickets. I didn't know if you'd want to go…"

"I love ballet," she said huskily. "I wanted to study it when I was a child, but…I never had the opportunity." She looked back at Don. "Okay, he can go. Just until breakfast, though. I won't get to have him around for very long, because we start shooting again the day after New Year's."

"You're joking!" Cash exclaimed.

"I'm not. The producer told us that his director has

to start shooting a new film in Europe in March, so he's in a hurry to get this one in the can." She sighed.

"You'll get bruised even more," Rory groaned.

She shrugged. "What can I say?" she asked, and then grinned. "I'm a star!"

RORY PACKED an overnight bag and went next door. Cash returned to his hotel to change into a suit, while Tippy went grasping through her entire wardrobe looking for just the right dress. She'd only found it when Cash was at the door again.

She caught her breath at the sight of him in evening clothes, with a spotless white shirt and black tie, finely creased trousers and shoes so polished that they reflected the ceiling. His hair was loose at his neck, slightly wavy and jet-black. He looked devastatingly handsome.

"You're going in a housecoat, then?" he asked, nodding.

She pulled it closer. "I was looking for the right dress."

He checked his watch. "You've got five minutes to find it," he pointed out. "I have reservations at the Bull and Bear for six o'clock."

Her jaw fell. "That's one of the most exclusive restaurants in the city…"

"At the Waldorf-Astoria," he added for her. "I know. The ballet starts at eight. I'm ready. If you're not going in that—" he indicated the ankle-length blue housecoat "—you'd better get cracking."

She left a vapor trail getting into her bedroom.

She wore an off-the-shoulder white velvet dress with a black bow, and topped it with a black velvet coat with a white lining. She left her hair long and used the faintest trace of makeup. She put on diamond earrings and a diamond necklace and bracelet. Without looking again in the mirror, she went out to join Cash.

He was browsing through her bookshelf when he heard the door open. He turned, and his face froze.

She felt suddenly insecure. "Should I wear something else?" she asked nervously.

He just looked at her, his dark eyes narrow and quiet. "I saw a painting in a gallery once," he murmured, moving toward her slowly. "Of a fairy dancing in the moonlight, laughing. You look like her."

"Was she wearing a velvet coat, then?" she asked facetiously.

"I'm not joking." He framed her face in his big hands. "I thought she was the most seductive creature I'd ever seen until right now." His eyes fell to her soft mouth. "You take my breath away…!"

His hard lips settled on her mouth, slowly, gently, so that he didn't frighten her. He drew her against him lazily, not forcefully, and his lips toyed with hers until he felt her tense body relax, until he felt her lips slacken. She took a jerky breath and slowly settled close against his hard chest. Her hands slid up to the nape of his strong neck. He could feel their coldness against his skin.

He lifted his head scant inches so that he could look into her beautiful pale green eyes. She was frightened. But she wasn't fighting to get away. If anything, those eyes were glittery with desire.

"I won't hurt you," he promised quietly.

"I'm not afraid of you," she said breathlessly.

"Are you sure?" he taunted at her mouth. He bit at it in quick, ardent little kisses that had an explosive effect on both of them. He caught her hips suddenly, riveted them to the powerful thrust of his body. She gasped, shivering at the sudden rush of hot pleasure that seethed in her veins at the intimate contact.

"Yes, you know what that is, don't you, baby?" he ground out against her mouth. His hands tightened and his mouth hardened on her lips. "Do you want to feel it inside you?" he whispered at her ear.

"Cash!" She struggled helplessly, really frightened when she couldn't get away.

He realized it, finally, and loosened his grip. "Sorry," he bit off.

She didn't move. Her eyes searched his. "Me, too. I forget…men…lose control," she whispered.

"I don't," he replied curtly. "Not ever. Not until just now."

She stared at him with wide, fascinated eyes. The stark confession should have frightened her. It had the opposite effect. He didn't realize that it made him seem more vulnerable to her. It exorcised her fear in one long sigh.

"It's all right," she whispered, and managed a soft smile. "I'm not frightened anymore."

His fingers teased around her softly rounded chin. They moved to her mouth and toyed with her soft lips. He explored her, his fingers like an artist's brush, touching and tracing…tormenting.

Her body rippled as his arm drew it closer. But her lips lifted and her eyes closed, in blatant invitation.

"You taste like cotton candy, Tippy," he breathed as his mouth settled gently over her parted lips. "I could eat you alive…"

She felt the hardness of his lips brushing at hers, teasing and lifting, searching. She followed them blindly, hanging against him like a dove, living from second to second in his loose embrace. He wasn't threatening. He wasn't frightening. She loved the touch of his body against hers, the clean, crisp scent of his aftershave. She loved the way he held her, with tenderness but also with strength and confidence.

Odd little tremors began to work through her legs, up her spine. She moved closer to Cash, uncertain. Her hands behind his neck began to link. Her body lifted, involuntarily, into closer contact. She would have died to have him.

He felt those responses and lifted his mouth from hers to search her confused eyes. "You want me. I know it, but I won't take advantage. You're safe," he breathed. "It's all right to let go. I won't hurt you. I won't force you. All right?"

She was still uncertain, but she nodded faintly and closed her eyes, waiting.

Her trust in him made his knees weak. He knew instinctively how hard this was for her, to give up control of her body to a man, after what she'd suffered in her youth. He clamped down hard on his own rising desire. He wanted to be tender with her. He wanted her to feel such pleasure that she'd never be able to look at another man as long as she lived…!

His mouth brushed hers softly, and then insistently. He let her responses guide him, drawing back slightly when she stiffened, pressing his advantage when she pushed closer to him. Seconds rushed by in a heated pulse of pleasure that grew and grew.

She moaned softly when his mouth grew hungry on her lips, and her body lifted up against his with real need. He felt the desire funnel up in her, felt her own hunger kindle from contact with his.

Yes, he thought feverishly, she wanted him. Even if she didn't know it yet. He reached around her and lifted her completely off the floor in his embrace, and his mouth became passionate on her soft lips.

She shivered at the need in him that she could feel like a living pulse. His mouth was fierce in its possession of her lips, his body began to tauten. She heard him groan huskily into her mouth as his arms tightened roughly at her back.

She should have been frightened. He might never lose control with another woman, but he was quickly losing it with her. She was flattered at the need she sensed in him. She recalled dazedly what he'd told her once, about it having been a long time between women. He was hungry and she was apparently willing. What if he didn't want to stop? What if he couldn't stop?

He felt her enthusiasm wane and he drew away from her at once, letting her slip back to her feet. He lifted his head, watching her, his face wiped clean of expression. Only his glittery dark eyes were alive in it.

She swallowed hard. "Just checking," she managed weakly.

"To see if I really could stop?" he mused with a smile.

She nodded, embarrassed.

He traced her swollen mouth. "You're not what I expected."

"Neither are you." She hid her face against him for a moment, remembering the blatant question he'd asked her earlier. Even in memory, it aroused her. She thought of feeling him deep inside her body. She shivered with exquisite pleasure. But just as she started to say something equally blatant to him, he drew back.

He bent and kissed the tip of her nose. "We'd better go. We're going to throw everything off schedule."

She looked up at him, hesitating. She felt hot all over, strained, hungry. Her eyes were full of unsatisfied need. "If I asked you…"

"Yes?" he prompted.

She swallowed and forced herself to speak. "If I asked you to make love to me…"

He pressed his thumb against her swollen mouth. His eyes flared. "I want to! You can't imagine how much. But I don't start things I can't finish."

"But I could finish this," she said with painful emphasis. "I could, with you!"

His body actually shuddered. He put her away from him. He didn't dare accept that invitation. He should be shot for what he'd already done and said tonight.

"Well, you're not going to. Not tonight. I offered you dinner and the ballet," he said brusquely, moving to the door. "Only that!" He glanced at her. "Are you coming?"

She felt ashamed that she'd made such a rash offer, and to Cash Grier of all people. She was furious at him for making her feel that way. He'd started it, after all. Throwing his perfect body at her like that and then slapping her down when she got aroused! Were all men like that?

"Dinner and the ballet," she agreed curtly, wrapping her coat around her tightly and buttoning it up to her chin. "And don't worry, I won't try to seduce you in the front seat of the car!"

He glared down at her. "Thanks. I was really worried."

She swept by him in a fury.

They ate without knowing what, and Tippy felt guilty, because it was delicious. They went from the elegant restaurant to the ballet, where she sat beside Cash and never saw what was happening on stage except for noting the beautiful colors and how they reflected on the dancers. She was angry. She was elated. She was eaten up with physical desire that she'd never felt before in her life. She was blinded by her hunger for him. She wanted to jump on him and tear his clothes off where he was sitting. Outraged and mortified by her own helpless urges, she ignored him throughout the performance.

As if he understood completely what she was feeling, he didn't say a word or even touch her until the ballet was over and they were filing out of the theater. He took her arm to help her across the street to the parking garage, but she was like steel to the touch.

He unlocked the door and she got inside, reaching idly for her seat belt. He glanced at her as he started the engine and pulled out of the parking space. He felt remorseful about refusing what she'd offered him. But he was honest. He had nothing to give. Nothing at all. It would have been unfair to take advantage of something she couldn't help. He was flattered that she could feel such attraction for him, but he didn't trust it. He didn't trust her. He was still stunned that he'd spilled his darkest secrets to a woman who was, after all, little more than a stranger. Except that she didn't feel like a stranger. She felt…familiar. Too familiar.

He whipped the car out into traffic with muted violence.

She noticed. She turned her evening bag over in her lap and looked out the window at the crowded streets with their floods of neon lights and glimmering messages on billboards.

"Don't get conceited, Grier," she said sharply. "I'm sure there are at least five or six other men on the planet who could make me feel like ravishing them on the sidewalk."

He made a rough sound in his throat.

She didn't look to see if it was laughter or something else. "Besides, I can always take a cold shower and go in for team sports…"

The car jerked under his hands as he tried to cope with what he was feeling. "Will you give it a rest?"

he asked after a minute. "We both know you'd start screaming the minute I laid hands on you with intent."

She started. "Is that what you think?"

"I've been in law enforcement and the military most of my life," he said, slowing in traffic for a turn. "I know more about rape victims than you do."

She didn't say anything else, but she was watching him, waiting.

He glanced at her as he made the turn. "You may have the best intentions in the world, but it's not going to be that easy for you to be with a man—even a man you think you want. One of the roughest rape cases I ever testified in was a similar circumstance. A young girl who'd been raped tried to make it with her new boyfriend. But she couldn't go through with it and he couldn't stop."

"What happened?"

"She started screaming about the time her parents came home. They had the boy arrested. She tried to recall the charges, but it was too late. He did get probation—it was a first offense—but he never spoke to her again. She really loved him. She just couldn't have sex with him."

She folded her arms together over her coat and shivered.

"You get the picture?" he asked tersely.

She nodded. Her eyes went back to the passing storefronts.

His lips flattened together. "I couldn't live with it if I lost control and forced you, okay?" he admitted finally.

Her caught breath was audible. "But I offered," she said huskily.

He glared at her. "What would that mean if I left you with more scars than you've already got?"

Her anger evaporated and she studied him quietly. "I've never felt like this with anyone since it happened," she confessed. "I was very attracted to Cullen, but he found women repulsive. Even so, it wasn't like this. I'm on fire," she said with a nervous little laugh. "I ache all over. It's almost like pain. All I can think of is how it would feel to be with you in a bed all night."

His hands tightened on the steering wheel until they turned white, while he tried to convince himself that this was a disaster waiting to happen.

"But if you're not interested, you're not interested. I guess you're worried about that marriage thing. I don't have any plans to propose to you, no matter how good you are in bed, if that would change your mind," she promised.

He laughed in spite of himself. "You don't understand."

"You're impotent?" she murmured dryly.

He glared at her. "I am not impotent."

"You're saving yourself for someone you haven't told me about?" she persisted.

"Hell!"

"I'm only trying to explain to you that I want your cooperation in a science project," she continued, unabashed.

"A what?"

"A science project. Anatomy." She grinned.

He was losing ground. This wasn't good. He had to keep his head, because it was a sure bet that she was losing her own.

"I won't even ask you to leave the lights on."

He frowned. "Why would I want them out?"

"Well, a man of your age," she murmured, glancing at her polished nails. "I mean, you might have inhibitions about your body." She peered at him through her lashes.

He felt himself go taut. He wondered if she even realized how arousing this sort of conversation was.

"I have a great body, thanks."

"In that case, we can leave the lights on."

He gave an exasperated sigh as he turned onto her street and pulled up in front of her apartment, with the engine still running. He scowled at her in the glare of the streetlights.

"You want to do it right here, with the engine running?" she exclaimed in a hushed tone, looking around.

"I do not!" he bit off.

"Then, shouldn't we go upstairs?" she prompted.

"I haven't checked door to door, of course, but I'm sure my neighbors are easily shocked."

He met her level stare and tried to weigh the consequences logically. But his mind wasn't cooperating. His body was making it impossible to think at all. Just the sight of her in that white gown, with her bodice plunging and hinting at the beautiful curves underneath made him ache. It had been a long time. Too long. He was ripe for a reckless night in bed. But not with an abused woman who was barely one step removed from virginity.

"Last chance," she said breathlessly, her nails biting into her evening bag as she fought inherent shyness to make the outrageous offer.

He sighed angrily. "Listen…"

She held up a hand. "You're just bristling with excuses," she gleaned. "I'm sorry, but it's no use. You don't want to. Okay. I understand. Thanks for dinner and the ballet. I know it didn't look like it, but I really did enjoy them."

She opened the door and got out, smiling forcefully. "Are you going to be around tomorrow? It's Christmas Eve."

He frowned. "I don't know."

"If you are, I'm having turkey and dressing and all the trimmings," she said.

He was confused and upset. He'd never been in a situation where he was so torn between two alternatives. He'd never wanted a woman so badly, either. But he thought her outlook was overly optimistic. She'd never really dealt with her past.

"Have you even had therapy?" he asked abruptly.

"You think I need therapy because I offered you sex?" she exclaimed.

"Hell!" he burst out. "Can't you be serious for a minute?"

"I've spent my whole adult life being serious, and it's getting me nowhere."

"You need counseling," he insisted.

She glared at him. "I don't need counseling. All I need is…well, never mind what I need. You're not interested."

"You haven't faced your past," he said flatly.

"Oh, yes, I have. Despite what you think, I can live with my past. Can you?"

She turned and started up the steps. She was angry, but her body was still throbbing like a wound. She couldn't quite control that, or her unsatisfied desire. He thought she couldn't function as a woman. She knew she could, with him, at least. But if he wouldn't believe her, there was little hope in showing him.

She paused as she unlocked her front door to look back at him. He was still sitting in the car, scowling, with both windows up and the moon roof closed. The car was still running, too.

She waved and went inside. It was the hardest thing

she'd done in years. She knew she might never see him
again. The funny thing was that she'd been telling the
truth. Her body was throbbing with desire. She wanted
him so much that she was almost shaking with it. Any
other man would have had her in the bedroom before
she could get the whole invitation out. And she had to
run across a man who was too concerned with her
hang-ups to accept a blatant offering!

CHAPTER FIVE

CHAPTER FIVE

CASH WATCHED HER GO in the door with his heart in his throat. That beautiful, desirable woman wanted him. But she was inside, and he was sitting out here in the cold with the engine running. And why? Because he was afraid that once wouldn't be enough. He was afraid that he'd finally met the one woman he couldn't walk away from, and he didn't want to take the chance that lovemaking would lead to obsession. He'd already had a taste of what passed for love in a woman's mind. It had destroyed his life.

But Tippy wasn't just any woman. She had a past of her own to live with. She understood him, perhaps better than anyone else alive. He remembered Christabel Gaines listening to him, sympathizing with him. He'd gotten drunk on her caring kindness.

But it hadn't been love, not on her part. It had been friendship. It wasn't like that with Tippy. She aroused a rage of passion in his body, in his mind, in his heart. He wanted to know how it would be to have her. He ached to know.

While he was trying to convince himself that he should pull the car out into the street and go away, his body was turning off the ignition and opening the door. He was rigid with desire, so tormented that he couldn't think past relief. All his arguments were being consumed in a veritable maelstrom of aroused passion.

He rang the bell without giving himself the opportunity to run for it.

There was an answering buzz. The door was unlocked. He went through it and up the stairs, his heart pounding madly with every quick step. He wouldn't think about tomorrow. Not until he had to.

She was waiting for him at the door when he reached it. She'd taken off the coat, but she was still wearing the shoulderless white velvet dress. Her glorious red-gold hair was around her shoulders, falling in soft waves on her creamy skin. She was breathing quickly, despite the faint trace of fear in her soft eyes that she couldn't contain. Her skin looked like silk.

He moved into the apartment and closed the door. On an afterthought, he reached behind him blindly and threw the lock.

She backed away from him. At first, he thought she was changing her mind. But she was moving toward the bedroom. He followed her slowly, his face giving away his hunger for her.

He followed her into the room and closed that door, locking it, too. He stood and looked at her, vaguely aware of the neat coverlet of the double bed behind her and the closed windows and curtains that flanked it.

She swallowed hard. "The…light," she faltered, flushing, because it was a little embarrassing, despite her bravado earlier.

His eyes narrowed. "Do you want it out?"

She nodded.

"There's something you have to know, before this starts. I don't have anything to use."

Her eyes sought his. "I don't care."

His heart jumped wildly. He thought of Jessamina, Christabel's little girl. He thought of a child. Tippy wasn't refusing him because he hadn't anything to prevent a child. She loved children. He permitted himself to think, for an instant, of a little girl with red hair and green eyes, and his heart began to race.

"We're both insane," he choked.

She nodded slowly, her lips parted huskily. "Turn out the light. Please."

It was the last thing she said.

HE FOUND HER IN THE semidarkness with his hands, and then with his mouth. She melted into him. She felt the zipper in the back of her dress being slowly lowered, and then she felt his hands on her bare skin. She gasped at the incredible sensation it produced.

"Yes," he murmured at her ear. "You feel it, too, don't you? It's like electricity when I touch you. I've never touched skin like yours. It feels like flower petals, warmed by the sun," he whispered huskily. His hands smoothed up her back and then down again, slowly taking the dress and half-slip and panty hose with them. "You aren't wearing much under this," he whispered amusedly.

Her breath was coming in jerks. The touch of his hands made her knees go weak. "You can't wear much under a dress like this," she confessed.

His mouth was working its way down her body, along with his hands. She felt it on her breasts and she shivered.

He paused, his mouth hovering just over a taut nipple. "Frightened?" he whispered softly.

"No!" She jumped when she felt his warm lips open and pull at the nipple. Her hands caught in his thick, dark hair and she moaned.

He laughed gently. "You like that? And we've barely begun."

She didn't understand. Not then. But as he found more and more of her with his mouth, and then with his hands, and the passion began to burn high and bright, the words slowly made sense.

He had all the time in the world. He didn't rush. He lingered over every satin-smooth part of her, exploring, teasing, testing, while she alternately moaned and wept at the rush of sensation that made her boneless and famished. She ached for him. Her body was his. She belonged to him. Every brush of his mouth on forbidden places, every slow movement of his hands was pulsing ecstasy.

He felt her move against him and he smiled at her soft belly, enjoying her responses, her soft cries of pleasure, enjoying the sensation of oneness that it gave him to feel her nudity against his.

She jerked when she felt him against her, but he soothed her and comforted her, his mouth teasing gently at her lips while he moved slowly into intimacy between her long, trembling legs.

"Remember what I asked you?" He eased his mouth between her full lips as he began to penetrate her tenderly. "I asked if you wanted to feel me inside you." He caught his breath harshly. "You do, don't you?" he bit off. His eyes closed. "I want to feel you, too, as close to me…as I can get you!"

"Cash…!" she exclaimed, shivering, and her hands tightened on his muscular upper arms. "You're so big…!"

"Shh," he whispered into her mouth. "We're going

to fit together like two spoons, despite what you're thinking. It isn't going to be stark or violent. I know too much to rush my fences. I won't hurt you, baby. Relax. That's it. Just relax. I'm driving. You're riding. Okay?"

She laughed huskily at the images that flooded her mind. Then he moved slowly, sensuously, and she felt his tender, soft invasion. She started to stiffen, but it wasn't hurting. It wasn't violent. It wasn't even…urgent. It was… Her eyes closed and she began to moan softly as the long, slow movements provoked nerve endings she didn't even know she had into pleasure.

His hands were under her now, one at her neck, the other under her slender hips, lifting her gently into the motion of his body. "That's it," he whispered huskily. "Making love is like singing the blues. The slower it is, the better it is."

He nibbled her upper lip softly while he moved on her, lazily, tenderly. With every soft motion, she felt him deeper in her body, the shocked pulse of pleasure beginning to grow and flare up inside her as her body stretched to accommodate him. She gasped at the heat and power of him.

"I…feel you," she whispered, clinging closer.

"I feel you, too. Silky skin, soft breasts, sweet mouth…I can't get…close enough, Tippy!"

She felt the same way. Her breath whimpered his

name out as the sensations grew more violently pleasurable. She shivered with ecstasy every time he moved. It was incredible!

His mouth covered hers as the movements increased in depth and power. She shivered. It was.... beautiful! She could feel him inside her. She was expanding. He was...potent. She'd never dreamed...!

Her mouth opened under his as her body opened for him. She felt him fill her. She could barely contain him. Stars were flashing behind her closed eyelids as the pleasure became a flame. It was burning her, pulsing, rising, exploding in every cell of her body. She sobbed, her arms frantic as they reached around him. Her legs curled over his powerful thighs, feeling the muscles as he increased the power and rhythm of his slow invasion.

"I...never...knew!" she cried rhythmically. "Please. Please don't stop, don't stop, don't...stop!"

His mouth moved against her throat hungrily. "I can make it even better. Slide your legs inside mine," he bit off breathlessly. "Hurry, baby!"

She didn't understand, until she followed the urgent command. And then her body began to burst with unexpected pleasure. She continued to sob helplessly, her teeth suddenly biting into Cash's muscular shoulder, her body in an arch of pleasure that was surely enough to break bones...

Somewhere in the back of her mind she heard his

voice at her ear, husky and hoarse and fierce, whispering, "Give me a baby, Tippy…!"

She shot off into the sun, shattering with ecstasy, a tiny helpless scream of pleasure ripping from her throat as she went unconscious for a space of seconds. When she regained her ability to think, she heard him groan at her ear and she felt the harsh, helpless shudder of his powerful body above her as he found his own fulfillment. It never seemed to end. She held him, comforted him, while he convulsed in her arms. She kissed him tenderly, her heart full, her body full, belonging as she'd never belonged to anyone in her life.

He collapsed on her finally, his heartbeat shaking her damp body in the darkness. She clung to him with her eyes closed. Don't let it end, she whispered silently. Don't let it end. Don't let it end….

She didn't realize that she was whispering it to him, or that the sound of her husky voice pleading for his body had caused a sudden, impossible arousal.

She'd heard girlfriends talk. She knew that a man's body wasn't capable of what his was already doing. She opened her mouth to tell him, but he was moving on her again. This time, he wasn't slow, or hesitant, or tender.

His hand caught in her hair and his mouth crushed down over hers. His hips pushed down against hers insistently, with a quick, sharp pressure that lifted her sensitized body into sudden, agonizing fulfillment.

She cried out helplessly into his devouring mouth, her legs gripping his hips, her arms holding him furiously against her. He felt her instant satisfaction, but his own came more slowly. He hated her for what was happening to him. He couldn't stop. He couldn't hold back. He was desperate to taste that unbridled ecstasy he'd just had with her. He had to have it again. He had to!

His body riveted hers while his mouth grew even more invasive, more insistent on her mouth. It was taking so long…!

"Slow…down," she whispered into his mouth, her voice tender, breathless. "Slow down. It's all right. It's all right!"

"Damn you…!" he bit off, his voice throbbing with the desire he couldn't hide.

"It's all right," she whispered again. "I want you, too. I want you so much, so badly. Don't rush. Don't resent what you feel. Slow down, Cash. I'll do anything for you. Anything! Tell me what you want."

The ardent little speech made the sense of helplessness go away. He felt more in control. The pace of his lovemaking slowed into tenderness.

"Tell me what to do," she whispered again at his ear, clinging to him. "You can have…anything you want!"

His mouth covered her eyes, her cheekbones, her nose. His breath shook with every kiss. "I've never had it like this," he said harshly.

Her fingers traced his mouth, his chin, his strong neck. "I never knew it could feel like this," she whispered. "I thought it always hurt…."

"Doesn't it?" he murmured at her breasts. "It hurts…so good!"

"Yes!"

He rolled over, holding her above him while his hands guided her hips. He could hardly see her face, but he could feel her faint embarrassment. "Move up a little. That's it…!"

She obeyed him, feeling his body grow even more potent. She groaned.

"What's wrong?" he asked quickly.

"I don't know…anything!" she ground out. "I watch movies, I read books, but I don't know how…!"

"I'll teach you what you need to know," he said huskily, pulling her down to him. "You're perfect just as you are," he added as his mouth found her lips. "The most perfect lover…I've ever had!"

That reminded her that she wasn't the first of them, and she started to speak, but he rolled over again, pinning her, and the pleasure exploded in little bursts. She gasped.

"It's been years," he ground out at her breasts. "And even the best…was nothing compared to this!"

She caught her breath. He meant it. She could tell.

"I want a child," he whispered helplessly as his

body moved into total possession. "Oh, God, Tippy…I want a…child!"

She went under like a drowning swimmer. She heard him whispering urgently as the pleasure began to seep into her, her body following him mindlessly as he positioned her, taught her how to touch him, how to take him. It was the most beautiful few minutes of her entire life. Right up until the last helpless little shudder of fulfillment, she never thought she could live through it…

TIPPY WAS VAGUELY AWARE that he was dressing. She heard the movement of clothing on skin. She blinked. It wasn't morning. She looked at the clock. It had big numbers so that she could see it without her glasses. It was four in the morning.

"You're leaving?" she asked blankly.

He didn't answer. He finished dressing and sat down in the armchair beside the bed to put on his shoes.

"But…it isn't even dawn," she persisted.

He still didn't answer her.

She heard him stand up. The bedroom door opened, letting in light from the living room that they hadn't stopped to turn off when they first came home. He turned and looked at her in the light, at her creamy skin over the blue and pink floral sheet she held to her breasts. She looked…loved.

His face was hard, devoid of feeling.

"Can't you say something?" she asked, insecure and trying to hide it.

"We were both irresponsible," he bit off. "This was stupid. But you started it."

She sighed. "Oh, Lord, it's the hair shirt and the flail," she murmured, throwing herself onto her back.

He couldn't believe he'd heard her say that. He glowered at her. "I am not marrying you!" he continued angrily. "But if there's a child, I'll be responsible for it. And I'll want to know!"

She stretched, drawing the sheet deliberately down to her waist so that the rosy tips of her breasts were visible. She knew he was looking at them. It made her feel odd. Sensuous. All woman. She'd never felt like that in her life. She felt as if she belonged to someone, for the first time in her life. She smiled to herself. "Will you, really?" she murmured, glancing at his set features.

He couldn't help looking at her. He drew in a harsh breath. "You have the most beautiful breasts I've ever seen," he said involuntarily.

She kicked off the covers and arched up to give him a better view. "How about the rest of me?" she asked huskily.

"I'll die trying to forget." He turned away again.

"Why do you have to?" she asked. "I haven't asked you for a single thing."

His eyes closed. "I don't want ties," he said harshly.

"Fine. Don't expect me to buy you one for Christmas."

He glanced at her and bit off a laugh. "Damn it!"

She stretched lazily. "Wouldn't you like to stay until dawn?" she asked.

"It wouldn't do any good if I did. I'm wasted. And I imagine you are, too."

She sighed. "A little."

His eyes were involuntarily possessive.

"All my friends have lovers, and they say that no man can do it two times in a row," she remarked.

One eyebrow rose. "They're right."

She stared at him.

He shrugged. "Abstinence," he said stubbornly.

She kept staring at him.

He cleared his throat. "Abstinence and the right woman."

Both eyebrows went up.

"What do you want from me?" he asked quietly.

That put things in perspective, because he had suspicion written all over him.

"I have money in the bank," she pointed out, pulling the cover back over her slender body. "I don't have lovers. Except this once, of course. I don't need a cook or a bodyguard. Draw your own conclusions."

He'd been fielding women for years because he was rich and it usually showed. It did here. But Tippy was right, she had money and fame—although in her line of work there was no such thing as job security. She had no reason to want him. Except for himself. Or for sex, he amended, recalling that she'd never made it with a man of her own volition. Was that the draw? First time euphoria?

"That's it, of course," she said, as if she could see into his mind. "You're my first real lover and I'm overwhelmed by how good it was. So naturally I'm panting to keep you around as long as I can."

He glared at her. "Stop that. I don't like people reading my mind."

She shrugged. "Okay."

"And this was a one-night stand. Period."

"Then why did you want me to get pregnant?" she asked reasonably.

His eyes widened. He hadn't realized… He really glared now. "Men say all sorts of things to women to arouse them!"

"Ah. So that was it." She nodded. "Nice touch. It really raised the threshold."

"I'm leaving," he said coldly.

"I noticed."

"I'm going home."

"I'll send you a Christmas card."

"There isn't time. It's day after tomorrow."

"In that case, Merry Christmas."

"Yeah. You, too."

"Are you going to say goodbye to Rory?" she asked.

His hand hesitated on the doorknob. He hadn't thought about Rory. The boy was looking forward to Christmas Eve with him.

"We can be civil to each other for one meal. For Rory's sake," she said. She smiled. "I promise not to bend you back over the dining-room table and have you in the mashed potatoes and corn-bread stuffing. If that helps."

He wanted to yell. He wanted to laugh. He didn't know what the hell he wanted. "I'm leaving."

"You said that," she said, unspeakably delighted. He was confused, overwhelmed, totally at sea, and she knew why. He felt something for her. Something powerful. Now he was going to fight it to the bitter end. But somehow she felt an optimism that she couldn't explain.

"I'll be back for lunch," he said finally. "Just for lunch. I'll be packed and ready to leave town after."

"Okay."

He hesitated. He looked back at her with dark, quiet eyes. "I didn't hurt you?"

"Of course not," she said softly.

He sighed. Some of the anger drained out of him as he looked at her in the pale light. "Even at the last? I was rough. I didn't mean to be."

"I know that. I wasn't afraid. It was glorious!" She managed to smile. "I never thought…" She shrugged. "It was…almost unbearable."

He nodded. "For me, too." His eyes narrowed as he studied her. "But it was still irresponsible. I should have used something."

"I'll remind you next time," she promised.

The glare was back. "I've told you, there isn't going to be a next time!"

"That's what you said this time."

"I'm really leaving."

"Don't speed," she chided.

He gave her a cold glare and slammed out of the apartment. Below, she heard the roar of a wildcat and the furious acceleration out of the parking spot. No wonder they called them Jaguars, she thought, wincing at the screeching tires.

TIPPY DANCED AROUND the apartment, cleaning and polishing and cooking, feeling happier than she'd ever been before. She was crazy about Cash. She couldn't get the forbidden images out of her mind as she relived over and over again the feverish pleasure of his body against hers in bed.

Hiding it from Rory was difficult. He wouldn't understand what was going on. Or he might. But she didn't want Cash to become lessened in the boy's eyes. She didn't want him to think that Cash had taken advantage of her, or hurt her.

"You're cheerful today," Rory commented when she took the turkey out of the oven.

"I feel good," she mused.

"Nice date last night, huh?" he murmured, his eyes twinkling.

"Nice," she agreed.

"We heard some maniac drive off about dawn," he mumbled without looking at her. "There are some pretty bad tire tracks in front of the apartment."

"Cash and I had a…disagreement," she said without meeting his eyes. "Just a little one. He's still coming to dinner today."

"Sis, he's not exactly what he seems," Rory said, solemnly for a nine-year-old. "He's had some really hard knocks and he has no close friends at all."

"Your commandant knows him. I forgot."

Rory nodded. "I'm crazy about Cash. But I don't want you to get hurt."

He was saying things she'd only thought. Hearing them made her stiffen. She was living in a fool's paradise. She'd seduced Cash, she was daydreaming about happily ever after. And her nine-year-old brother knew what was going on better than she did. Was she actually thinking that an outcast who'd lived an outcast, dangerous life would rush to get involved with a woman? Especially after a disastrous marriage that had left mental scars he was still carrying?

Cash wasn't thinking about happy ever after. He'd even said so. He hadn't wanted to touch her in the first place. She'd played on his weakness and his need. She'd led him right to her bed and he hadn't been able to resist. But that didn't mean he loved her. Not even that impassioned husky plea for a child meant love. It meant that he was lonely and jealous of Judd Dunn and hungry for a child. But…what if he was hungry for Christabel's child? Did he still love her? Had he submitted to Tippy's advances out of rejected desire for a woman he couldn't have?

The whole face of things changed in an instant. She went cold. All the joy drained out of her like rain out of clouds.

Rory actually winced. "I'm sorry," he said. He went to her and hugged her, as hard as he could. "I'm sorry!"

Tears stung her eyes. She was too proud to shed them. She held her little brother close and felt cheated. Absolutely cheated.

"We're going to have a great Christmas," she said after a minute, wiping away the tears unobtrusively to smile down at him. "You want to cook the biscuits?"

"You want to be able to eat them?" he shot back.

She laughed. She and Rory had always been a great combination, even from the age he'd been when she'd acquired him from her mother.

"That settles who cooks, I guess. If Cash shows up while I'm in the kitchen, you can entertain him."

He gave her a wry look and wiggled both eyebrows. "That's my department, all right. Let's see if I can find my juggling balls and my top hat…"

She tossed a dishrag in his general direction as she turned to get out flour and olive oil and milk. When she was alone, her face fell. She had no idea if Cash would even show up, after all, despite his affection for Rory. The prior evening had been an unmitigated disaster and it was totally her fault. If she hadn't put Cash in a position where he had to do something about their mutual physical attraction, they might still be friends. And from there, she might have captivated him for real. Now her dreams of happiness had boiled down into a furtive night of passion, which Cash with his greater experience would dismiss as he'd said he would—a one-night stand.

If only, she thought, she could go back and undo the major mistakes of her life. But the only way open was the future.

CASH DID SHOW UP, just as Tippy was chewing off her nails with everything already on the table.

Her heart skipped as the buzzer sounded. Rory ran to see who it was, and Cash answered.

"I'll buzz you right in!" Rory enthused, pushing the button.

Tippy was wearing a simple pair of emerald velvet slacks with a white silk top, her hair tied back with an emerald green scarf. She looked festive, but casual. She didn't expect that Cash would dress up.

And she was right. He was wearing black again—

slacks, T-shirt and leather jacket. He looked at her without seeing her, and forced a smile for Rory's benefit.

"It looks great," he said.

"It's nothing fancy, just plain food. Sit down. Rory, say grace," she murmured quickly, taking her place.

Rory did, glancing furtively from one adult to the other with a long sigh.

It was a quiet meal, compared to the ones that had gone before. Tippy felt terrible, because she'd ruined not only her Christmas and Cash's, but Rory's as well. They ate in a long silence until everyone was finished.

"I offered to make the biscuits," Rory told Cash, "but she said she wanted to be able to eat them afterward."

Cash chuckled. "Are you that bad a cook?"

"Not with most things," Rory said. "But I have a hard time with bread."

"Me, too," Cash confessed. "I used to make a passable biscuit, but these days I just buy them in tins and heat them up."

"Tippy doesn't. She does them from scratch."

"A woman of talent," Cash said without looking at her.

It was a good thing. She went scarlet and jumped up to get the cherry pie she'd made and open a small pint of vanilla ice cream to top it with.

Her hands shook. Cash saw it and cursed himself

for losing his head the night before. She was taking the blame for everything, when it was his own damned fault.

She fixed three bowls of dessert and passed them out with a frozen smile. "This is a bake and serve pie. I didn't have time to do one from scratch, but these are pretty good."

"Everything was good, Tippy," Cash said, his voice deep and apologetic.

She didn't look at him. "I'm glad you liked it."

He ate his pie, feeling two inches tall. She was going to blame herself for everything. After he left, it would be even worse. She'd convince herself that she was little better than a call girl, and she wouldn't go near him again.

He blinked, amazed that he knew her that well. He'd accused her of reading his mind, but he could see right into her own. It was eerie. It was as if they were…connected.

"This is really good, Tippy," Rory said. "Want me to wash up?"

"I don't mind," she said at once.

"Let Rory do it. I want to talk to you," Cash said firmly, getting to his feet.

"I really should—" she protested.

He caught her hand and pulled her into the living room, out of sight of the kitchen. He looked down at her solemnly.

"Nobody's to blame," he said firmly. "It just happened. Don't beat yourself to death over it. Whatever happens, I'll handle it."

She swallowed and then swallowed again. She couldn't look at him without hearing his voice, husky and deep at her ear, while he whispered to her in the darkness.

He framed her face in his hands and forced it up to his searching eyes. He winced when he saw her eyes.

"Let me go, please," she whispered, tugging away from him. "I'm not a child. You don't have to worry that I'll…that I'll chase you, or anything."

He felt sick to his stomach. He'd done untold damage, much worse than he'd suspected. "I never would have thought that."

She moved back, forcing a smile. "I hope you have a good trip home. Please tell Judd and Christabel hello for me. I expect she's very happy now, with a husband who wants her and two little babies to look after. She's going to make a wonderful mother."

"Yes, she is," he said, and he couldn't help the tenderness in his voice. Christabel had been special to him.

Tippy knew that, and she was jealous. She hated herself for it.

She glanced up at him and away. "Well, I'll just go and help Rory with the dishes. I'll send him out to say goodbye first. Thanks for bringing him home. And for taking me out on the town."

He was angry now, and it showed. His eyes were blazing. He hated being in this position. He didn't know what to do or say that wouldn't make things even worse, and that infuriated him.

Before he could think of anything, she was gone and Rory was standing in her place, looking curiously at Cash.

"I wish you could stay longer," he told the tall man. "It's the best Christmas I ever had."

Cash was touched. He was already fond of the boy. He held out his hand and shook Rory's firmly. "If you ever need me, Tippy has my number. Or if she's not around, just call the Jacobsville Police Department and somebody will find me. Okay?"

Rory smiled at him. "I won't need you. But thanks, Cash."

"You never know." He glanced toward the kitchen. "Take care of her. She's a lot more fragile than she looks."

"She's okay," Rory said. "It's just that nobody ever paid her much attention except if they wanted something from her. It's natural that she might go a little overboard because a man liked her for herself, you know?" He grimaced. "I'm messing it up again. I don't know how to put it into words…"

"I understand what you mean, Rory," he said and laid a big hand on the boy's shoulder. "She'll get over it."

"Sure she will."

Neither of them believed it, of course.

"Take care of yourself. I'll see you again," Cash promised.

Rory grinned at him. "You, too. Stay out of fights."

Cash's eyebrows raised. "I will if you will."

Rory smiled self-consciously. "I'll do my best."

"And so will I. See you."

"Sure. See you."

"Goodbye, Tippy," Cash called from the front door.

"Have a safe trip," she called back, and said nothing else.

Cash opened the door and went through it. When it closed, he felt as if he'd left part of himself inside.

CHAPTER SIX

CHAPTER SIX

TIPPY FELT HEARTSICK after Cash left. She missed him and she hadn't really known him long enough to feel that deeply. But they'd skipped a few steps along the way. Her heartbeat accelerated every time she thought of his handsome face. She wondered how she was going to live without him in her life.

Rory went back to school after the first of the year and Tippy resumed work on the film. She began having some odd bouts of illness, and when she consulted her pocket calendar, the one she circled for her periods, she noticed that her long night with Cash had been at the worst possible time. More than that, her period was late. And it was never late, despite the very physical challenge of her job.

She worried about the stunts she was required to

do. Didn't they say that it was dangerous to do physical labor during the first trimester? Or was that just
an old wive's tale?

A month after Cash's departure, she bought a
home pregnancy kit and used it. The results were predictable, and vaguely terrifying. She couldn't call
Cash and destroy his life. She already felt protective
of the tiny life inside her.

She was going to have a baby. Would it look like
her, or like Cash? she wondered dreamily. Or would
it look like some ancestor neither of them even remembered? She thought of diapers and formula and
two-o'clock morning feedings with pure delight.
Rory would love having a niece or nephew.

But she'd have to quit work. Not at once, but
when she started showing. It was no big thing for a
Hollywood star to have a child out of wedlock. But
it was for Tippy. It would give her mother a weapon
to use against her. Despite her own murky past, she
could go to the tabloids and say that Tippy slept
around and wasn't a good guardian for her little
brother.

There was another consideration. Cash didn't
want marriage. He was adamant about being a
loner. He'd meant their encounter to be a one-night
affair, despite his hunger for a child. It had probably been just as he said, something to bring the heat
up between them. Men did say things in passion

that they didn't mean. Tippy had heard other women talk about it, even if she didn't know from her own experience.

Her problem was what to do about it. She couldn't hide it for forever. At some point, she'd have to see a doctor. There were vitamins that a pregnant woman had to have. She'd have to eat properly as well—something else that would impact her career. She wasn't allowed to gain more than five pounds during the filming of the movie, and that was written into her contract. She needed the money so badly, for Rory's school tuition and her own rent and utilities and food bills. She couldn't afford to lose her job.

But she wanted her child, just as much. She sat in the evenings after work and fantasized about it. She would have someone of her very own, someone of her own flesh and blood and bone to belong to. She would be a mother. It was an awesome responsibility. It was a heady joy as well. She patted her flat stomach gently and thought about the day when she would hold her child in her arms. She sighed, closing her eyes on dreams.

THE REALITY WAS A LITTLE LESS euphoric. The second assistant director, a gung ho young man named Ben, took over while the first assistant director took a break to handle a personal problem. Ben insisted that she run the length of a board between two buildings and land with a breakfall on the roof of the location set in Manhattan. There was a drop, not a big one, and the chances were slim that she'd fall. Still, she put a protective hand over her flat belly, feeling it was too risky.

"I can't do this," she said firmly.

"You make the jump or you're out of work," Ben said coldly.

"I'm pregnant," she began. "Hire a stunt double."

"No dice! I'm already over budget and my job's on the line. I'm not paying for a stunt double, and there's no need for one. The jump is perfectly safe."

"Can you guarantee that no harm will come to me or my baby?"

"How many times do I have to say it? You'll be fine!" he snapped.

"Well if you're absolutely positive…" Still she made her position clear. "If this jeopardizes my pregnancy you'll grow old paying for it. That's a promise!" she warned.

"Yeah, yeah, like you have any pull with my boss, when he's directing A-list actors!" he retorted. "Get to it!"

She went back to the scene, her mind far removed from the hustle and bustle of the set, from cameramen and sound men and makeup technicians and the location manager. All she could think about was what she had to lose if anything went wrong. Cash didn't even know. She was going to have to tell him, and speak to Joel Harper about this arrogant little ape who'd caged a job with him.

For the meantime, she resolved herself to finish the scene. She closed her eyes, said a small prayer, and made the running jump. She misjudged the distance without her glasses and went down. The fall left her in a tumbled heap with a terrible pain in her stomach. She screamed.

SHE WAS AMBULATORY, but Joel Harper, just arrived on the scene in time to find her bent over double, called for an ambulance at once. They rushed her to the emergency room while Ben tried to explain his actions to Joel, who was calling him names in a steady unprintable stream all the way to the hospital.

"She was pregnant, you idiot, why do you think I've been so careful with her for the past week?" Joel demanded. "If she loses the baby, she can sue us for every damned dime I have, and collect. And she'd be within her rights! Damn you!"

"But, sir…" Ben protested, white-faced.

"You're off the picture," Joel told him icily. "And you'll never work on another film of mine! Get out of my sight!"

Ben walked away cursing his own fate. But he didn't leave. He stood nearby, waiting for word of Tippy's condition.

Joel Harper waited patiently until the doctor came out to speak to him.

"Is she married?" the doctor asked.

"No," Joel said. "She has a young brother…"

"She lost the baby," the doctor said curtly. "She was six weeks along, by the look of it. She's inconsolable. I had to sedate her."

Joel was shattered. He looked at Ben, who'd heard every word and was looking shaky. "You son of a bitch," Joel said, enunciating every word as he went for the younger man and grabbed him by the collar. "She lost her baby because you forced her to do a stunt she should never have had to do in the first place!"

"She volunteered to do it!" Ben lied. "I didn't force her! She didn't care about the baby!"

"In a pig's eye!"

Ben saw the intent in the older man's face. He cut his losses. He turned and ran. Neither man noticed the man standing nearby with a pad and pen, who started scribbling excitedly and jerked out a cell phone. A reporter for one of the bigger tabloids had followed a wounded prison escapee and his captors into the emergency room in hopes of a scoop. But now he had something better. Much better.

"Give me the rewrite desk," he said. "Harry? Take this down. Tippy Moore, goddess of models, sacrificed her baby today for the sake of a movie contract…!"

THE TABLOIDS SOLD IN EVERY grocery store in the country. Even in Jacobsville, Texas. Cash Grier had stopped by the local Jensen Supermarket to pick up some eggs for an omelet after his duty shift. The tabloid carried a photo of Tippy Moore at her most glamorous with a headline in red ink denouncing the career-minded model for sacrificing a baby on the altar of selfishness.

Cash almost choked. Tippy had been pregnant, and the child was almost certainly his. She'd been just at six weeks, the tabloid read, and it had been that long since Christmas Eve.

"Terrible, ain't it?" an older woman said, noticing his fascination with the headline. "She was here making some movie last year. Pretty little thing. I guess women these days don't care much for home and family. Poor little baby. But maybe it's better off. I mean, what sort of mother would a woman like that make?"

Cash hardly heard her. He paid for his eggs, white-faced, and went home. He didn't turn on the television or the lights. He sat there in the dark while history repeated itself.

TIPPY WAS SO BROKEN UP over her miscarriage that she couldn't cope with going back to work, even though she was out of the hospital in less than twenty-four hours, with no other physical damage. Joel Harper postponed the additional scenes until she could return, hiring a stunt double and apologizing daily for his assistant director's incompetence. He'd filed a complaint against the man himself, and he'd badgered Tippy to get an attorney and file suit.

But Tippy didn't care. She was inconsolable. She couldn't even call Cash and tell him how sick she was about the loss. He'd have seen the tabloids by now. He'd think she did it deliberately, just as his ex-wife had done it deliberately. He'd think she didn't want his child. Maybe even that she was getting even for having him walk out on her. She wasn't. She'd wanted the child, so badly.

In the end, Joel Harper was so concerned that he called the commandant at Rory's military school and explained the situation to him. The commandant put Rory on the first plane for Newark on Saturday, at Joel's expense, and Joel met him at the airport.

"How is she?" Rory asked at once.

"Have you read the tabloids?" Joel replied as he escorted the boy to a black stretch limo waiting outside in the parking lot.

"Yes," Rory said glumly. "Actually, I should say, they've been read to me by the other boys."

Joel grimaced. "I wouldn't have asked you to come, Rory, but she's not herself."

"I know that," Rory told him. "My tenth birthday was yesterday, and she didn't phone me. That's not like her. She always sends me something, and she always calls."

Joel sighed as he put the boy into the limo. "She's still in depression and she can't snap out of it, even to work. She needs someone with her."

Rory was trying to be stiff-lipped, but tears brightened his eyes.

"You know who the father is, don't you, Rory?" Joel asked. "Do you think he'd come to see about her?"

"Maybe," Rory said. "But I want to talk to her first, before I call him."

Joel was amazed at the sensibility of the young man, who seemed so mature for his age. "Okay," he agreed. "We'll wait."

Tippy had been sitting around in a T-shirt and sweatpants in her apartment, watching an old movie. But she stood up at once when she heard Rory's voice, and ran to the buzzer to let him in. She held out her arms when he reached the door. She cried like a child, while Rory patted her back and tried to sound comforting. Joel paused long enough to say hello, and then he left, promising to return the next afternoon to put Rory on a plane back to Maryland.

Rory sat down on the sofa beside his sister, worried now that he could see how haggard and strained she looked. Her eyes were so full of pain that he could hardly bear to look into them.

"Joel wants me to call Cash," he began slowly.

"No!"

"But, sis—" he pleaded.

She cut him off. "Listen to me. Promise me you won't get in touch with him. Promise me!"

"But it's in all the tabloids," he protested. "He's going to know already…"

"Rory, this will be hard for you to understand," she said huskily, "but he was married and his wife…got rid of their child. He's never gotten over it. He doesn't want to get married again, and he doesn't really want a child. But he'll blame me for losing it, just the same. He'll…hate me." She closed her eyes on a wave of pain. "I wanted my baby. I wanted him, so much! Cash will never believe it. He'll hate me forever, Rory, because I didn't refuse to do the scene. He'll think I did it deliberately, don't you see? We can't call him. It would only make things worse. I expect he's hurting, too, now that he knows, even more than me." She sighed. "We can't hurt him anymore."

Rory didn't think Cash would blame her. The man he'd briefly gotten to know was bigger than that. Of course he was.

So it came as a shock that Cash refused to speak to him when he called the Jacobsville Police Station while Tippy was in the shower. Rory hung up, feeling alone and scared. He never said a word to Tippy about the phone call.

CASH WAS BACK AT WORK after a day's absence at home just after he read the tabloid account. He seemed not to be fazed by it all, but he was suddenly quick-tempered and hard to talk to. Not that anybody knew why. They didn't know that he was the father of Tippy Moore's child.

Judd Dunn suspected, of course. But he didn't want to risk a knock-down-drag-out fight with Cash by asking him.

Just the same, he was surprised days later when he overheard one of the men telling someone that Cash had left orders not to put through any calls from anyone named Danbury.

Danbury was Tippy's real last name. She'd told Judd, when she was making the movie out at the ranch he shared with his wife Christabel.

"Who was that?" Judd asked, concerned.

The officer shrugged. "Some kid named Danbury."

"Did Cash tell you not to accept calls from kids, too?"

The officer glared up at him. "If you want to tell him and risk having him put a fist through your nose, go ahead. He's already had one bite of me today, and I'm covering my rear!"

Judd walked into Cash's office without knocking and studied the older man quietly before he spoke.

"You look white in the face," Judd told him.

Cash didn't look up. "I'm busy."

Judd closed the door and perched himself on the

corner of the desk. "She wouldn't have done it deliberately."

Cash's eyes were terrible. "Why not? My ex-wife did!"

Judd's surprise widened his eyes.

"Women don't want babies, they're too damned much trouble. They want careers!"

"Sure," Judd said, losing his temper. "That's why Tippy took her little brother in and raised him."

Cash stared at him without speaking. But something touched his face.

"It's not the boy's fault, whether or not she's responsible," Judd said coldly. He stood up. "You shouldn't take it out on him."

"I haven't said a thing to him," Cash said defensively.

Judd scoffed. "Your desk sergeant just hung up on him and said you told him to," he said, nodding at the dismay on Cash's face. "Try calling him back, why don't you, and see if he'll listen to you. If he called you, it can only be because he's worried about his sister." He glared at his friend. "I guess she got pregnant all by herself."

He turned and strode angrily out the door. Cash felt sick at his stomach. It had been a shock to learn that Tippy was pregnant and hadn't told him. He'd had to read about it in the tabloids. It had been a bigger shock to read about her deliberate stunt work leading to the miscarriage. He'd told her that he'd take responsibility for anything that happened, but she hadn't even called him.

And why would she, he asked himself miserably, when he'd done everything in the world to make her think he didn't want either her or a child. He couldn't have made his distaste for their intimacy more evident. Tippy had low esteem already, and his attitude hadn't helped. Rory must have been worried to take a chance on calling him at work. Apparently Rory wasn't angry, and certainly he suspected that the baby's father was Cash.

But his helpful colleague out there, put off by Cash's ongoing bad mood, had told Rory that Cash wasn't accepting any phone calls from him. So now Rory would think Cash had deserted him, too.

He didn't even bother phoning back. He didn't want to talk to Tippy, or about her, not just yet; not until he could come to terms with his horror at what she'd done. He knew her career was important to her. He hadn't realized that it was the most important thing in the world.

Now that he knew, he could stop hating himself for what had happened. He'd actually thought about going back to her a time or two, of trying to make a relationship work between them. But it had come to nothing. He couldn't force himself to take a chance. Maybe that was a good thing, considering how it had worked out. She obviously placed her career before any relationship, even before a child. It was graphic proof that she didn't want anything more to do with Cash Grier.

IT TOOK A COUPLE OF WEEKS for Tippy to get herself back in any sort of shape to go to work. She was drinking, for the first time in her adult life, to stop the memories and the pain. She was hiding it from the people she worked with—and from Rory. She hadn't seen him since the weekend Joel had brought him to see her. He'd finally confessed that he tried to call Cash and that Cash had told his men that he wasn't speaking to anybody named Danbury. Tippy was even more depressed after that.

Her mother had read the tabloids and phoned her at once, just after Rory's visit. "Now you're going to see what I can do," she told Tippy, slurring her words—obviously she was using again. She never seemed to stop. "I'm going to get my son back, or you're going to pay through the nose to keep him!"

"I'm between jobs," Tippy lied. "I don't have any money. You'll have to wait until I get a royalty check from the first movie."

"Which will be when?"

"I don't know. Next year."

"No good. I need money now. You listen to me, girl, I'm not going to sit down here in Georgia starving while you ride around in limousines and eat at fancy restaurants! I deserve something for all the hell you put me through, you and that little brat!"

Tippy clenched her hand on the phone. "You deserve to burn in hell, you witch!" she raged. "You did nothing for either of us but help your sick boyfriend abuse us."

Her mother laughed. "I was just helping you grow up," she drawled. "You'd have gotten to like it eventually."

"I'd have killed you both, eventually," Tippy said coldly. "Sam's a loser, just like you."

"You've got money and we need some. You give it to us, girl, I'm warning you, I'll do something desperate!"

"Why don't you go to the tabloids and tell them how your boyfriend raped me when I was twelve years old?" Tippy asked harshly. "Maybe I'll tell them myself!"

There was a pause, as if the other woman was trying to think through a fog of drugs. "You were older than that…."

"I was not," Tippy choked.

"I want some money!" came the harsh reply. "I shouldn't have to work, when you're rich! You owe me. I gave you that boy!"

"You sold him to me for fifty thousand dollars!" Tippy screamed into the receiver.

"That was just a down payment. I want more. I

need money. You don't know what it's like," she rambled drunkenly. "I got to have it. I got to. You better send me some money, or I'll tell Sam to get it however he can. Sam's got connections in Manhattan. He can make a lot of trouble for you. You'll see."

"You miserable excuse for a human being," Tippy said under her breath. "How can you live with what you are?"

"You just send me a check, or else." The line went dead.

Tippy had been furious for days after that phone call. What must it be like to have a parent love you, want you, protect you, she wondered. Surely in the world there were good women. She only wished there had been one, just one, in her life.

Now her mother wanted more money and she didn't have any to spare. She was out of work, and no paycheck would be coming in until she went back on the job. But in the meantime, she didn't have enough for Rory's tuition or money to pay rent and utilities.

She began to laugh hysterically. She was going to starve and Rory would end up in a foster home, while her mother went running to the tabloids to tell everyone on earth how her ungrateful daughter was mistreating her.

She took a whiskey bottle out of the cabinet and filled a tea glass with it. It was the weekend. She wasn't working and she could do what she pleased, she told herself. If she was going to lose everything, maybe she could numb the hurt just a little…

SPRING BREAK CAME IN EARLY April. Tippy had pawned some of her jewelry to pay Rory's fees through until the summer, and he came home on the train to spend his week off with her. But it was a changed Tippy who met him at the station.

She was thin as a reed and shaky. She smiled and hugged him, but her eyes were blank and there were deep, dark shadows underneath them. She looked like the walking dead.

"Are you back to work?" he asked worriedly.

She nodded. "We finish up next week," she said dully. "Joel got me a stunt double. Too little too late." She laughed huskily. "Well, what the hell. Better late than never!"

"Tippy, are you okay?" he asked.

"Of course I am!" she said enthusiastically. "We're going to have a great time together. I made a cake with a happy face on it."

"I'm just a little bit too old for happy cakes," he ventured.

"Nonsense. We're going to have fun. We'll be just like a…like a family." She swayed a little on the way to the cab.

"You've been drinking!" he accused softly, and

with evident surprise. "Tippy, you know you shouldn't drink. Look at our mother!"

That comment made her uneasy, but she laughed it off.

"There's a tendency toward alcoholism," he pointed out.

She laughed again, this time a little wildly. "Rory, I just had a couple of drinks to unwind, for God's sake. Don't start lecturing me." She hugged him. "There's my sweet boy… I'm glad you're home."

"Me, too," he said. But he didn't smile.

There was a phone call on Rory's first night home. He answered it and the caller hung up at once. Tippy had Caller ID, but the number had been blocked. It might have been Cash, he thought optimistically. He hadn't tried to call the man back, but perhaps Cash had been thinking about them and decided to check on them.

"Have you heard from Cash?" he asked her abruptly.

Her face closed up. "I have not!" she said angrily. "And I do not want to hear from him! If he'd given a damn about me, he'd have called here weeks ago!"

"You haven't phoned him?"

She glared at him. "Why would I want to? He hates me."

"You don't know that."

"Yes, I do," she said with utter certainty. She

poured a little whiskey into a glass and tossed it back. "And I don't care."

But she did. It was killing her. Rory winced at the look on her face, at the thinness of her body. He wished he were older, that he knew what to do. But he had no idea.

She had another drink and just as she did, there was a knock on the door.

Rory answered it. His friend Don was there, looking puzzled. "Rory, we just came back from the store, and there's a guy waiting downstairs who says he knows you. He wants you to come down and talk to him."

"Cash!" Rory exclaimed. "Is it Cash?"

The boy shrugged. "I couldn't tell. I only saw your sister's friend once. This guy had a hat pulled down over his eyes and he's wearing a long coat…"

"It must be Cash!" Rory said excitedly. "I'll go down and meet him. Don't tell my sister, okay?" he added quickly.

"Whatever you say. Want to come over and go to the ice rink with me and mom tomorrow?"

"We'll see. Thanks, Don!"

"No problem."

Rory paused at the door. "I'm going next door for a minute," he called to Tippy. "Be right back!"

"Okay. Don't go off anywhere without telling

me!" she called after him, belatedly remembering her
mother's threat of trouble.

"I won't."

He closed the door and went down the stairs.

AN HOUR LATER, Tippy noticed that his few minutes
had stretched too long. She put down the liquor glass
and tried to get her mind to work. He'd said he was
going over to Don's apartment. She phoned the apartment next door and spoke to Don's mother.

"But he was never here," came the shocked reply
from the other woman. "Did he say he was coming over?"

Tippy felt her heart sink. "Yes!"

"Wait a minute." She called her son and there was
a mumble of conversation. "I just asked Don," the
other woman said worriedly. "Tippy, he says that a
man came to the door downstairs and asked for Rory
to come down. Rory thought it was that friend of
yours, Cash isn't it? But Don didn't recognize him.
He said the man had on a coat and hat and he looked
mysterious."

Tippy thanked her and hung up. Terror lodged in
her throat. She knew at once, without being told, that
her mother's vicious boyfriend had Rory. She knew
it! But her mind was foggy and she couldn't think.
What must she do?

The phone rang again and she picked it up.

"We've got Rory," came a familiar, terrible voice from the past. "We want a hundred grand by morning. Or you get a dead body back. Don't call the feds. We'll phone you in the morning with instructions. Sleep tight, sweetie," he added sarcastically, and hung up.

Tippy was scared to death. She knew it was Sam, and she knew he meant what he said. There had never been a time when she wasn't afraid of him, long after she'd run away from home. The man was Rory's father. Rory didn't know that. But she couldn't let him hurt the boy. And he would. He had no paternal feelings for anyone.

Her hands trembled. She grabbed her purse and thumbed through the numbers in her appointment book for Cash Grier's. He probably wouldn't speak to her, but she had to try.

She punched in the number of his cell phone, that he'd given her long ago when she left Jacobsville for New York after the film shoot. She wasn't certain that it was still current.

It rang once. Twice. Three times. Four times. Her lips moved in a silent prayer. Be there. Please be there!

It rang five times. Six. Her heart sank. He wasn't going to even answer...!

"Grier," came a cold, deep voice over the line.

"Cash!" she exclaimed. "I have to talk to you. I need help!"

"Help? You need help? Damn you, Tippy!" he burst out.

"Just listen," she said firmly, trying to get a grip on herself. "Please. This is serious!"

His voice was icy. "I have nothing to say to a woman like you, Tippy. Don't you ever call me again as long as you live."

"Cash, for God's sake…!" she choked desperately.

The line went dead. She punched Redial but nothing happened. He wasn't going to answer. And she knew it would do no good, no good at all, to try other numbers, like the police department's there. Cash didn't know about Rory, and he wouldn't let her tell him. She knew he would have tried to help, if he'd known. But he wouldn't listen.

She cursed roundly, grasping at options. She had to save Rory! On a sudden whim, she tried Judd Dunn's number, but nobody answered, not even Christabel.

Those options gone, she poured a cup of cold coffee into a cup and drank it down quickly, hoping to clear her mind. Her only other hope was to raise the ransom money. Joel. Joel Harper! If she could get in touch with him…!

She tried his home number, but the answering machine turned on. She tried the studio. None of his staff was there, she was told. They'd gone with Joel on location to set things up for his next film, now that

Tippy's was almost in the can. The location was in the wilds of Peru, and even his cell phone wasn't accessible right now. Apparently the group was in some location where there were no relays.

Tippy tried an officer of the studio, but was told that he was out for the week. It was fate, she told herself miserably. She couldn't get help. She was on her own. She thought about calling the police, but how did she get in touch with someone who wouldn't jeopardize Rory's life by rushing in with guns blazing? She had no idea what to do next.

She put the phone down with a dead sigh. She couldn't possibly get the amount of money Sam wanted by morning. She had no more than a thousand dollars in her savings account, and her credit cards were maxed out. She'd pawned her jewels to pay Rory's fees. There was nothing left. She had nothing left to borrow money on.

There was only one possible way to handle it. She had to offer to exchange herself for Rory and tell Sam to contact the motion picture company about the ransom. They wouldn't know that Joel was out of the country. If she played her cards right, she could convince them that she was worth more to them than Rory. She'd convince them that her studio would pay handsomely for her release.

Her company wouldn't pay it, of course, because they wouldn't have any more luck than she'd had trying to find someone with the authority to raise the ransom. But the subterfuge would save Rory.

She got another drink and sat by the telephone all night, waiting for Sam to call her back. She thought about willingly putting herself into Sam Stanton's hands again. She remembered all too well her fear and pain and anguish when the man had raped her, all those years ago. She was still terrified of him, of his violent temper. He would be uncontrollable when he found out that he couldn't get money from her or her bosses. He would kill her, if she was lucky. The alternative didn't bear thinking about. She had another drink and wondered how things might have been if she hadn't seduced Cash, if she hadn't risked her child, if, if, if…

The bottom line was Rory's safety. Her little brother was still a child, and she loved him. He deserved to live.

She poured out the last of the whiskey. "Okay, kid, you can do it," she told herself. She raised her glass in a toast. "To more guts than brains, and going down in a blaze of glory," she murmured.

When the phone rang, she made her suggestion to Sam in cold blood and with mock confidence. He thought about it, talked to someone, and finally agreed, giving her an address.

"Get a cab, and don't call anybody," he threatened. "I can still kill the kid before anybody gets to me. You got that?"

"I've got it, honey," she drawled in her best sarcastic manner.

"Don't waste time." The line went dead.

She mentally reviewed all the martial arts she'd learned. As an afterthought, she picked up a balisong knife she'd had for the part she played in the movie. She didn't really know how to use it, but it had a long and lethal blade. If she got a chance, any chance at all, she was going to make Sam Stanton pay for everything he'd done in his miserable life. Cash could read all about *this* in the tabloids, she thought coldly. And she hoped his conscience tortured him every time he thought of her!

CHAPTER SEVEN

CASH TOOK A CAB TO TIPPY'S apartment from the airport. He hadn't wanted to spend the time driving all the way from Texas, especially after Tippy's frantic phone call. He didn't know what had happened, but he had a cold, uneasy feeling in the pit of his stomach, as if he sensed something terrible was wrong. He had to find out.

He couldn't get her voice—her tormented voice—out of his mind. It had haunted him ever since he'd spoken to her. In the end, he'd picked up the phone and called her back, just to be sure she was okay. It was her phone. But it wasn't Tippy who answered it.

What took Cash to New York was the voice that answered the phone when he called her apartment.

The voice was a man's, brusque and all business. Cash asked for Tippy, and there was a cold silence.

He was asked what he wanted. Cash, his blood running cold, said he wanted to speak to Tippy Moore. There was another pause, then he was told that she wasn't available, to call back the next day, and the line went dead.

Cash had held the receiver in his hand long after the man hung up. He felt sick all the way to his soul. Something had happened to Tippy. Men were in her apartment, monitoring phone calls. People in law enforcement. He knew it by the very tone the man had used. He'd used it himself in kidnapping cases he'd helped solve.

He couldn't get to the bottom of this situation by phone. He told everyone he had a family emergency, took a leave of absence, left Judd in charge, and got on the next plane to Manhattan.

He'd gone over and over that last call in his mind. Tippy's apartment had been staked out. They were watching for someone, for something. He thought about Tippy's mother and Rory's father and the threats she'd said they made. What if they'd kidnapped Rory? That would certainly explain Tippy's almost hysterical tone. She'd called him for help, and he'd cursed her and hung up on her. He closed his eyes on a wave of pain. If anything had happened to Rory or Tippy because of his refusal to help, he couldn't live with it. But…if Rory was in trouble, why hadn't Tippy answered her own phone?

He got out of the cab, paid the fare plus a tip, and took two steps at a time getting to the door. He pushed the buzzer.

"Yeah? Who is it?" a voice demanded. It was the same voice that had answered the phone earlier in the day.

"I'm an old friend of Tippy Moore's," he lied pleasantly. "We work in movies together."

There was a pause, and a boy's anguished voice. "Let him come up. Please!"

Rory! Cash ground his teeth together trying not to lose his temper. Rory was there. He hadn't been kidnapped, but he sounded frantic. Something had happened to Tippy. Something bad.

There was another pause. "All right, come up."

The door unlocked as he was buzzed in. He went up the stairs like a madman, forcing himself not to behave like one when Tippy's door opened.

Rory ran past the suited men waiting, and threw himself into Cash's arms, sobbing wildly.

"What's wrong?" Cash asked softly, holding the boy close.

"You know the boy?" one of the men asked.

Cash studied him. The man was familiar. He couldn't remember…then it came to him. The man was FBI, an agent he'd worked with many years past.

"What's going on here?" Cash asked without reacting.

"That's need-to-know. You don't."

"Can't he have coffee with me?" Rory asked quickly. "He's a good friend of Tippy's!"

"Do you know where she is?" the suited man asked suspiciously.

"She's at work, I guess," Cash lied glibly. "Isn't she?" he prompted Rory.

The boy's eyes were haunted, but he wasn't allowed to answer.

"Sure. She's at work. You got five minutes, then you're out of here," the older man told Cash. "We're waiting for a call."

Cash followed Rory into the kitchen and turned on the taps to disguise his voice. He turned to Rory with cold eyes.

"Spill it. Quick," he told the boy.

"Sam kidnapped me for ransom," Rory said under his breath. "Tippy didn't have the money, so she traded herself for me." His voice choked. "She told Sam to ask her company for the ransom. She can't pay it. She's got no money coming in at all until they release the movie."

Cash's heart stopped. "They'll kill her," he said involuntarily.

"She knows that. She kissed me goodbye when they let me go, and she told me she knew what she was doing, that it didn't matter about her." Rory swallowed, hard. "Since she lost the baby, she doesn't care about anything. She told me to come home and don't think about her. She said if they killed her it would just stop the pain... Cash!" he exclaimed when the man's big hands caught his arms bruisingly hard.

Cash let him go with a mumbled apology. "The tabloids said she did the dangerous stunt on purpose!" Cash bit off.

"That's a lie. The assistant director swore it was safe," Rory muttered. "When Mr. Harper found out what the man did, he fired him. But it was too late by then...."

Cash's eyes closed on visions of horror. Every harsh word he'd said to Tippy came back to haunt him. She was going to die. It was his fault. She'd called him to save Rory and he'd insulted her and hung up on her. She hadn't had any other way to save the boy except to trade herself for him, and to the one man on earth she had real reason to fear.

"Snap out of it, Cash!" Rory said suddenly, shaking him. "We've got to save her!"

Cash's face was like paste. He was dragging in breath after strained breath, trying not to think of what she might be going through even now.

"Cash!" Rory persisted, looking more adult than the adult beside him.

Cash let out a long breath. "It's all right," he said quietly. "I'll take care of it."

"I don't think those guys know what they're doing," Rory said worriedly. "They're just sitting around waiting for the phone to ring, but I don't think Sam's crazy enough to call here. He was going to call Tippy's film company. But Joel Harper is out of the country on location and can't be reached, and there's nobody else with the authority to pay any ransom without his consent. The kidnappers will kill her. I know they will."

"How did Stanton get you?" Cash asked quickly, because the men in the other room were suddenly quiet.

"He told my friend next door that he wanted me to come down. I thought it was you." Rory looked away. "Sam's got a cousin who lives on the lower east side, not too far from here. His father runs a little bar. He's in some gang or other, and he has mob connections."

"What's his name?" Cash asked.

"Alvaro something. Montes, I think. The bar's called 'La Corrida,' over somewhere near 2nd Street."

Cash looked toward the doorway, where the suited men were looking at them suspiciously. One was dark and only a little older than Cash himself. The other one was taller, grayer, and in his fifties. He had a face like cold steel.

"That's your five minutes," the taller one told Cash. "You look familiar," he added.

Cash grinned. "Maybe you've seen me in a movie. Did you ever watch *The Dancer?* I played the waiter…"

The man looked disgusted. "I don't watch musicals."

Cash glanced down at Rory with caution in his whole look. "When your sister gets back, we'll have that game of chess I promised you," he said evasively. "You aren't staying by yourself, are you?"

"No, he isn't. He'll be safe with us," the older man said coldly.

Cash pulled out a business card and handed it to Rory. "I run a small business nearby," he told the men with a smile, "sort of between movies. The boy can call me if he ever needs a place to stay, while Tippy's on location."

The suspicious looks grew more suspicious. "Let me see that card," the shorter one said.

Rory glanced at Cash, who took it back and showed it to the men. It read, Home Away From Home, Smith's Hideaway, Brooklyn, N.Y. There was also a phone number. "This you—Smith?" he asked Cash.

"That's me. Easy name to remember," he added with a pleasant grin, and thanked his lucky stars he'd thought to bring those old business cards with him.

The man handed it back to Rory. "He'll be in touch if he needs you," he said curtly to Cash. "Now beat it."

"Take care of yourself, Rory," Cash said, and he nodded slowly, as if to tell the boy that everything was going to be okay.

Rory nodded back, but he didn't believe it. He had no idea how Cash would go about rescuing her all alone. This was far from a routine job.

CASH WAS THINKING THE SAME thing as he left the apartment, and he already had his cell phone out. He punched in a speed dial number on the special cell phone he kept for emergencies.

"Peter?" he asked when a voice answered. "It's Grier. Fine, you? I need a little help."

"Such as?" came the reply.

"About ten ounces of C-4, a K-bar, some rope, a .45 auto, a couple of flash-bangs, and transportation to Brooklyn."

There was a burst of laughter. "Sure, no problem, I'll just waltz down to the local market and pick it all up. Where are you?"

HALF AN HOUR LATER, Cash climbed into the car two blocks away and shook hands with his protégé, Peter Stone. The younger man was a professional mercenary these days. He'd been in Micah Steele's group, but was now working security with Bojo, another former member of the group, in the Middle Eastern nation of Qawi, for Sheikh Philippe Sabon.

Peter was in the country visiting relatives, between assignments.

"Imagine you, working as a hick police chief," Peter chuckled.

"Imagine you, fighting international terrorists," Cash shot back.

Peter shrugged. "We do what we can." He became serious. "What's up?"

"A friend of mine has been snatched for ransom. I'm going to get her back."

"Her?" Peter echoed. "You, caring enough for a woman to rescue her? She must be something special."

"She is," Cash managed curtly. He averted his eyes. "She traded herself for her kid brother. She told the kidnappers they could get the ransom from her film company, but she knew they wouldn't pay it. There's nobody in the country who can negotiate a payment. She knew that, too."

"Gutsy lady," Peter said solemnly.

"Gutsy. And she'll be dead if I don't do something. The man who snatched her is the worst kind of scum."

"Don Kincaid is in town," Peter told him. "And I can get in touch with Ed Bonner if I need to. He used to be Marcus Carrera's local boss, back before Carrera reformed…"

"I'll only ask Carrera as a last ditch option," Cash told him. "He counts favors."

"I know what you mean," Peter said wryly. "I still owe him one, and I'm sweating bullets wondering what he'll ask for."

"Maybe it will only be for some exotic fabric," Cash chuckled.

"Don't ever joke about his quilting habit," Peter said at once. "There's a guy in the hospital who's sorry he ever brought it up!"

"We have a lawman in Texas who quilts and knows Carrera," Cash told him. "He was on a quilting show on TV. There's a guy in my department who used to work for him until he made a cute remark about men making quilts. But he's okay now," Cash added. "In fact, his new front teeth look real natural."

Peter chuckled, and turned the car into an alley. "Where do we go from here?"

"To a little bar called 'La Corrida.'"

"I know it!" Peter exclaimed. "The guy who runs it, Alvaro Montes, is from Spain. His father was a bull-fighter. Died in the ring, just the way he wanted to."

"Is he a scalawag?"

"Not him," Peter said easily. "But he's got some shady relatives. Including his no-account son," he added coldly. "There's a guy who needs an attitude adjustment."

"Funny you should mention him," Cash told him. "That's who we're after."

"Do tell!" Peter grinned. "Let's go see Papa

Montes. Maybe he can tell us where his boy would hold a hostage if he had one."

"Listen, I'm in no mood for a barroom brawl…"

"It won't be like that," Peter assured him. "You'll see."

THEY WENT INTO THE SMALL, badly lit bar. A tall man with gray sprinkled black curly hair looked up from the counter as they walked in. The bar was empty, except for one old man at a corner table.

"Peter," the owner greeted him with a warm smile. "I didn't know you were back in town!"

"Just for a few days, Viejo," he told the older man and grinned. "This is my friend, Grier."

The bar's owner hesitated. His eyes narrowed as he looked at Cash. "I know of you," he said quietly.

"Most people do," Peter replied easily. "A friend of his has been kidnapped."

"And you come here, to see me." The older man closed his eyes and sighed heavily. "No need to ask why, of course. It is that cousin, that man from the South, who comes here to make trouble for us. Last time it was gunrunning. Is it something that bad?"

"I'm afraid so, maybe worse," Peter replied. "I think you know where he would go if he had a hostage."

"A hostage." The old man closed his eyes. "Yes, yes, I know where he would go," he added slowly.

"To a warehouse where I keep my spirits and good wine," he said coldly, "a few blocks from here." He gave Peter the address. "You will try not to involve my son in this?"

"Your son is already involved," Cash said without apology. "And if anything has happened to the woman, he will regret it."

The older man winced. "I have been a good father," he said heavily. "I have done everything I could to teach him right from wrong, to separate him from friends who were on the wrong side of the law. But once he left home, I lost control, you see. Do you have children?" he asked Cash.

"No," Cash said in a tone that didn't invite comment. "Will your son have anyone else with him, besides the cousin?"

The man shook his head. "His brother is an attorney. Perhaps a fortunate thing. My other son has never given me heartache. He was always a good boy."

"I've worked in law enforcement long enough to know that children go wrong even when their parents do everything right. It's a matter of individuals, not upbringing, for the most part," Cash said.

"Gracias," the bar owner replied quietly.

"See you, Viejo," Peter said. "Thanks."

The older man only nodded. He looked very sad.

"He is a good man," Peter told Cash when they were in the car again. "He sacrificed to bring up

those boys. Their mother died when the youngest
was born. She was good people, too."

"So is Tippy," Cash snarled, impatient to get down
to business. It was going to take a lot of stealth and guts
to get her out alive. Even with help. He didn't dare
think about the consequences if he wasn't in time.

"I brought along your old threads," Peter volunteered. "It'll be a night to remember."

"I don't doubt it," Cash said.

THE WAREHOUSE WAS ON a back street, and one of the
streetlights had been shattered, probably with a rock.
There was a group of young boys wandering around
making catcalls. But when they saw Cash and Peter
in their working gear, they found a reason to go in
the opposite direction.

"Don't worry about them," Peter said easily. "Nobody's going to interfere with us in this neighborhood. Not at any price. How do we go in?"

They'd already cased the warehouse and located
all the exits.

"Over the roof and in through the ventilation system," Cash said. "Then from the second floor over
the rail and down into the warehouse itself."

"Try not to break too many bottles, okay?" Peter
groaned. "Viejo doesn't have much money, this is
probably his entire fortune."

"I'll do what I can. Let's go."

"What about the feds?" Peter asked solemnly.

"Good thinking." Cash took out his cell phone and made a call.

THEY CLIMBED TO THE ROOF with the aid of grappling hooks and then quickly and quietly worked their way down through the ventilator shaft to the top floor.

With tiny receivers in place in their ears and mikes at their lips they could communicate without yelling, and at a distance. Cash went first, a length of nylon rope coiled over one shoulder, a K-bar knife in its sheath at his waist, along with a .45 automatic. He was all in black, like Peter, with a ski mask over his face.

He paused on the walkway to look down onto the warehouse floor. Among the barrels and wine racks, he caught a glimpse of a woman lying prone on a piece of cardboard. Above her, three men were arguing. One of them had a bottle. It was broken. He was waving it at one of the other men. No sound at all was coming from the woman. Cash's heart stopped in his chest as he looked down at what he could see of her. If they'd hurt her, he'd kill them. He wouldn't be able to stop himself.

He motioned to Peter to go across and around to the other side of the warehouse. The man nodded, indicating his own coiled rope. It took an eternity for Peter to silently make his way between the boxes. Once, he paused and waited until the sound of a passing truck masked the step he had to take over a piece of plastic.

Peter made it to the position and gave the thumbs-up sign to Cash. They both fastened the nylon ropes to the iron rails of the second story. Cash pulled out his automatic. Peter did the same. Cash stood up on the railing, watching Peter follow suit, and they both rappelled down at the same time with loud yells to disconcert the men below.

"What the hell…!" the taller of the men on the ground floor exclaimed.

"Shoot. Shoot!" the second man yelled, waving a pistol. He threw off a couple of shots in Cash's direction, but Cash was an old hand at dodging bullets. He dropped from the rope, rolled and fired.

The second man went down, holding his leg and groaning. Peter had the other one in a choke hold from behind. The third one had cut his losses immediately, and sprinted for the exit. He was through it before Cash could get a good look at him.

Cash holstered his weapon and ran to Tippy. When he got closer, he could see that her face was covered in blood. Her blouse was red with it, too, and torn. Bruises were visible all over her creamy shoulders and back. She wasn't moving. She didn't even seem to be breathing.

In that instant, Cash recalled seeing Christabel Gaines lying on the ground after being shot by one of

Judd's enemies months before. The same sick panic gripped him again, but this time with more force.

"Tippy," he ground out, rushing to kneel beside her and feel for a pulse at her throat. His hand was shaking.

For a few painful seconds, he thought she was dead. He couldn't feel her heart beating. Then, all at once, the pressure rebounded on his fingers and he felt a faint, fluttering beat.

"She's alive," he called to Peter. He whipped out his cell phone and dialed 911.

SHE WAS STILL UNCONSCIOUS when the ambulance and the police came, along with two suited men. By that time, Peter had gone with all the equipment, including the change of clothing that Cash had worn, and with every bit of evidence that would tie the two men to the scene of the crime. They weren't going to find a weapon that would match the bullet in the taller kidnapper's thigh, though.

But Cash had phoned Tippy's apartment at the same time, to alert the FBI to what was going on. They arrived with the police.

The taller of the two suited agents pursed his lips when he saw Cash on the warehouse floor, sitting with Tippy's bloody head in his lap while the paramedics brought in a stretcher. Uniformed policemen were at the door and crime scene investigators were already at work on trace evidence.

"Now I remember where I saw you," the tall agent told Cash drolly.

"No, you don't," Cash replied firmly.

The man scowled. "See here…"

"You see," Cash returned harshly. "These men kidnapped my fiancée. No way was I going to sit by a phone and wait for a call. Unfortunately I missed all the action. Gunfire had already been exchanged by the time we arrived on the scene."

"You can't interfere in government business!"

"The hell I can't," Cash replied tersely. "Try me!"

"I'll call headquarters and they'll have your butt in a sling by morning," the agent said furiously.

"I'll call headquarters and you'll be selling pencils out of a cup on Broadway!" Cash retorted.

The younger agent pulled him to one side and whispered something emphatically. The taller agent backed down. "You'd better not be around by morning."

"I won't be," Cash said quietly. His attention turned back to Tippy, who was sucking at breaths as if they were coming with painful effort.

The two agents moved closer and looked down at the handiwork of the kidnappers. "What the hell did they do that for?" the older one demanded angrily. "She wasn't any threat to them!"

"The one who got shot likes hurting women,"

Cash said without looking up. He couldn't erase the image of Stanton standing over her with a broken bottle when he'd come in.

"Oh, yeah?" The agent went to the man who was tying a ripped piece of his shirt around his thigh to stem the bleeding.

"Get me on an ambulance, you butt head, I've been shot! One of those masked guys put a bullet in me!" Sam Stanton demanded arrogantly.

"That's okay, boys, he's only nicked here!" the agent called to the paramedics. "Do her first!"

"Damn you!" Stanton groaned.

Cash glanced at the agent. "Thanks," he said huskily.

The other man shrugged.

The paramedics examined Tippy even as they loaded her onto the ambulance. Cash climbed into the back with her, and held her hand tightly. He was scared to death and trying not to let it show. He thought about Rory, all alone. He hadn't asked the agents what they'd done with the boy. He prayed that they'd left him with the neighbors, his friend's parents.

But when the ambulance rolled into the emergency entrance, there was Rory, waiting with the two FBI agents.

Cash could have hugged them. Rory ran to the stretcher, his face pale, his eyes red and swollen. "Tippy!" he cried.

Cash caught him, hugging him close. "She's alive," he said at once. "She's bruised and cut and concussed, and she looks terrible. But she's going to be fine."

Rory looked up at him, desperate to believe. "You wouldn't lie to me?"

"Never," Cash said flatly. "I'd never do that. She's going to be all right. I promise you she is."

"What about Sam?" Rory asked miserably.

"Ask those guys," Cash told him, and he smiled wearily at the agents. "They're waiting to transfer him into federal custody, along with his accomplice, when he's treated for a gunshot wound. There was another one, but he got away. Maybe they can track him down."

"Sam got shot? All right!" Rory said fervently. "You guys shoot him?" he asked the FBI.

"Sorry," they echoed.

"Don't look at me," Cash lied, straight-faced. "I don't carry when I'm out of Texas. It's against the law."

The FBI gave him a look that would have stopped traffic. Cash smiled like an angel.

"Stanton doesn't know who shot him," the agent continued, with a suspicious look. "And he said there were two guys, not just one."

"He'd obviously been drinking," Cash said innocently.

The older agent sighed. "Obviously," he said. "You know a guy at our district office named Callahan?"

"I'm not sure," Cash said, grinning.

The agent just shook his head.

Rory caught on that Cash was hiding something and tried not to smile.

"What's the rap for kidnapping and assault these days?" Cash asked the feds.

"Time enough that they'll be wearing long gray beards when they get out," the taller agent promised him. "We'll try to make them tell us about the one who got away tonight. And I swear to God, I'll be at every parole hearing for the rest of my life, after that guy goes up, reminding them what he did to that young woman."

"You're a prince," Cash said.

The other man shrugged. "I work for the government," he replied. "We're all heroes."

"You are in my book," Rory said genuinely. "Thanks."

"Just doing our job," the shorter man replied. But he smiled.

THE EMERGENCY ROOM DOCTOR came out to speak to Cash. Tippy had a concussion, as Cash already knew, and even though she was now conscious, she would have to be watched closely for the immediate future. In addition to the numerous cuts on her face and upper body, she had sustained blunt force trauma to her ribs, which was cause for concern. It bruised the lungs. This could not only cause bleeding or hemorrhage, but in a worst-case scenario, it could even cause pulmonary failure. They would have to do MRI scans of her head and chest, and X rays as well to ascertain the extent of the damage. She would have to remain in the hospital for several days. The doctor had ordered the various tests, and as soon as they knew something definite, they'd contact Cash.

Cash grimly told the doctor he wasn't going anywhere, he'd be in the waiting room as long as necessary. The doctor asked if he was a relative. If he said no, they might deny him access to her. For Rory's sake, he had to prevent that.

"I'm her fiancé," Cash said quietly, keeping up the cover story he'd told the feds. He added, "She's a former model. But right now, she's a motion picture actress working on her second film. Her first one premiered last November and was a smash hit. Her face," he said somberly, "is her livelihood."

"I'll make sure they call in a plastic surgeon for consultation right away. We'll have to clean the cuts carefully and stitch them and apply sterile dressings, to prevent infection. But I can tell you from what I've already seen that I'm fairly sure there's no severe damage to her face," he said gently. "Her lung is what concerns us most at the moment. We'll keep you posted."

"Thanks," Cash said quietly.

"All in a day's work," the doctor assured him with a smile.

Cash found Rory, with the two agents, and assumed responsibility for him. He took Rory into the cafeteria, bought him a soft drink, and told him what was going on.

"I like that," Rory said after a minute. "That you're honest with me," he added when Cash looked curious.

"I wouldn't insult you by being anything less," Cash replied.

Rory glanced at him curiously. "Why wouldn't you talk to me when I called you in Texas?"

Cash felt sick. He hated the question, because it made him feel small. "One of my officers didn't put the call through. He thought it was what I wanted." He stared into his black coffee. "I believed what I read in tabloids," he said with self-contempt.

"Tippy's not like that," Rory told him firmly. "She'd never sacrifice a baby for a career, no matter how rich or famous she could get. She told me one time that fame and fortune were no substitute for somebody who loved you."

Cash should have known that. Trust came hard to him.

"She'll get over it," Rory said suddenly. "She just needs time. You're…going to stay until we know for sure?"

"Of course," he replied matter-of-factly.

Rory relaxed a little. "Thanks."

Cash didn't answer him. He was thinking of Tippy's condition, and how precarious it was. He didn't dare think ahead even an hour.

Rory had finally drifted off to sleep in a borrowed hospital bed when the doctor came to tell Cash the results of the tests. As he'd figured, there was a badly bruised lung and some bleeding. They'd siphoned off the fluid and stitched up her cuts—which the plastic surgeon felt would heal quite nicely since there was no muscle or nerve damage. Now it was a matter of waiting, to see if the lung damage progressed and keep watch over the concussion. Tippy was moved to ICU overnight for constant monitoring.

Cash knew too much about head and lung injuries not to worry. He sat beside the bed in ICU, breaking regulations right and left, holding her hand. They'd given her something for the pain and she drifted in and out. She didn't seem to know him at first.

He wasn't leaving her. If he'd listened instead of giving her hell, she wouldn't be here. He knew it. The knowledge hurt him. She could have died. She still might. He didn't share that terror with Rory, who was sleeping peacefully down the hall, thinking that his sister was fine.

Cash didn't sleep at all. It wasn't until dawn that her green eyes opened and became alert. She winced and choked, trying to breathe. It hurt. She put her hand to her bruised rib cage and groaned.

"Easy," Cash said gently. "Lie still. What do you want?"

She looked up into worried dark eyes. She was dreaming. She smiled faintly, murmured, "So I've died," and went back to sleep.

He pushed the button for the nurse. She came quickly, listened to Cash's update, and smiled as she went to call the doctor for further orders.

"It's not a dream," Cash whispered at her forehead, kissing it fervently. "I'm here, and you're alive. Thank God. Thank God!"

She thought she heard Cash's deep voice. He sounded frightened. But he hated her. He wouldn't be here. Someone had hit her, so hard, so many times. She remembered finally just crying for mercy, pleading for her life. She couldn't fight. There was no use in it. She wanted Cash, but he hated her. She'd lost their child. He'd never forgive her. She was only dreaming again.

Tears slid out from under her closed eyelids.

"Hates me," she choked. "He hates me!"

"No!" he said hoarsely. "He doesn't!"

Her head moved restlessly on the pillow. "Leave me be," she managed in a wispy, weak tone. "It doesn't matter what happens to me."

"Yes it does!"

He sounded desperate. She was certainly dreaming now. He was pleading with her. He wanted her. He was sorry. She had to forgive him. She had to live!

Wait… She must be hallucinating. He'd told her to go to hell. And she had. There was no better description for what had happened to her in that warehouse, in the darkness. She was broken and bruised and cut to pieces, and the future seemed so bleak. Work wasn't enough anymore. Even Rory wasn't enough. She was tired of the struggle. She had nothing but pain to look forward to. She started crying, groaning again when it hurt her lung. Her voice rose just as the nurse came back in quickly.

Cash was shuttled out of the room protesting and cursing for everything he was worth. It sounded like she had lost the will to live. She was trying to give up and die. He couldn't let her go!

"She's going to be all right," the nurse assured him crisply. "You sit down and let us take care of her. She's not going to die. She's not! You believe that."

The woman was a veteran of many traumas. She looked into the man's dark, tortured eyes and saw more than he meant her to.

"She's not going to give up," the nurse told him quietly. "I won't let her. I promise. You'll have time to make it up to her." She let go of his hand and smiled at him. "You should try to sleep. She's going to be fine. We won't let her slip away. All right?"

He began to relax, just a little. He was so damned tired. He was so scared… "All right," he said after a minute.

She led him to the waiting room and pushed him down into a chair. "I'll come for you, when she's in a room and settled."

"You're moving her out of ICU?" he asked, dazed.

"Of course," she replied with a grin. "We don't keep recovering patients there!"

She turned and left him, just in time to miss the wetness stinging his eyes. She would live. Even if she hated him, she would live. He closed his eyes and leaned back. Seconds later, he was sound asleep.

CHAPTER EIGHT

CHAPTER EIGHT

THE NEXT THING CASH KNEW, Rory was shaking him.

"Come on, Cash, she's awake! She's goofy, because they're giving her stuff for the pain, but she's got her eyes open. Gosh, she looks awful!"

Cash's dark eyes slid open. He blinked as his gaze centered on the smiling boy. "She's awake?" he parroted.

Rory nodded. "I only just woke up. It's almost eleven in the morning. Come on."

Cash got to his feet slowly, wincing as he stood up. "I'm getting too old for that kind of work."

Rory studied the tall man quietly. "You went in and got her, didn't you?"

Cash nodded. "I called in a marker. One of my

buddies came along, but you don't know that," he added firmly.

Rory nodded. "Thanks."

Cash averted his eyes from the gratitude. He still felt responsible for what had happened to Tippy. He dreaded facing her.

But he walked into the room with Rory, prepared for anything.

TIPPY WAS BARELY CONSCIOUS. Her face hurt. Her body hurt. She was aware of lacerations that seemed to cover most of her. There was a tube in her arm. She was getting oxygen through tubes in her nose. Her ribs hurt. But when she saw Cash and Rory standing beside the bed, she wasn't certain she was really seeing them. She'd been having a dream. Cash was kissing her and whispering that she had to hold on. She had to live. She knew it had been a dream, because Cash hated her.

Her mind went back to her last terrible memory, of Sam Stanton standing over her with a bottle, swearing at the top of his lungs that she'd double-crossed him and she wouldn't live to brag about it. She could still feel the impact of the bottle on her back and shoulders, on her rib cage, where it felt bruised. She'd put up her hands to shield her face as he blindly swung it at her. Something had hit her in the head and she started to fall just as Sam threw the bottle and it shattered on the concrete floor. Her face felt swollen and painful and tight, but the cuts didn't feel very deep. Perhaps she'd fallen in the broken glass, and that was how her face got cut. Now she seemed to be alive, but she could hardly get even a shallow breath of air. She knew Rory and Cash were there, but she could barely hear them.

Cash paused by the bed and caught his breath audibly at what he saw. Her poor face had cuts that had been cleaned up and medicated. There were no stitches in them. He knew from his own experience that cuts weren't sutured unless they were dangerous cuts. He thanked God that hers were superficial. They would take months to heal completely, but they were obviously shallow and unlikely to leave permanent scars. Her lung was the biggest danger. If it hemorrhaged, she could die.

There were cuts on one of her arms, the one the IV wasn't in. That one did have stitches. He knew that she'd had concussion from the way the medics had raised her head instead of lowering it when they arrived on the scene. But she was still breathing, and she could get immediate help if she needed it. Thank God.

Rory walked right to the bed and held his sister's hand without flinching. "You're going to be fine, sis. Just fine."

"Sure I am," she said. Her voice was groggy from

drugs. "My head hurts so much!" she moaned. "I've been sick twice already. And my side hurts…"

She lifted her eyes and looked past him at Cash. She didn't react at all. She just looked at him.

"Do you need anything?" he asked quietly.

She took a shaky breath and lowered her eyes to her hands. "I need you to take Rory back to the apartment and have him bring my insurance card here, if you don't mind," she said grimly. "The doctor who admitted me just got through doing rounds. He says I've got badly bruised ribs and mild concussion. I have to stay in the hospital for at least three days, to make sure I don't develop pneumonia from the ribs—they've got me on antibiotics just in case. The concussion was mild, and the CAT scan didn't show any damage—at least not anything that worried them. The cuts weren't very deep, thank goodness. He thinks they'll heal perfectly without any plastic surgery—but it will take several months for them to heal completely. After that, they'll see if they think I need it."

Cash's face was like rock. "Why did Stanton do this to you?" he asked.

She moved and grimaced as the movement hurt her ribs. It was hard to breathe. Hard to talk, too. "He was angry because he couldn't get in touch with anybody who was willing to pay ransom for me," she said heavily. "He said he'd make sure I never worked again, but he was too high to realize that he wasn't hitting hard enough to kill. He slammed the bottle down on the warehouse floor just before I fell—I expect he was planning to cut me some more with the bottle neck."

"He was standing over you with it," Cash recalled. "But I think falling into broken glass is what gave you those cuts."

She laughed coldly. "They won't heal overnight, regardless of how I got them. I won't be working for a few months. Joel Harper may have to replace me in the film."

She didn't add that she was going to be destitute if that happened.

"All you need to worry about is getting through this," Cash told her quietly. "I'll take care of everything else, including Rory."

"Thanks," she said tautly.

"I know you hate having to depend on anyone," Cash replied. "So would I, in your place. But you'll have enough to do, just letting the damage heal."

"Now I know what they mean by 'cut and paste,'" she murmured.

"What else do you need from the apartment?" Cash asked.

"Besides my insurance card? My gowns and a robe, some underclothes and my bedroom shoes," she said. "Rory will know which ones. Some loose change for the snack machine, and something to read."

She still wasn't looking at him. He moved closer to the bed, noticing how she tensed at his approach.

"Rory, could you give us a minute?" he asked the boy.

But before Rory could answer him, Tippy's eyes went to Cash's face. There was no emotion in them. "There's no need for him to leave," she said. "You and I have nothing to say to each other, Cash. Nothing at all."

He let out a harsh breath.

"If you'll just bring my things, I'll be grateful," she said. "Rory, the policeman who was in here said that one of the men got away. You can't possibly stay here in the hospital with me. And you can't stay at the apartment, or with Don," she added when he started to argue, "without putting his family in jeopardy. I'm sorry you'll miss the rest of spring break, but you really need to go back to school, so the commandant can keep you safe. Cash, would you talk to the commandant and explain what's going on?"

"Of course," he said. He turned to Rory. "She's right. You're safe in Maryland. You won't be here."

Rory grimaced. "I don't want to go," he said.

She caught his hand and held it tight. "I know. All we have is each other," she managed, and she smiled. "But I'm going to be all right. I promise, I won't give up. Okay?"

He swallowed hard. "Okay."

"Summer isn't so far away," she reminded him with a weak smile. Her face, once so beautiful, was a mass of cuts. "We'll do something special for vacation this year."

"We could go to the Bahamas," he suggested.

She nodded. "We'll see. Go with Cash and get my stuff. You can pack yours at the same time. You'll need to phone the airport and get a ticket. My credit card was maxed out but I'll write a check to Cash to reimburse you."

"I'll take care of all that," Cash told her. "You don't need to pay me back."

She wanted to argue, but she couldn't. She was momentarily helpless. She grimaced as she moved.

"What's wrong?" Cash asked perceptively.

"Bruised ribs," she said huskily. "It still hurts when I move."

Cash's eyes were blazing. He was sorry he hadn't aimed to kill the man instead of just shooting him in the leg.

"Go on," Tippy said, closing her eyes. "I'm going to try to sleep for a little while. Thanks, Cash," she added quietly.

He felt two inches high. It hurt him to look at her. If he hadn't hung up on her…

"Come on," Rory said, tugging Cash's hand.

He gave in to the boy's persuasion and followed him out of the room. He didn't look back. It hurt too much.

TIPPY'S APARTMENT WAS A MESS. The federal agents had obviously looked around for any hint of an intruder's presence. Cash and Rory spent quite a while replacing and repacking her things. While they were about it, they packed Rory.

"I know you don't want to go," Cash said quietly. "But I can't take care of you and Tippy at the same time."

Rory was quiet. "She won't let you take care of her," he commented as he put a shirt in his suitcase.

"She's going to have to. There isn't anyone else," he said matter-of-factly. "I'll get her through the next few days. Then I'm taking her home to Texas with me."

Rory glanced at him. "She won't go."

He sighed. "Yes, she will. I know she hates me. I don't blame her. But she's got nowhere else to go. She can't stay by herself."

"You're a chief of police," Rory reminded him. "If she stays with you…"

"I've already thought about that," Cash interrupted. "I'm going to have a nurse stay with her day and night while she's there, so there won't be any gossip."

Rory slowly packed another shirt.

"Look, as soon as school's out, you can come out, too," he said. "You can stay with me, too."

Rory looked up at him. "I could?" he asked huskily.

Cash smiled. "You'll have to do your share of the

housework, though," he added. "Tippy won't be able to do anything strenuous for at least six weeks, which means I'll be doing all of it until you show up. I hate vacuum cleaners. I'm on my third one this month."

Rory's eyes widened. "Why?"

Cash looked uncomfortable. "The hoses get tangled. The cords get caught under the hose. They're like elephants. You have to drag them around by the trunk."

Rory laughed. It was the first time since the ordeal with the kidnappers had begun.

"You can laugh now," Cash said. "Wait until you're tangled up in ten feet of hose and the cord wraps around your ankles and trips you. That's why the last one got retired suddenly." His eyes narrowed. "I should have shot the damned thing, instead of just stomping on it."

"I like vacuum cleaners," Rory said. "I don't mind vacuuming."

"Great. Consider that your part of the housework."

"I can cook, too," Rory said surprisingly. "I'm really good at barbecue. I make my own sauce."

Cash smiled at the boy. "I'll let you try it out on me."

Rory smiled back. "Thanks, Cash. For everything."

Cash sat down on the bed and folded his hands between his knees. "You're no kid, Rory," he said solemnly. "You're mature for your age, so I can tell you this. I made a terrible mistake with Tippy. I wasn't ready for a long-term relationship, but I gave in to temptation without thinking things through. I guess you know already that it was my child she lost."

Rory nodded. "She really wanted it."

Cash swallowed hard. He couldn't meet the boy's eyes. "I would have wanted it, too, if I'd known."

"She said you'd told her there was no future for both of you," Rory said. "She said she'd keep the baby and raise it, just the same. She was buying baby clothes and stuff when she fell on the job." He winced. "She just went all quiet and started drinking really hard afterward. It was in all the papers, too. That just made it worse." He looked up. "You can't let her drink. Our doctor said both of us have a tendency to become alcoholics on account of our mother. She doesn't need to be drinking."

"Thanks for telling me," Cash said. "I know about the dangers of alcohol. I won't let her get on that path."

Rory drew in a long breath. "Thanks. It was worrying me."

"She's going to be all right. I promise."

Rory nodded. "Okay. You'll call me once in a while and tell me how she's doing?"

"I'll phone you every day. And she'll call you, too."

"The recuperation's going to be bad, isn't it?" the boy asked.

"Yes," Cash replied. "But she's got grit. She'll get over this and bounce back."

"Somebody needs to try to call Joel Harper," Rory said.

"I'll track him down," Cash promised. "Everything's going to be all right."

Rory turned away as tears stung his eyes. "It's been a hard couple of days," he said gruffly.

Cash stood up and put both hands on the boy's shoulders. "Life is like an obstacle course," he said. "You get through the challenges and you get a reward, every time."

Rory turned around, surprised. "That's what Tippy always says."

Cash smiled. "We're both right. You'll see." He thought about hugging the boy, to comfort him. But he wasn't used to touching people. He had the impression that Rory wasn't used to it, either. Clearing his throat abruptly, he turned back to the suitcase. "Now let's get packing."

Rory was grateful that the older man hadn't offered him comfort. He was able to control the tears. He forced a grin. "You bet!"

TIPPY WAS STILL GROGGY that evening, but her mind had started to work again. The drugs were keeping the pain down, and they'd given her something for nausea. She wasn't thinking clearly, but she was better than she'd been earlier in the day.

It was torture to see Cash in her room. She remembered too well his harsh words, his refusal to listen to her. She remembered her terror when she knew that Rory was missing. She could still hear Sam's voice on the phone as he made his final ransom demand, and Tippy offered to trade herself for the boy. Once the kidnappers let Rory go and they realized they weren't going to get any ransom, she recalled the pain and terror when Sam turned to her menacingly and said she'd pay now...

The door opened and she looked up, the frightening memories put at once to the back of her mind. Earlier, Cash had brought her insurance card and clothes, then she'd said goodbye to a tearful Rory and Cash had taken him to the airport to put him on a plane for Maryland. She'd lost track of time while he'd been away.

"I came back earlier, but you were asleep and I didn't want to wake you," he said quietly. "I've been in the cafeteria."

"I've been asleep for a long time," she said slowly. "I feel a little better."

"Good. I just talked to the commandant," Cash said as he neared the bed. "He picked Rory up at the airport and drove him back to the school. They won't let anyone take him out except you or me. He's going to be safe."

She let out a long breath. "Thank God they didn't hurt him. I was so afraid of what Sam might do."

"So you traded yourself for him." His breath was audible. "He could have killed you."

"It wouldn't have mattered, as long as Rory was safe."

Cash slid his hands into his pockets and stared at her with his lips compressed while he fought back rage at his own inadequacy. She wouldn't meet his eyes. "You know you can't stay alone, don't you? Not with that other lunatic on the loose. Stanton is sure to have told him where you live."

She swallowed, hard. "I can get a room in a hotel somewhere…"

"I'm taking you back to Jacobsville with me."

"No!" she said harshly. "Not after what's been in the tabloids!"

"I'm going to have a live-in nurse until you're back on your feet," he continued, as if she hadn't spoken. "There won't be any gossip."

"You…would do that?" she asked, surprised.

He nodded. "Rory pointed out that you couldn't stay alone with me," he said, tongue in cheek. "I'm the police chief. We have to think about my reputation."

"Obviously we don't have to worry about mine," she said drowsily. "I don't have one anymore."

"Stop that," he said curtly. "Nobody believes what they read in tabloids!"

"Nobody except you," she agreed and she looked straight at him.

He couldn't argue with that, but it hurt to hear it. He jingled the change in his pocket. "I told the staff we were engaged."

"What for?" she asked coldly, trying not to let a helpless flutter of excitement show.

"They wouldn't let me into ICU any other way. You were there until they ran twenty tests and patched you up, when they first brought you in," he replied. "I wasn't going to be kept out. So we can tell people we're engaged when we get to Jacobsville, too." He studied her flushed face. "That would shut up any gossip."

"You don't need to sacrifice yourself on my behalf," she said with a hint of her old spirit. "I won't be around long, anyway, if these cuts can be covered up with makeup when my ribs heal and the bruises fade. I'll have a movie to finish when Joel Harper gets back in the country."

He moved closer. "I did a stupid thing," he said through his teeth. "Two stupid things. I gave in to temptation and then I believed what I read in the tabloids. You wouldn't be here if it wasn't for me. You called to ask me to get Rory back, didn't you?"

She nodded without looking at him.

He jingled the change in his pocket again. He hadn't apologized in years.

"You told me how you felt, in the beginning," she said heavily. "I didn't listen. I pushed you into what happened, Cash. I don't even know why I did it, but if there's anybody to blame, it's me."

He scowled. "Rory said you were going to keep the baby."

She turned her face away, wary of letting him see the wetness in her eyes. "None of that matters anymore."

But it did. He could feel the pain that radiated from her. "The only thing that does matter is getting you back on your feet," he agreed. "And keeping you safe until we have to testify at Stanton's trial."

"I've been expecting a call from my mother," she said coldly. "I guess Sam hasn't gotten in touch with her yet. She'll blame me for his being in jail."

"No doubt," he agreed. "The FBI is looking into the possibility that she conspired with him to do it. If they find enough evidence, they'll charge her with conspiracy, and she'll go to trial, too. Kidnapping is a federal offense."

"I didn't think of that," she said abruptly. "There's still a man at large, too."

"Yes. That's why you have to go to Texas with me. Judd will be around, or I will, all the time. You won't be vulnerable."

That was what he thought. "Christabel won't… mind…having me around after all that business with Judd?" she worried.

"Christabel and Judd are like two little kids in a candy shop since they married—especially since the twins came," he said. "They won't mind. Nobody's jealous of you anymore."

She sighed, wincing when it pulled her ribs. "How do you like living in such a small town?" she asked. "You were like a duck out of water when I was there."

He hesitated. "I'm not sure. At first, I did it for a joke. My cousin Chet needed help and talked me into it. I was sure I'd hate every minute. But I was tired of cybercrime and sick of my life." He sighed. "I've been an outsider in Jacobsville ever since. But the job is…interesting. Varied. Never boring. And I feel as if I'm really doing some good. I've cornered the market on drug violations. Apparently Chet didn't want to make any waves, so he turned a blind eye to some of the higher level dealings. I called in the DEA and started staking out bars."

"You'll make enemies."

"I've got plenty already, thanks. We've got an acting mayor and at least two city council members who'd bring firewood if they offered to burn me at the stake." He pulled up a chair and sat down. "But if I can keep a secretary, I might give it another year."

"You need to look for a woman who isn't afraid of snakes and doesn't throw things back at you," she pointed out.

"That would be a change."

She rubbed her fingers over her mouth. "I'm so dry."

He got up and poured water in a glass, lifting her head so that she could sip it.

"I never knew how good water was until today," she said with a husky, broken laugh.

He eased her head back down and put the water glass on her side table. "You've got guts. Trading yourself for Rory was the stuff of legends."

"You'd have done the same thing I did," she replied, closing her eyes.

"Sure, but I'd have had a K-bar in my boot and a hide gun in an ankle holster," he retorted.

"My ankles are too thin for a holster."

"I noticed."

She drifted for a few seconds. "I had to ask for something else for pain," she explained. "I'm afraid to go to sleep, but I think I'm going to."

He moved his chair closer and caught her slender fingers into his. "I'll be right here," he said, his deep voice comforting. "Go to sleep."

She tried to smile, but she couldn't quite remember how. She sighed and drifted off.

THE SMELL OF POTATOES and chicken brought her wide-awake. Cash was removing metal covers on a tray that he'd positioned on the sliding table.

"For hospital food this doesn't look half bad," he mused, glancing at her. "You have ice cream for dessert, too."

She struggled to reach the button that would raise the head of her bed. He did it for her and moved the sliding tray over her legs.

"You need to go and get something to eat, too," she told him.

"I just did, while you were sleeping. You're going to have to be in here for several days," he said. "The doctor said we'd take it one day at a time, and see how you do. Then I'm taking you to Texas. Those stitches come out before you leave the hospital, but you'll still need a checkup down the line. He's referring you to a friend of his in San Antonio, and he's going to consult with him on your progress."

She gaped at him. "How did you arrange that?"

"I just asked."

She shook her head. "You're amazing."

"I hated the idea of flying you back up here for your two-week checkup. It's too risky right now."

"Okay."

"No argument?" he mused.

"I'm too tired."

"Eat your supper."

He handed her a fork. She drew in a long, slow breath and began to eat. She wasn't really hungry, but it was good food.

"I got in touch with Joel Harper," he added, not telling her that it had taken several international phone calls and even a couple of threats to chase the man down. "He's run into a hitch in the film he's working on, so it will be at least three months before he's back in the country. He said not to worry about your insurance. He'll pay what it doesn't, as an advance against your salary," he added.

She almost cried with relief. "Thank God," she whispered. "I was so worried…"

"Don't let that chicken go to waste," he said. "I had it down in the cafeteria. It's good."

She lifted another forkful to her mouth. "It's an Italian dish. I can make it myself, when I have time."

"Rory can make barbecue."

She lifted her eyes to his face. "Yes, he can. How did you know?"

"He told me." He toyed with his sleeve. "He's quite a boy."

"I think so, too."

"I told him he could come out and stay with me, too, as soon as school's out."

She hesitated. "I don't know. I'll probably be back at work, then."

"Probably not," he returned. "It's just barely April. Joel won't be back until July or early August."

She sighed, finishing her chicken. "I thought you didn't like ties."

"I'm not wearing one, am I?"

"You know what I mean."

He crossed one long leg over the other. "You can

watch the political process up close," he said evasively. "Calhoun Ballenger is running against one of our oldest state senators for the Democratic nomination. The primary's the first Tuesday in May. It's shaping up to be a very hot race."

"I don't know much about politics."

"You'll have fun learning," he said with a gentle smile.

"Think so?" She opened her ice cream.

"You didn't eat your sweet peas," he pointed out.

"I hate sweet peas."

"Vegetables are good for you."

"Only vegetables I like are good for me," she corrected. She spooned ice cream into her mouth. Chewing was uncomfortable, she had some bruises along with the cuts on her face, but the ice cream just melted on her tongue.

"We have an ice-cream parlor in Jacobsville," he said. "They sell every flavor under the sun. I'm partial to strawberry."

"That's my favorite, too." She finished and put the cup and wooden spoon back on the tray, grimacing when she shifted.

"Rib hurt?" he asked.

She nodded, leaning back against the pillows. "I wish I had a gun and five minutes alone with Sam," she said huskily. "To my credit, I did try one of those roundhouse kicks when he found out he couldn't get any money for me. I even managed to block his first punch. Then he grabbed that bottle and I lost ground. I'd love to show him how it feels to have bruised ribs and concussion."

"He's got a nice bullet wound," he told her.

She frowned. "He got shot?"

"Yes, he did. I slipped, or he'd have had more than a bullet wound."

Her lips parted. She stared at him wide-eyed. "*You* got me out…that's what the FBI agent meant when he said they had some interference. You came after me!"

"Yes," he confessed. "I didn't have a lot of faith in the agents they assigned to your case. They were sitting in your apartment with Rory waiting for a phone call that might never have come. I tracked Stanton and his cronies down, with a little help from a former colleague."

"I wondered," she said softly. "I couldn't get anybody to tell me what happened."

"They didn't know," he said simply. "Since there's no evidence to connect me to the shooting, the feds and I have an arrangement. I cleared my presence with a higher-up who owed me a favor. He ran interference for me with the police and the other government agents. At any rate, I don't want the complications involved in admitting I was the shooter. It could cause a scandal and negatively impact my reputation as a police chief in Jacobsville."

"Oh."

"So we're all pretending that Sam shot himself, and he was too drunk to see where the shot came from," he said, leaning back in his chair. "Lucky Sam to still be standing at all after what he did to you."

"He was very angry," she recalled, shivering.

"Did he force himself on you?"

"He was too busy hitting me to think about sex," she sighed heavily. "One of his friends tried to stop him, to his credit, but Sam was out of control. He'd been using something, I don't know what. His eyes were glazed and he was higher than a kite."

"Which man tried to stop him?" he asked.

"He had blond hair," she murmured. "That's all I remember."

"The one who was arrested with him was blond. One got away. The dark-headed one, I think."

"Maybe." She blinked. "My mother has a lot to answer for," she said. "If I were vindictive enough, I'd give the tabloids a story they'd never forget."

"You'd never get over it, either," he said. "Don't even be tempted."

She looked over at him with sad eyes. "They couldn't do much more damage to me than they've already done."

His face clenched. "I was stupid enough to believe them," he replied. "Most of this is my fault."

She shook her head. "Things just happen," she said

heavily. "My mother was behind this. I know she was. She'd already phoned me and made threats. I didn't believe she'd risk her own son for money. Silly me."

"Has she always been an alcoholic?"

She nodded. "All my life. I was calling bail bondsmen when I was eight, to get her out of jail. She'd been arrested for soliciting, for public drunkenness, for DUI, for theft…you name it, there was a charge. She latched on to one man after another to get money to support us. But eventually she stayed drunk too much even to do that. I had a paper route to buy my school clothes." She winced. "That was before Sam came to live with us."

"He's a loser, if there ever was one," he said coldly.

"Don't I know it. My mother thinks differently."

"There's no accounting for taste."

She laughed drowsily. "That's what I always say." She closed her eyes. "I'm so tired."

"You've been through a lot. Too much."

"You won't let Rory get hurt?" she asked suddenly.

"You know me better than that."

She did. He might not want Tippy for life, but he was already fond of Rory. He wouldn't let the kidnappers get the boy again.

"You don't think they'll make bond, do you?" she asked.

"Not if I can help it," he assured her.

What he didn't say was that sometimes a judge could be coaxed into believing a suspect, and setting reasonable bond. If Stanton could find a way, he'd get out. And if he did, he'd make a beeline for the woman who'd put him in jail. He'd have nothing to lose.

Cash was going to have his work cut out for him, keeping Tippy and Rory safe. But he was going to. He wasn't going to let anything happen to either one of them ever again.

CHAPTER NINE

CHAPTER NINE

TIPPY FACED THE POLICE the next morning. She held Cash's hand while she gave them a statement. It was the first step to recovery, she told herself. Just one more little obstacle to get through. They took photographs as well, with a digital camera, for evidence of the treatment she'd received at Stanton's hands.

Cash sat with her the whole time, going through endless cups of coffee. It was a straightforward procedure, but it took longer than he'd expected. He went with the investigators back to their precinct to write out a statement of his own. He couldn't tell the whole truth, but he told as much as he felt comfortable with.

"What about Tippy's mother?" he asked the lead investigator after they'd talked for a few minutes.

"She said her mother was behind the kidnapping, in order to get money from her," the older man said.

"That's right. She's a drug addict."

The investigator's pale eyes shimmered with anger. "You'd be amazed how many we get here, most involved in burglaries or holdups or murders. We had a guy last week, eighteen, got high on acid and beat his grandmother to death. Never remembered doing anything, but he'll go to prison for life if they convict him."

"I know," Cash replied. "I'm in law enforcement myself. I've spent the last few months rooting out drug money. You probably know where it comes from."

"Yeah," the other man nodded. "From respectable citizens who want to make a lot of easy money and don't care how."

"Bingo."

"I've always thought I'd like to work in a small town," the detective mused. "Is the money good?"

Cash chuckled. "If you like beer. It won't get you champagne."

The older man's eyes twinkled. "I hate champagne."

"Then you might want to try it. You can do a lot of good on a small scale."

There was a brief pause. "I heard some things about you from my lieutenant. He was in covert ops in the Gulf War."

Cash's eyebrows lifted. "Was he really?"

"He's got a nephew named Peter Stone. Lives in Brooklyn."

Cash gave him a wry look. "My, my, what a small world we live in." He grinned.

The lieutenant grinned back.

HE GOT A CAB BACK to the hospital. Tippy was sleeping again when he went into her room and sat by the bed. He was anxious about her. The interview must have been as much an ordeal for her as the wounds had been when she first got them. It was painful and she had a long way to go before she would recover from her injuries, to say nothing of the emotional scars that had been added to the ones she already carried. He hated the guilt. It was his fault. His fault…!

"Why…do you look like that?" she asked drowsily.

"Like what?" he asked.

Her lovely green eyes opened as wide as she could get them to. He was so handsome. She loved looking at him. She knew that he only felt guilty because he'd let her down, but it felt like heaven to have him this close and concerned about her.

"You look…lost."

He leaned forward. "I can't get away from my past," he said after a minute. "Everywhere I go, people know about me."

"That can't be a bad thing."

"Can't it?" He studied her hungrily. "I'm sorry about that interview, but they can't go forward without evidence."

"I'll have to testify against them, too, won't I?" she asked.

He nodded. "But I'll be right with you. Every minute."

She managed a weak smile. "Thanks." She shifted, grimacing again. "I'll bet you've had worse than this—concussion, cuts and bruised ribs, I mean."

"Broken ribs, broken teeth, gunshot wounds, cigarette burns, bruises all the way up and down…"

She caught her breath.

"…Facial cuts and fractures," he added. "But mine had to have stitches, and there wasn't time for plastic surgery." He touched the faint white marks on his cheeks.

"I was certain that he'd done major damage to my face," she said huskily. "There was so much blood. But the doctor said they were relatively minor cuts. They didn't destroy nerve or muscle. I was lucky."

"Extremely lucky," he agreed. "But I'm…sorry," he ground out the word, "that I wouldn't listen to you."

She drew in a few quick, shallow breaths to avoid the pain of deep ones. "You thought…I was chasing you. It's okay."

His eyes closed hard. "I don't trust people."

"I know that. Neither do I, much."

He looked at her with cold memory in his eyes. "They say bullets are dangerous. But the most dangerous thing on earth is love. It guts you, if you let it."

She put a hand to her ribs and groaned when she couldn't get her breath.

He got up from the chair. "Here." He took her spare pillow and put it gently on her chest. "When you have to cough, hold the pillow close. It makes it easier."

She tried, and it did. "How did you know that?"

"Two broken ribs. One punctured my lung," he said simply. "It took weeks to get back on my feet. I had pneumonia as a consequence."

Her eyes opened wider. "That's what the doctor was worried about, with me. He says when you breathe…shallowly…the stagnant air doesn't get forced out of your lungs and it can lead to infection."

"Exactly. That's why they're giving you antibiotics and making you drink so many fluids."

She managed a smile. "You know a lot."

"I've broken most of the major bones in my body at one time or another," he said simply. "If I hadn't been in such good physical condition, I could have died at least twice."

Her pale eyes searched his dark ones. "Rory thinks you're the greatest."

He moved restlessly. "I like him, too."

"You really don't like people getting close, do you?"

He shook his head. "I'm not comfortable sharing things." His eyes narrowed as he studied her. "It was too soon, what happened."

"Yes. Much too soon, and my fault," she added.

"It takes two, Tippy," he said quietly. "We both jumped in without looking."

Her eyes searched over his face like loving hands. "I bought baby clothes," she said with a painful laugh. "Stupid."

"Rory told me."

She closed her eyes. "Everything happened at once. The job became unbearable with the new second AD," she said, remembering the arrogant little second assistant director and what he'd cost her. "My mother made threats. I lost my baby." She ground her teeth together and a tear she couldn't stop rolled eloquently down her pale cheek. "I started drinking."

She felt his hand grip hers, hard, and hold on.

"Rory told me that, too. He's worried about you. Listen, I know about drinking. I've done my share of it. You can't keep it up. You think it will stop the pain, but it only worsens the impact when you sober up."

"I found that out."

"It doesn't even numb the pain, after a while. I ended up in rehab," he added matter-of-factly.

"After…your wife left?" she probed gently.

He nodded curtly, averting his eyes.

"You loved her."

He glanced at her and frowned. "I thought I did," he said involuntarily. "Maybe it was my pride, more than love."

She smiled gently and closed her eyes. His big, warm hand felt so comforting. Her long fingers curled into it trustingly as the medicine finally began to work again, numbing the pain, driving away the fear...

She was asleep. He watched her with turbulent eyes. His emotions, once so easily controlled, were beginning to get the best of him. He'd let her get right next to his heart, right under his skin. But he still didn't quite trust her enough. He'd hurt her badly. He'd chased her out of his life, and then had to come back to save her. She felt gratitude certainly. But she'd been traumatized by her recent experience, and he couldn't be sure of anything she said or did at the moment.

The doctor said it would be four to six weeks before she was well enough to work again. Her stitches were easier, they'd be out within five days. But it would also take longer for her emotions to stabilize. Meanwhile, he would take care of her, protect her, spoil her. Then, when she was whole again, they'd take stock of their situation.

That was what his mind said. But his body was tormented as it recalled the sweetness of her body against his in bed, the hunger of her kisses, the aching pleasure she'd given him in the darkness. He'd never touched skin so warm and perfect, he'd never wanted a woman so much. That one night had haunted him. It would haunt him forever. If he lost her…

He let go of her hand and sat back in his chair, worrying. He'd faced that problem already. He'd gone back to his job and tried to put her out of his mind. But he'd never succeeded. He'd felt like half a man ever since.

Now she was hurt and she needed him. Rory needed him. He'd never had to take care of anyone, not like this. He'd cared for wounded comrades in battle. He'd cared for buddies under the gun in covert raids. He'd saved civilians from peril in the course of his duties. But he'd never been needed on such an intimate level in his life, except by his mother, when he was very young. He hadn't been able to protect her from death. But he'd saved Tippy.

He studied her sleeping face hungrily. Didn't they say that a saved life belonged to the rescuer? He thought about having her in his house, providing for her, taking care of her. He thought of Rory living with him, looking up to him, coming to him for comfort, for reassurance, for affection. Rory had only had Tippy. There hadn't been a man in his life, except at military school.

He felt suddenly afraid of the responsibility, uncertain of his ability to shoulder it. He'd never had to consider the welfare of another person in his adult life. He hadn't been responsible or accountable to anyone except himself. That was going to change. Tippy was going to be dependent on him for weeks. So was Rory, while his sister was unable to take care of him.

Life was taking on a new form. He wasn't sure he was going to like the changes. But they would be interesting.

Only a few years ago, his life had been in flux. He'd wandered from job to job, never comfortable, never happy. He hadn't fit in with his co-workers. He hadn't found anything that made him secure.

Now, he had a job in a tiny little town that seemed hardly significant. But he was surprised to find how much it fulfilled him. It gave him a feeling of satisfaction he'd never had when working in the military or in big city police departments. He checked on elderly residents, to make sure they were all right and set up neighborhood watches. He spoke to grammar school classes about drug prevention. He assisted local and state authorities with drug raids. He reassured citizens who were robbed. He comforted people whose children attacked them in drug-crazed frenzies and helped them cope with the terror and emptiness of being both victim and parent. He stood beside frightened women who had to go to court to testify against brutal husbands. He instigated patrols in dangerous areas. He taught gun safety and self-defense classes for local citizens. He badgered the acting mayor, Ben Brady, to go before the city council and fight for better patrol cars and a bigger budget for night surveillance on crime-ridden neighborhoods.

Brady wouldn't do it. He was more concerned with his uncle—state senator Merrill—and his re-election campaign, than any city business. Cash was sorry their last mayor had been forced to resign after a heart attack. Certainly, Brady was going to have a hard time keeping the mayor's job, since a former well-loved mayor, Eddie Cane, had entered the race and was Brady's only competition to keep the job. They were both Democrats. It wasn't going to be much of a surprise at the primary in May. And the man who won it would be virtually unopposed at the November general election.

Nobody much liked Brady. He was narrow-minded and he did anything Senator Merrill—or the senator's daughter, Julie—told him to do. Cash knew things about them that most people didn't. Very soon, there was going to be a political scandal in Jacobsville that would raise the roof at city hall. But aside from that problem, the other councilmen and the city manager liked Cash and worked well with him on his projects, well, except for the two who were loyal to Brady—but Cash privately thought Brady intimidated them. His officers had warmed to him over the months. They were beginning to feel like family. Jacobsville felt more and more like home. He'd been an outsider his whole life until now.

His eyes returned to Tippy's sleeping face. This woman had gone from active enemy to intimate friend in a space of months. He'd become part of her life, and she'd become part of his. He didn't understand his own feelings anymore. He'd been crazy about Christabel Gaines. Her innocence, her kindness, her sense of humor, her independence and strength of will had attracted him. But Christabel had never known the sort of life he'd led. She would have been sympathetic to his nightmares and his horrific past, but she'd never have understood them. Tippy would. She hadn't been through wars, but the traumas of her youth had predisposed her to understand his.

Funny, he thought, how he'd been so positive that she was a sophisticated, sexually liberated sort of woman when he first met her; he'd been sure she was a man-eater. But her real personality was one of fragility, vulnerability, yet she was no shrinking violet. She was strong and fiercely protective of people she cared for. Her turbulent upbringing had been one of pain and terror.

He didn't know if he could ever share his past with her. It was far too brutal and cold. But if he could, he didn't think it would repel her. She had an empathy that he'd rarely encountered, and that annoying sixth sense that gave her an unwanted insight into his deepest feelings. He hated having her read his mind. She saw far too much.

He laughed softly to himself. He was getting fanciful. It was late, and he needed a night in a real bed, not in a chair. But when his eyes slid softly over her body in the bed, he knew he couldn't leave her. He didn't want to consider why he felt that way.

HE'D DRIFTED OFF WHEN the last nurse went off duty. When he was aware of his surroundings again, the new nurse was shaking his shoulder gently.

"Sorry," she said when his eyes came open. "But we have to give Miss Danbury her bath."

"Oh. Sure." He got up, stretched and yawned, and gave Tippy a quick glance. She looked far worse this morning. Her bruises were breaking out like measles, and the cuts were very red. She looked less like a model than the star of a horror film. He hoped they wouldn't let her see a mirror. "I'm going to find a hotel room and catch an hour or so of sleep, then I'll be back. Okay?" he asked gently.

She hesitated. "You don't have to come back…"

"If I don't, you'll check yourself out and go home," he murmured.

She flushed. "I would…not!" she exclaimed, wondering how he'd guessed her thoughts.

"It works both ways, doesn't it?" he mused enigmatically, thinking privately that he could read her mind a little, too. "Don't let her out," he told the nurse firmly. "I'll phone the nursing desk on this floor as soon as I'm checked in and give you a number to call if she puts a foot outside this room. Better yet, I'll give you my cell phone number."

"Yes, sir," the nurse said with a grin.

Tippy glared at him. "That's not fair. I can heal at home as well…as I can…heal here," she said, hating the spaced words, because it hurt to talk and breathe.

"You wouldn't make it to the elevator with those lungs," he pointed out, "not to mention the aftereffects of that concussion."

"He's right," the nurse said, chuckling at her glare. "Now, now, we're going to start giving you breathing treatments this morning. We don't want pneumonia."

"No, we don't," Cash said firmly.

"You're enjoying this," Tippy accused. "I feel like the Prisoner of Zenda!"

"That was Stewart Granger, who was much taller than you, and just as belligerent," he pointed out.

"I am not belligerent!" she snapped.

Cash and the nurse exchanged glances.

"You stop that!" Tippy grated. "This is not…fair. Two against…one!"

"She can't help it," he told the nurse. "She doesn't

want you to see that she's crazy about me. What she really wants is to follow me home."

"I do…not!" Tippy raged.

"Yes, you do, and I'll let you, the minute the doctor says you can be checked out," he promised.

"I am not…a book!"

He chuckled. "Have a nice bath and do what they tell you to. If you're very good," he added, "I might bring you a present when I come back."

She tried to glare and didn't quite make it.

"I don't take bribes," she muttered.

"Rory said you like cats," he told her. "Stuffed cats with sweet faces."

"You'll never find a stuffed cat around here," she stated.

"Think so?" He glanced at the nurse, who was nodding enthusiastically and mouthing "gift shop."

Tippy started to argue some more, but she really did like stuffed cats.

He smiled at her. His dark eyes twinkled. She met his eyes and couldn't manage another single protest. He affected her breathing as much as the badly bruised ribs.

And he knew it, the beast. He gave her a wicked wink and walked out before she could come up with a response.

"What a dishy man," the nurse said as she went into the bathroom to fill the plastic basin she'd brought with her. "Lucky you!"

Tippy didn't answer her. She wasn't sure how much luck was involved in her present situation, or how long Cash's conciliatory attitude would last. She was betting that it would give out about the time her wounds healed and she was ready to work again. By then, his conscience would be in better shape, too. She knew he was beating himself mentally for not listening when she'd phoned him after Rory was kidnapped. He was only doing penance. Once she was back at work, he'd forget her as easily as he'd forget a hangnail.

THAT EVENING JUST ABOUT supper time, Cash had gone to talk to someone he knew in law enforcement about the third kidnapper, who was still on the streets. He left a pretty marmalade stuffed cat with whimsical features by the bedside to keep her company. While he was gone, Tippy had an unexpected visitor.

A very large man, built like a wrestler, came in the door. An equally big man paused inside the door, mumbled something to the other man, and went outside to stand at the door.

The visitor approached the foot of the bed. He had thick wavy black hair and large brown eyes, in a broad face with an olive complexion. He was wearing a navy pin-striped suit that looked as if it might have cost as much as Tippy's apartment. His white shirt was spotless, crowned by a blue plaid tie that emphasized his olive complexion.

He gave Tippy a curious scrutiny and his heavy brows drew together angrily.

"Who are you?" she asked uneasily.

"Marcus Carrera," he said in a deep, gravelly voice. His brown eyes narrowed. "You don't know me, huh?" he added, and a faint smile touched his wide, chiseled mouth.

"Actually, I've heard of you through a dear friend of mine, Cullen Cannon," she added, and tried to smile back.

"Cullen was one of the most decent guys I ever knew." He slid his big hands into his pockets. "One of the rats who did that to you works for me. He did this on the side, of course, and I didn't know until this morning."

Tippy pushed the button that raised the head of her bed a few inches. "Do you know where he is?" she asked huskily. "I'd like to take a baseball bat and have a little talk with him."

He laughed, surprised. "No, I don't," he replied. "But if I find him, I swear I'll have him delivered here in a net and I'll furnish the bat."

Her smile grew. "Thanks."

His dark eyes didn't miss a scratch or a bruise on the part of her that showed above the white sheet and tan blanket. "They've got the other two in the city lockup," he murmured. "I talked to a judge and the assistant district attorney who's handling the case," he added. "They'll have a better chance at getting sainthood than they'll have at getting out on bond."

"Thanks," she sighed.

"I hate having anybody close to me messed up in something like this," he said with pure disgust. "Even when I was on the wrong side of justice, I never would have approved of something like this."

"Wrong side?" she asked.

The door opened and Cash came in, staring with narrow eyes at Tippy's guest.

"Hello, Grier," Carrera said pleasantly. "There's a guy in the local lockup who swears you shot him."

"Me?" Cash replied innocently. "I would never shoot another person. Honest."

Carrera burst out laughing and held out a big hand.

"What are you doing here?" Cash asked, shaking his hand. "And is that Mr. Smith outside the door?"

"Yep," he replied. "He worked for Kip Tennison, but when she married Cy Harden, she didn't really need him anymore. He's been with me ever since."

"He's a character. Does he still have the iguana?"

Carrera grinned. "He does. It's five feet long now. He keeps it in his room at the resort on Paradise Island. If we ever have problems with unruly customers, I send him down with the lizard. It's usually enough."

"I'm not surprised. Why are you here?"

Carrera sobered. "One of my guys was in on this kidnapping plot. I didn't know it," he added quickly when Cash's eyes started flashing. "I only found out this morning."

"Do you know where to find the guy?"

"No, I don't," Carrera replied. "But I went to the assistant district attorney on this case and gave him everything I had on the SOB."

Cash did a double take. "Excuse me?"

Carrera glared at him. "Why are you shocked? I am not a gangster! I own casinos and hotels, now. That's all!"

Cash cleared his throat. "Right."

"Just because I did a few little bad things once..." Carrera began.

"Some gamblers from South Dakota were found in, shall we say, unspeakable conditions in a backwater of New Jersey—"

"If Tate Winthrop told you I was responsible for that," Carrera interrupted.

"Actually, it was his boss, Pierce Hutton."

"He lives in Paris! What does he know?" the older man muttered.

"Then there was the Walters man who embezzled funds from the elderly mother of one of your staff who mysteriously wound up in an oil barrel floating down the Hudson River..."

"Listen, I don't own an oil barrel," Carrera interrupted again, "and for the last time, I am a law-abiding citizen these days."

"Have it your way," Cash said. "What do you know about the guy who helped Stanton nab Tippy's little brother?" he persisted.

"Not enough to track him down," the other man replied darkly. "If I did…"

"You're a law-abiding citizen," Cash reminded him.

"Well, yeah." Carrera pursed his lips. "But I know lots of guys who *aren't*, who owe me favors."

"You wouldn't believe what sort of favors he usually asks for," Cash told Tippy with a twinkle in his dark eyes.

Tippy gave the older man a piercing stare.

"Not *those* sort," Carrera growled. He shrugged his broad shoulders. "I like exotic fabric. Actually, I like antique cloth better."

Tippy was staring at him as if she wasn't sure she was hearing correctly.

"I quilt," Carrera said belligerently. "In fact, I win competitions. Some of my stuff is in an art gallery in the village right now."

"He's not kidding," Cash told her. "He's internationally famous for his designs." Cash grinned. "Didn't they find a body in one, once…?"

"Not in one of mine," the older man shot right back. "I wouldn't waste one of my babies on any hoodlum."

Cash laughed. So did Tippy.

"I won't stay," Carrera said. "I just wanted to see

how bad they hurt her. You'll be okay," he assured Tippy, motioning to his cheek, where two jagged white lines were visible against his olive complexion. "These went all the way to the bone, so they left scars. Yours won't."

"Thanks," she said.

He shrugged. "I won't stop hunting the guy. To answer your earlier question, his name is Barkley. Ted Barkley. He's a mechanic. A real mechanic," he emphasized. "He can fix anything, which is why I kept him around. He's got family somewhere in south Texas, so if you take her back home with you, keep an eye peeled."

"I'd like to know about the family," Cash said.

"Thought you would." Carrera pulled a folded piece of paper out of his inside jacket pocket and handed it to Cash. "That's the same info I gave the assistant DA. The guy's also handy with a gun, so watch your back. He'll do anything for money, and I mean anything. Stanton may not have much, but that son of Montes is heavily into money laundering, and he'll have people he can borrow it from. He won't want you to testify at that trial. If he can have you killed, he will."

Tippy caught her breath audibly.

"He'll have to go through me to do it," Cash assured her. "Stop worrying."

Carrera gave him a measuring glance. "If you need help, you can call me."

"I don't have any exotic fabric on me."

Carrera grinned and clapped Cash on the shoulder. "That's okay. You can owe me."

"Thanks," Tippy said.

He winked at her and left the room.

"Is he really reformed?" she asked Cash when he left.

"He really is. I know something about him that I can't tell you, but I can guarantee that he's on the right side of the law." He looked at her poor bruised, cut face with sad eyes. "Nobody's going to hurt you again, ever. I swear it."

She took that at face value. He was ridden with guilt and he felt sorry for her. It wouldn't last. She knew it, even if he didn't. She just smiled and said nothing.

CHAPTER TEN

CHAPTER TEN

TIPPY'S LUNG WAS CAREFULLY monitored until the doctors were certain that she was on the mend. She continued on the antibiotics and avoided looking at herself in the mirror. She looked like a second-rate horror show, she mused, and she was glad that she didn't have to appear in public for the time being.

She did worry about that third kidnapper who was still on the loose, and the danger of having a contract put out on her by Stanton or his cousin.

"Do you think Mr. Carrera was right?" she asked Cash one evening at the hospital. "About that cousin of Stanton's trying to have me killed?"

Cash was reticent. He had been for two days, ever since Carrera's visit. "Anything is possible," he said. "But you'll be in Jacobsville."

"I've heard it said that a hit man can strike anywhere."

He cocked both eyebrows. "Jacobsville has barely two thousand people. The vice president came through it last year. He stayed for a few nights to visit one of the Hart brothers—they're his cousins. The secret service tagged along and tried to blend in."

She listened, curious.

He laughed softly. "They're great guys. I've known several of them, and they really care about how they do the job. But they thought the way to fit in was to look like cowboys." He shook his head. "Here were these guys in department-store cowboy hats, wearing brand-new denim jeans and brand-new boots and spotless Western-cut shirts. One of the Hart's cowboys walked up to one and asked if he'd like to come out on the ranch and help cut some cattle. The fed said he didn't know how to butcher beef."

Even Tippy understood that the reference was to removing specific cattle from a herd, not actually cutting them up. She laughed softly.

"So they got back into their suits and went on with the job." He shook his head. "The point is, you can't walk into a small town, where generations of people have grown up together, and not be recognized as an outsider. In a city of a half million, maybe you could. But in a town the size of Jacobsville, you're noticed."

"That's a little more reassuring," she agreed.

"I'm not going to let you get hurt again," he reminded her firmly. "That's a promise, and I don't give my word lightly."

She shifted and winced. Her ribs were still uncomfortable, but at least the headache was gone.

"Do you have a television?" she asked.

"Yes. A television, a radio, a CD-player and two bookcases full of mystery and detective novels, along with a healthy ancient history section and even some science fiction novels. If all that fails," he added with a grin, "I've got some great videos. All the *Star Treks,* all the *Star Wars,* as well as most of the *Lord of the Rings* trilogy and the *Harry Potter* movies."

"Those are Rory's favorites," she exclaimed.

"What do you like?"

She thought about that. "Sherlock Holmes, old Bette Davis movies, anything with John Wayne, and those fantasy and science fiction movies you collect."

"I like Bette Davis movies myself," he confessed. He moved closer to the bed and looked down at her face clinically. "The cuts are looking better already. The bruises aren't," he added with a sigh. "They've gone purple and yellow. You look like you've been in one hell of a fight."

"You ought to be on the inside of these bruises," she murmured facetiously. "I never got hit that hard, even on the streets when I was twelve."

He scowled. "You were beaten?"

She averted her eyes. "I had a couple of close calls before Cullen picked me up," she said. "And that's all I'm saying about it," she added belligerently.

He put his hands deep in his pockets, still scowling. "You don't trust me even now, do you?"

"I trust you to be human," she replied. "Most people are sympathetic when someone gets hurt. That doesn't mean much after they heal."

He hadn't realized she was so cynical. So was he, but he didn't think about it much. He considered Carrera's warning and had some minor misgivings about his ability to protect Tippy. He couldn't be at home all the time, and there was always the slight possibility that a hit man could sneak in at night without being seen locally. He knew how possible that was, from his own agonizing past experience.

"You look tormented," Tippy remarked quietly.

He blinked and his face closed up. "You're the patient here, not me."

She cocked her head and studied him quietly. "You don't share anything, either, do you? Your past is a closed book. You live with your nightmares, all alone in the dark."

His eyes glittered. "I don't trust anyone close enough to share them. Including you," he lashed out involuntarily.

"Especially me," she agreed. "I see too much,

don't I? That's what really set you off, the night before you left New York."

He turned away from her and stared out the window. It was raining again, typically April weather in New York. He didn't like having Tippy look inside his mind. It was disquieting, because it denoted an intimacy that was already establishing itself between them.

"Okay, I'll stop visiting your brain when you aren't looking," she murmured dryly.

"I'm a private person," he said without looking at her.

"I knew that the first time I saw you. But it didn't apply to everyone. I remember the day you were talking to Christabel at her ranch," she recalled, and her voice changed. "Your voice was so tender—it was almost like you were talking to a small child. You offered to take her to town for a hamburger. You'd let her ride in your car and turn on the siren, you said."

He turned, shocked that she remembered that.

She avoided his searching gaze. His attitude toward Christabel had hurt her. She'd never understood why, until recently. She'd been jealous. It was stupid, because this was a man who didn't belong to people. He was always the outsider, the loner. He kept everyone at arm's length. But he indulged Christabel always. It didn't take a mind reader to know that he'd have sacrificed anything for her, including his own life.

"She put up with a lot from me," Tippy was saying out loud, without realizing it. "I was totally unfair to her. I never felt it more keenly than when she was shot. I'd told her some hurtful thing about Judd, and if she died, I'd have had that memory to live with."

He moved back to the bed, frowning. "I didn't know that."

She toyed with the sheet over the faded floral fabric of her cotton gown. "Joel's assistant director was overbearing and he reminded me of Sam Stanton. I was afraid of him. Judd was my protection, my guardian angel. I was afraid if he got seriously involved with Christabel, I'd be on my own." She looked up at him ruefully. "I was, too. Except for you." Her eyes were dazed. "I couldn't believe it when you grabbed his hand and made him stop harassing me."

"I don't like bullies," he said simply.

"Yes, but I was the enemy," she reminded him.

"Not after Christabel got shot, you weren't," he told her. "You knew exactly what to do for a gunshot wound. I didn't realize that at the time." His eyes narrowed. "How?"

She smiled wanly. "A lifetime of watching medical shows on television." She yawned. "I'm very tired. I think I could sleep a little."

He watched her impossibly long eyelashes close and stood staring down at her with his heart in his

eyes. She was the most surprising person he'd ever
known. He was glad he'd have time to try and make
up for his mistakes when they got back to Jacobsville.

He'd phoned his office already, to give Judd a
progress report on Tippy and give the other man an
idea of when he was coming home. It wouldn't be
long, he thought, the way Tippy was progressing.
Not long at all.

AND IT WASN'T. Within three days, she was out of the
hospital and Cash was packing things for her.

She noticed that he was uncomfortable in her bedroom, where they'd shared that one long night of
pleasure. She didn't mention it, and neither did he.

When her clothes were packed, he cleaned out
the refrigerator and carried the contents to Rory's
friend Don and his family down the hall. Then he
turned off everything at the switch and made time to
talk to the landlord, to make sure Tippy would still
have her apartment when she came back.

Tippy realized that Cash wasn't inviting her into
his house for life. Just the same, it stung to have him
so concerned about making sure her apartment lease
didn't lapse in her absence.

He was going day by day, not looking ahead. He
tackled the details as he did every move he made,
with precision and skill and economy of motion.
Tippy watched him covertly, her eyes hungry on the

powerful lines of his body, on his handsome face as he opened drawers and folded blouses.

"You're very good at packing," she remarked.

He glanced at her and grinned. "I've lived out of a suitcase most of my life, first in military school, then in the military itself. I'm efficient."

"I noticed." She looked around her with a sigh. "I'm going to miss my own space," she confessed. "This is the first apartment of my very own that I've ever had. Before, I lived with Cullen in his penthouse and afterward, I shared one with another model. But this is my own."

He smiled. "You'll like my house. They say it's enchanted."

Her eyebrows arched. "Really?"

"The story was that a man built it for his wife, who had Scotch-Irish ancestry. Her people came from the Isle of Skye." He folded another blouse and put it in the suitcase. "Local legend has it that you never wanted to make that lady angry, because bad things happened. She wasn't a mean person, she just had this unwanted 'gift' of the 'evil eye.' They said she also had the 'second sight.'"

"Like me," she murmured. "But I can't put the evil eye on people. I'm sure of that, because if I could, Sam would be under the dirt instead of above it."

He chuckled. "You'd never be able to live with a death on your conscience."

There was a pregnant silence behind him. He turned, curious, but she was busily pulling books out of her bookcase, not even looking his way.

Her heart was beating her to death. She was glad that he couldn't see it. There were still things in her past that she didn't want him to know. Not yet, anyway.

"What are those about?" he asked when he noticed two books in her hands.

"One is Pliny the Elder," she replied, and laughed. "He wrote about nature, you know. I find his work fascinating. He was killed when Mount Vesuvius erupted in 79 A.D., trying to rescue people on a boat. The second book is by his nephew, Pliny the Younger, who wrote the only description extant of the eruption itself. It makes fascinating reading."

"I haven't read the Plinys."

"You can borrow mine while I'm in residence," she said with magnificent hauteur. "I feel an obligation to educate the ignorant during my convalescence." She put her forearm across her brow with theatric emphasis. *"Noblesse oblige."*

He burst out laughing.

She peered at him from under her long lashes. The sound fascinated her. She had a feeling that it was something he did infrequently. He'd been happy enough with Rory and Tippy at Christmas, but even then, there had been a reticence about him that was palpable. But right now he was happy.

He became aware of her rapt stare and turned toward her with a curious expression.

She smiled. "I like hearing you laugh," she said simply.

As if the remark made him self-conscious, he turned back to his task.

She told herself that it was a start. All she had to do was convince him that smiling used fewer muscles than scowling did, and that laughter was good for the soul. It might change his life.

HE TOOK HER TO JACOBSVILLE via Houston. The plane trip was uncomfortable, even though he'd purchased first-class tickets, against her wishes. He hadn't wanted people to stare at her. There were fewer people to do it in the front seats, and the steward and stewardess were discreet.

Tippy still felt the aftereffects of her concussion—confusion and headaches—and some chest congestion from the bruised ribs. He'd worried about flying her out, but after examining her the doctor had told Cash it would be better to fly than subject her to hours in a car even with frequent stops.

Judd Dunn met them at the Jacobsville airport. He met Tippy with a grimace and then a smile.

"I know, you think it looks bad, but you're going to be your old self again in no time," Judd assured her with a dark-eyed smile. He was out of uniform and Cash noted it. "It's my day off," he reminded Cash. "I've left Lieutenant Palmer in charge."

"Palmer and not Barrett?" Cash remarked, because the men were both veterans and capable leaders.

"It's Barrett's day off, too," Judd replied, and then cleared his throat. "He had something to do."

Cash stopped dead beside Judd's big SUV, with Tippy's suitcases dripping from both big hands. "No," he said at once. "No, you wouldn't. You wouldn't send Barrett over to paper my house…!"

Judd looked highly offended. "I'm a police officer. In fact, I am an assistant chief of police," he added haughtily, with a grin at Tippy. "I would never do anything illegal."

"If I find one sheet of toilet paper, anywhere on my newly planted grass…" Cash began.

"Did you know he had such a suspicious mind?" Judd asked Tippy as he helped her up into the tall vehicle and gently into her seat.

"If you answer that, I'll make you liver and onions for supper," Cash said laconically as he stowed the luggage in back and then hopped up into the back seat.

Tippy glanced over her shoulder at him, wincing when the movement hurt her ribs. "I hate liver and onions!"

"I know." Cash smiled at her.

Judd chuckled as he started the big black vehicle and started out of the airport parking lot.

They pulled into the graveled driveway at Cash's house. It was a simple clapboard house, painted white with black shutters and a sprawling front porch with a swing and a rocking chair. There were rose-bushes all around the porch, along with seedlings that were just sprouting in the flower bed.

Cash helped Tippy out of the SUV while Judd carried the suitcases to the porch.

"Don't you put a foot in my seedbeds," Cash warned.

Judd stopped with one big, booted foot in midair and glanced at him. "What seedbeds?"

"The ones you're about to step on!" Cash muttered. "I planted zinnias in that one, and a mix of bluebonnets, Indian paintbrush, marigolds and daisies in the other one."

"You like to garden?" Tippy asked him softly.

He looked down into her wide green eyes and felt the world tilt. She had lovely eyes. Even in her bruised, cut face, they were exotic and fascinating. "I like getting dirt on my hands."

Tippy was equally lost in his eyes, feeling tingly all over from the intensity of his gaze. She wanted to move forward, to step right up against him and let his arms close around her. It wouldn't have done her ribs much good, but it was a temptation she hated having to resist.

"That's just what that drug dealer said when we

arrested him last year," Judd said without looking at the two people nearby. He'd avoided the flower beds and stuck the suitcases on the edge of the porch. "He planted two kilos of cocaine in *his* flower bed." He grinned. "I'll bet he was hoping it would grow."

Cash dragged his eyes away from Tippy's. "His mistake. He got ten years."

"Sadly, he'll be replaced. In fact, he already has been. Our new crack dealer has relatives in power in the city. You don't know that, of course," Judd cautioned her.

"Oh, I don't know anything," Tippy agreed at once. "Ask anybody."

"Stop that," Cash chided, touching his finger to the tip of her nose. "You're plenty smart enough."

Tippy smiled and flushed a little. Her eyes clung to Cash's like ivy.

Judd would have agreed that Tippy was no fool, but he felt keenly that he was trespassing in things that didn't concern him. At least Tippy and Cash seemed to be getting along well enough. That was a start.

"Christabel says you can both come to supper whenever you want to," Judd offered. "Tonight, if you like."

Tippy hesitated, looking up at Cash.

"She's had a hard few days, and the plane trip was no picnic, even if they were smooth flights," Cash told Judd. "But we'll take you up on it next week."

"Thank Christabel for me, too," Tippy added

gently. "I know it would be an imposition for her to have company with two infants."

"They're not quite infants anymore," Judd chuckled. "They're crawling."

"Already?" Cash exclaimed. "Jessamina, too?"

Judd glowered at him. "She has a brother. His name is Jared."

"I know that," Cash replied. "But he's yours." He swaggered. "Jessamina is mine. You wait and see."

Judd almost bit his tongue in two not suggesting that Cash could ask Tippy for a daughter of his own. The loss of their baby had devastated Cash. Apparently it had wounded Tippy as well, because her eyes clouded at the talk of Judd's children.

But she recovered quickly when she remembered Cash's pet. "Your snake!" she exclaimed. "Is it…in there?" she added worriedly.

"Don't worry," he said patiently. "I figured you'd go nuts with a snake in the house, so I gave Mikey back to Bill Harris."

"Thanks," she said, and meant it.

"I have to get home. But we should go inside first," Judd said quickly.

"All three of us?" Cash asked hesitantly.

"Definitely all three of us."

Judd went up onto the porch and opened the door.

"That's breaking and entering, Dunn," Cash admonished.

"It isn't if you have the permission of the owner."

"I'm the owner, and you don't," Cash rejoined.

Judd only chuckled.

They walked inside to a dining-room table piled high with food. There were covered casseroles, platters of ham and cheese, a huge salad, homemade biscuits and at least five desserts.

Lieutenant Barrett, slim and dark-headed, was holding a big bag, grinning. "Just made it in time, chief," he told Cash. "We had all the wives baking today, so you wouldn't have to cook when you came home. We know how you like Julia Garcia's biscuits and homemade preserves, too, so we had her put in a jar of blackberry jam and some grape jelly and a whole pan of biscuits. He's not as bad as the Hart brothers," he told Tippy, "but that's a man who really appreciates a fluffy biscuit."

"Lieutenant Garcia's wife makes the best ones around," Judd added.

"Thanks," Cash said, taken aback. "I didn't expect this."

"You've had a long week," Judd said simply. "We thought you'd be too tired to cook."

"I am. What about Miss Jewell?" he added.

"She'll be over as soon as she's got her things together," Judd said. "She said it would be about an hour from now. She's sort of a practical nurse who sits with sick people," he told Tippy. "Sandie Jewell is in her fifties, and she loves to cook. You'll like her. She saw your movie in the theater and thought it was grand. She'll pump you for information about the actor who was in it with you, though. She's a real fan of Rance Wayne."

Tippy smiled. "Okay," she said. "I'll try not to tell her too much about him, so she can keep her illusions." She touched her bruised face self-consciously. "Nobody's going to believe I was ever in a movie if they see me like this."

"Cuts and bruises fade, Miss Tippy," Lieutenant Barrett said gently. "You're going to be fine."

"Thanks," she said shyly.

"Well, let's be off," Judd told Barrett.

"I didn't see your car," Cash mentioned to Barrett.

"That's because I dropped him off with the food before I went to pick you up," Judd confided with a grin. "We didn't want his car to tip you off too soon."

"It was a surprise," Cash admitted, and he smiled. "Thanks. Tell Mrs. Garcia those preserves won't be wasted, or the biscuits either. I'll enjoy them."

"If you're quick enough, you will," Tippy said impishly. "I love biscuits with blackberry preserves. My grandmother used to make them for me when I was little."

"We'll leave before hostilities ensue," Judd said. He gave them both a wink. "Let's not have any calls about altercations from the neighbors, okay?"

"I never altercate," Cash said, deadpan. "I hear it causes blindness."

Tippy had to hold her ribs to keep them from killing her while she laughed until tears stung her eyes.

Cash grinned at her and then left to walk Judd and Barrett to the SUV.

HE WAS BACK LESS THAN five minutes later. He didn't tell her what he'd said to them, about the threat from Carrera's former employee and the risk of a hired killer coming after Tippy. But they knew to keep a close vigil on the house when he wasn't in it. He was also going to keep loaded guns around the house, in an unobtrusive way. He was also going to keep Tippy from knowing that in addition to sitting with sick people, Mrs. Jewell was a former special deputy with the local sheriff's department. Her son was a police officer who worked for Cash. The woman could handle a pistol almost as proficiently as Cash himself, and she was afraid of nothing on earth. If there was trouble, she'd keep Tippy safe when he wasn't around, until help came.

"This was so nice of them," Tippy murmured, looking over the loaded table. "I'm not used to this much food at one time."

"You need protein to help you heal," he pointed out. "Don't worry about any extra pounds. You've lost enough lately that you can afford to put on a little."

She turned toward him and looked up at him, bird-like. "Do you think I'm too thin? Honestly?"

He drew in a slow breath. "Your figure isn't my business," he said, as gently as he could. "I brought you here to protect you…"

She'd withdrawn mentally even before he got the words out. She smiled. It was a plastic smile. "I know that," she said. "I was just making conversation. Now where's that jam?"

Cash watched her take out paper plates and utensils from the sack that was included and remove lids from the plastic food containers.

"This looks wonderful," she murmured. Inside, her heart was breaking in two. She'd had hopes, dreams, that she couldn't put to rest, all about Cash. But he didn't want her permanently, and she had to find a way to face that. He might find her attractive, desirable, but that was surface stuff. He didn't want commitment. And she did.

"This looks like squash," she murmured.

Cash made a terrible face. "Where's my gun?"

She gave him a superior look. "Squash is a noble vegetable. Indians gave it to the white man. You have Native American ancestry. Therefore, you should love squash."

"The Indians only gave it to the white man to get rid of it," he said right back.

She laughed, putting a big spoonful of the delicious-smelling casserole on her plate. She brought it up to her nose and sniffed. "Mmm," she murmured.

"Yuch," he replied, moving away from the evil thing.

They filled their plates quickly and quietly. There had been no food service on either of the planes, unless you could call peanuts food. Cash poured sweetened tea from a jug into glasses filled with ice he'd found in his refrigerator. He put the jug of tea back in it.

"I'm glad they made tea for us. I love it," he commented as they sat down in adjoining chairs to eat.

"I'm not allowed sweet tea when I'm on the job," she said. "Calories."

"All food has calories," he retorted.

"Yes, but sugar has the nutritional content of cardboard."

"No wonder you're so slender."

"It isn't lack of food that does that, it's the pace." She shifted. The movement was still uncomfortable. "Filming is a torturous process. An action film like this one has all sorts of physical demands, from martial arts to stunts…" She recalled the fall, and the loss of her baby, and the explanation faded away.

He glanced at her lost expression. "Don't do that," he said gently. "Looking back doesn't solve any problems, it only causes new ones. Nothing you do can change what happened."

She lowered her fork to some potato salad and lifted it to her lips. "I was never pregnant before."

"It would have killed your career," he said curtly.

"They could have filmed around me," she said simply. "It wouldn't have been that hard. In fact, Joel actually wrote a pregnancy into one script when his leading lady announced her good news in the middle of filming."

He glanced at her curiously. She didn't sound like a woman who couldn't balance work with motherhood. In fact, she made it sound easy.

She noted his close scrutiny and laughed. "Don't worry, you're perfectly safe. I can't even remember the last time I tried to get a man pregnant."

She'd waited until he took a big sip of tea to say that. Predictably, the tea was airborne immediately.

She laughed while he cursed. She handed him two napkins and watched him mop up his white T-shirt. "Sorry," she said. "Couldn't resist it. You did look so somber."

He gave her a long look. "I don't get mad. I get even."

She chuckled. "I'll take my chances. It was worth it."

He lifted the tea to his lips again with a secret smile. Whatever her residence brought, it wasn't going to be boring.

CHAPTER ELEVEN

SANDIE JEWELL WAS FIFTYISH, tall, slender and dark-eyed, with wavy light brown hair cut short and a beaming smile. Tippy liked her at once. She was nobody's idea of the matronly female.

She checked Tippy's medication to make sure she kept it on schedule, although it was only antibiotics and a tablet that helped keep her lungs clear. She hurried Tippy off to her bedroom after supper, because she needed to rest after the long trip.

When Tippy was comfortably settled, Sandie closed the door and went into the kitchen to talk to Cash.

"Is she resting?" Cash asked, offering her coffee, which she accepted.

"She's tired," Sandie replied, "and there's a little more congestion in that lung. I'm going to get her up and walking in the morning, and fill her full of fluids to thin the secretions. Lord, she looks like a walking car accident victim!" she added, shaking her head. "I'll never understand what makes a man do that to a woman."

"We've both seen enough cases of domestic abuse," Cash agreed. "She has to be watched all the time. If Stanton does send a hired gun out here after her, we can't risk being surprised. I tucked your .45 in its case into the bathroom closet, up high, behind some towels. It's loaded."

"Thanks. If I have to use it," she told him, "I won't miss."

He smiled. "I know that. I appreciate you staying with her, Sandie. There's nobody I trust more."

"You going in tonight?"

"Thought I might…"

Just as he spoke, the phone rang. He picked it up quickly, before it disturbed Tippy. "Grier," he said at once.

"Chief, you'd better come over here," one of his officers said hesitantly. "There's some trouble."

"What sort?" he asked.

"Two of our patrol officers just made an arrest for drunk driving. They brought the perp in, handcuffed, and did a breath test. He failed. They're filing a citation. He's hopping mad and threatening to have their jobs."

"Who is he?"

There was a pause. "State Senator Merrill."

Cash took a long breath. This was any police officer's worst nightmare. Most politicians would fire any officer who dared to arrest them. Certainly, they'd do their best to make the arresting officer quit. Cash had seen it happen in a dozen cities over the years.

"The acting mayor phoned and told me to fire the arresting officers on the spot," the watch commander added.

"You're firing nobody, on my orders," Cash said at once. "I'll be there in ten minutes. You tell Brady he'll have to talk to me before any jobs are sacrificed, and that goes double for Senator Merrill."

"The senator's daughter is on her way here, too. She's thick with Jordan Powell."

Powell was a rich rancher. Very rich, and very high-tempered. Cash wondered if facing down a hit man wasn't an easier proposition than stepping into this lava pit.

"I'm on my way. Keep your cool," Cash told the man.

Sandie shook her head when he hung up the phone. "No need to tell me what's going on. One of our deputies got fired for pulling over a state legislator once. Never had a chance."

"These officers aren't walking," he said curtly.

Cash put on his uniform, took his service revolver and holster out of his desk drawer and put them on.

The bustle of activity made Tippy curious. She came out of her bedroom and down the hall, stopping short when she saw Cash in uniform. It was a shock, even though she'd seen him that way when she was filming in Jacobsville. It had been a long time.

"You look very nice. Are you going to work at this hour?" she asked.

He glanced at her. "Go back to bed. You need to be resting. I've got a small problem downtown. I'll be back when I can."

Tippy had to bite her tongue to stop from saying "be careful." She had a sudden, shocking glimpse of what it would be like if they were married and she had to watch him go to work every day, knowing he might not come home.

The knowledge was in her whole expression. Cash saw it and was disturbed by it. He checked his weapon and holstered it before walking to Tippy and taking her gently by the shoulders.

"This is what I do," he said softly. "I don't know a way of life that doesn't involve risk of some sort. In fact, I don't think I could live without it."

She couldn't help feeling that he was making a statement about their future. She managed a smile. "I know you're good at what you do. Judd told me."

His big hands lifted to frame her face. "I'm always

careful, and the only real risks I take are calculated ones. I'm not suicidal, even remotely. It's carelessness that gets you killed in this business."

She drew in a long breath and lifted her hands to straighten his tie. She smiled, because it was such an intimate, domestic thing to do. "Don't get killed," she said simply.

His heart jumped. He bent and drew his lips very softly over her full lips. She wasn't wearing makeup to camouflage her bruises, but she was still beautiful. She smelled vaguely of roses.

She lifted her face closer to his, her eyes closed, her mouth smiling. Her hands were on his chest now, because it was painful to lift them as far as his tie. She loved letting him kiss her. This was a slow, tender kiss tasting unlike the kisses that had gone before. This one wasn't urgent or passionate or ardent. It was gentle. It made promises.

"Go back to bed," he said when he lifted his head. His dark eyes were turbulent. "This may take a while."

"Okay."

He cocked an eyebrow. "Doesn't that sound docile," he chided, studying her guileless smile. "And the minute I walk out the door, you'll be cleaning the kitchen or trying to rearrange the cabinets."

"Not yet. It still hurts too much." She smiled demurely. "I'll wait until next week, at least."

He chuckled softly. "Don't get too comfortable," he murmured. "I'm a happy bachelor."

"There's no such thing," she replied smugly.

He gave her a daunting look, but she kept smiling.

"Did somebody rob a bank?" she probed.

"They're trying to fire two of my officers for stopping a politician who was driving drunk," he replied.

Her eyes opened wide. "Why?"

"Because he's a rich politician."

"Big deal," she said flatly. "The law is the law."

"Darling!" he exclaimed and kissed her firmly. He drew back at once, and chuckled at her expression. "Don't get your hopes up. That was an accident."

She cocked her head, curious.

He shrugged. "I like it when you take my side."

She grinned. "I know where we could get a ring," she said to irritate him.

He pursed his lips. "So do I, but we're not getting one."

Tippy spotted Mrs. Jewell at the kitchen door. "Mrs. Jewell, he's toying with my affections and he won't marry me."

Mrs. Jewell gaped at her.

"No, he won't," Cash agreed pleasantly. "And I am not toying with your affections. I only kissed you because you think I'm right."

"No, you didn't. You kissed me because you

couldn't help yourself." She struck a pose, despite the twinge of pain in her rib cage. "I'm simply irresistible."

"You need a guitar and a band and you can sing that," he pointed out.

She remembered the song he was alluding to, whose wonderful composer had died. "It was a great song."

"I thought so, too," he said. He gave her a wicked look. "Go to bed."

She wiggled her eyebrows at him.

"And you stop that," he added firmly. "Mrs. Jewell is going to protect me from you, so watch your step."

"You're really going to do that?" Tippy asked the older woman. "Don't you like me?"

Mrs. Jewell burst out laughing. Cash took the opportunity to shoot out the door while he was still one step ahead.

"I've known him almost a year," she told Tippy, as they listened to his car drive away. "Never saw him laugh as much as he has in the past few minutes. I think he's sweet on you."

"I'm hurt and he feels sorry for me," Tippy replied carelessly. "But he doesn't growl so much when I'm teasing him."

Mrs. Jewell's dark eyes didn't miss much. "Love him a lot, don't you?" she probed.

Tippy hesitated, then she smiled and sighed. "For all the good it will do either one of us. He's not a marrying man, and he sees me as a risk."

"What you are on the screen isn't what you are at home," the other woman pointed out.

"How perceptive of you," Tippy said, surprised. "Most people can't see that."

"I've had a lot of practice sizing up people," Mrs. Jewel said. "Now you get back in bed, Miss Tippy. You need rest, so that you can get better."

Tippy touched her face. The cuts were still sore and red. "I must look terrible," she said.

"You look like someone who's been hurt, dear," came the soft reply. "Those cuts and bruises will heal. So will your ribs. But you must rest and drink lots of fluids so that you don't let your lungs get any more congested. Flying in a pressurized cabin can't have helped them."

"It didn't, very much," Tippy confessed. "But driving that distance would have been so much worse. I've got medicine, and I promise I'll take it. I really want to finish this film, so I get paid." She noticed how the older woman was looking at her and felt anger about the tabloids' reporting of her earlier accident.

"An assistant director swore that jump was harmless and refused to hire a stunt double," she explained. "I didn't have a good feeling about it, but I didn't want to lose my job because I was being paranoid about risking the pregnancy. I didn't have much money coming in, and there was my little brother's school fees and my rent to pay. I'd done similar stunts without an accident so I foolishly trusted the assistant director and took a chance I should have refused to take. As a result, I lost my footing and fell. And I lost my baby," she added, almost choking on the words.

Mrs. Jewell winced. "I lost two," she said softly. "I know how it feels."

The two women exchanged looks. Words weren't even necessary.

"Go back to bed," Mrs. Jewell prompted. "I'll bring you something nice to drink and then maybe you can sleep."

"I won't until Cash comes home," Tippy said worriedly.

The other woman chuckled, herding Tippy toward the bedroom. "That's one man you never have to worry about. He can take care of himself. Wait and see!"

THE POLICE STATION, usually quiet with a skeleton crew on the night shift, was literally a hothouse of activity. Three patrol officers were standing around the desk at which the night secretary/bookkeeper worked. A senior citizen was weaving slightly and making threats of immediate action against two patrol officers—a male and a female—who were tight-lipped and worried. A beautiful young woman in expensive clothes was telling everyone what was going to happen if they didn't drop the charges against her father immediately.

Cash walked in, his very stride threatening. "Okay, what's up?" he asked curtly.

Everybody started talking at once.

Cash held up his hand. "Who made the collar?" he asked.

Lieutenant Carlos Garcia, a veteran officer who was in charge of the patrol unit, and Officer Dana Hall, a new female recruit, stepped forward. Cash knew them well. Garcia's wife was the county public health nurse, beloved by the local citizens. Dana's late father had been one of the most respected superior court judges in the circuit.

"Hall was riding with me," Garcia said quietly. "We observed a car weaving in and out of its lane and bumping the shoulder repeatedly. We followed him for a mile to make sure the complaint was valid. He almost hit another car head-on. That was when I threw on my lights and siren and pulled him over."

"Go on." Cash urged him to continue.

"Hall and I approached the car in a textbook manner, one on either side of the car, in case the suspect was armed. I asked to see his license and registration, but the perpetrator immediately stepped out and began making threats. I smelled alcohol on his breath, so I tested his reflexes by making him touch his nose with his eyes closed and walk a straight line. He couldn't do either."

"What happened next?" Cash probed.

"I then advised him that I was bringing him into the station for a breath test. He began cursing me and began resisting arrest. I subdued him while Hall handcuffed him. We brought him in, and administered the test. His blood alcohol is .15—which puts him well over the legal limit for alcohol consumption—so I issued a citation, locked him up and had our bookkeeper Miss Phibbs phone his daughter, at his request, to sign a property bond and secure his release until his hearing."

"You can't arrest my father for drunk driving the month before the primary election!" the senator's pretty blond daughter protested. "I want these officers fired. My father is not drunk!"

"Indeed, I am...am not!" the senator mumbled. "You're all fired!" he added, weaving.

"Since you've posted bond, you can go home in your daughter's custody," Cash told the older man pleasantly. "You'll appear in city court before the city judge to defend the charge. At that time, the judge will make a decision about the possible revocation of your driver's license."

"Our attorney will take care of all that, the minute I can get in touch with him. You can bet on it!" the senator's daughter said haughtily.

"You can't take away my license, I'm a senator!" the old man said belligerently.

"That will be for the court to decide."

"I'll have your job for this!" the senator raged furiously.

Before the situation could escalate, the acting mayor, Ben Brady, came into the station in a T-shirt and slacks that looked hastily thrown on. "What's going on?" he asked, and the arresting officers had to explain the situation once more.

"Bosh," Brady said huffily. "My uncle never drinks and drives. You can drop the charges and tear up that bond. This is all a mistake."

"It is not a mistake," Cash said firmly, moving closer to the mayor, whom he towered over. He looked threatening. "My officers made a legitimate arrest. They have the results of a breath-analysis test to back it up. The senator is over the legal limit for driving. He is being issued with citations for the offense. That's the law."

Brady turned red in the face. "We'll just see what our city attorney thinks about that!"

"He'd better think that these officers are hired to enforce the law," Cash returned. "And before you question that," he added when Brady started to speak again, "you'd better remember that Simon Hart is the state attorney general."

"Which won't help you…!" Brady raged.

"The Harts are my second cousins," Cash replied quietly, and there was a sudden stillness in the room. He hadn't made that bit of information public before.

Brady turned to the senator. "Uncle, I'm certain this is all just a mistake. Go along with what they want you to do for now. I'll set up a disciplinary hearing for the arresting officers next month and we'll get to the bottom of this. You won't object to that, I hope?" he asked the chief of police.

Cash only smiled. "Why should I? My officers did nothing wrong." The smile faded. "But they will not be suspended, with or without pay, until they are formally charged with misconduct and given the opportunity to defend themselves."

Brady looked as if he wanted badly to make that charge, but he was intimidated by Cash. "Very well," he said huffily. "Your people will be notified when to appear in city court."

"You'd better look for another job," Julie Merrill said hatefully.

"Oh, I have a job, Miss Merrill," Cash replied pleasantly. "I have no plans to resign."

"We'll see about that!" she scoffed.

Cash smiled at her. She actually took a backward step and rejoined her father and the acting mayor without saying another word.

MINUTES LATER, the office was cleared of civilians. Only the bookkeeper—smiling smugly—Cash and his two patrol officers were still in the building. He glanced at his two distraught officers. "What?" he asked, when he saw their expressions.

Garcia shifted uncomfortably. "We thought you'd want us to resign."

"That's right," Hall agreed.

"Like I can just go out and pick up two good patrol officers any time I feel like it in a town of less than two thousand souls!" Cash exclaimed.

"It's going to be messy," Garcia said. "I've seen this happen before. Old Sergeant Manley arrested a city councilman for drunk driving years ago, and they fired him. He was a year away from retirement. Chief Blake never said a word."

Cash met the other man's eyes evenly. "I'm not Chet Blake."

Sergeant Garcia managed a smile. "Yes, sir. We, uh, noticed."

Cash stood up, with Hall beside him.

"Thanks for standing up for us, Chief," Officer Hall said. "But we're willing to resign, if we have to."

"I'm not resigning," Cash said easily. "Neither is anybody else, for doing his job. Or her job," he added with a grin at Hall.

"They won't make it easy," Garcia persisted. "And we don't have legal counsel. We're such a small department that there's no attorney on staff."

"We might get Mr. Kemp," Hall ventured.

"I'll get legal counsel," Cash told them in a pleasant tone. "You're going to find that a lot of people around here are tired of politicians bypassing the law. We're going to put a stop to it. And nobody's quitting. Got that?"

They smiled, not really believing him, but more hopeful than they'd been when they walked into the room.

CASH WENT HOME, tired but satisfied. He should have been surprised that Tippy was still up, waiting for him in the living room.

"I told Sandie to make sure you went to bed!" he grumbled.

"Don't blame her," Tippy replied, wrapped up comfortably in a gown with a quilted robe covering up all of her, except her hands and feet and head. "She can't stay up late. Once she was asleep, I got up again. I felt like sitting up for a while, that's all," she lied. Actually, she'd been afraid that something had happened to Cash, and there was no way she could have slept until he was home.

He had one of the strangest feelings he'd ever known in his life. He couldn't remember a single time when his wife had waited up to see if he'd come home or not, even when he thought she loved him the most. He was completely alone. Now, here sat this gorgeous woman with red-gold hair and haunting green eyes, a woman who was idolized by men everywhere. And she was sitting up on his sofa waiting, because she'd been afraid for him.

He didn't say anything. He removed his pistol and its holster and put them away, frowning curiously.

"You're angry," she surmised.

He didn't look at her. "I don't know how I feel."

"You could lie down on the sofa and tell me about your childhood," she suggested with a wicked little smile.

He cocked one eyebrow and gave her a long look. "If I lie down on a sofa, you're going to be lying down on it first."

Her cheeks showed just a hint of embarrassment. "Bruised ribs," she reminded him.

"Oh, they'll heal," he replied. "Then look out."

"It's no use, you've already said you won't marry me," she said with a big grin. "I almost never play around on sofas with confirmed bachelors."

"Spoilsport."

He sat down in the easy chair next to the sofa with a heavy sigh and removed his neat tie, unbuttoning the top buttons of his blue shirt to reveal a spotless white T-shirt underneath it.

"Want to talk?" she asked, without pushing too hard.

He frowned. "I've never had anyone to talk about things with," he said conversationally. "The one time I was married, my wife hated my job."

She searched his eyes. "Something's upset you."

"Will you stop reading my mind?" he demanded, slinging his tie onto the coffee table.

"It isn't deliberate," she tried to explain. "And, if you want to know, it's more of a curse than a blessing. I can only read negative things, like danger and emotional unrest."

He leaned back and crossed his long legs. "You can tell when something's wrong with Rory, can't you?"

She nodded. "Since he was very small. I had it with my grandmother, too. I knew when she was going to die, and how." She shivered and wrapped her arms around her slender body. "I saw it in a dream."

"It must unsettle people when you tell them about it," he remarked.

She met his eyes evenly. "I've never told anyone. Not even Rory."

"Why?"

"I don't want to freak him out. I'm pretty sure he doesn't have the gift. My mother certainly doesn't," she added. "What will happen to her?"

"If she's involved, she'll serve time," he said. "Kidnapping is a federal offense."

She was quiet for a long time. "If they sent her to prison, maybe she'd dry out."

He smiled quizzically. "You don't think prisoners have access to alcohol and drugs?"

"They can't," she replied. "Not in prison."

He leaned back again and closed his eyes. He was

tired. "Honey, you can get anything you want in prison. It's another whole social structure, with its own hierarchy. Anyone can be bribed, for the right amount and the right reason."

"You're very cynical," she noted, still tingling from the endearment he probably hadn't even realized he'd used for her. They were all alone in the world, and talking like husband and wife. It made her feel warm all over.

"I know all about the world," he said wearily. "Most of the time, it's a dangerous, joyless place with few compensations for the pain of going through life."

"Family is a powerful compensation," she remarked.

He opened his eyes and looked at her coldly. "Family is more dangerous than the outside world."

She knew that. It showed in her quiet, haunted eyes.

He grimaced. He hadn't meant to attack her. It had disturbed him that she knew he was upset. He never talked about the job, except to other people in law enforcement. Tippy knew too much about him, and he didn't trust her. He didn't trust anyone.

She could see the future in his face. He would fight with every breath to keep her at arm's length, both physically and mentally. He didn't trust her not to hurt him.

"You even know what I'm thinking right now, don't you?" he growled.

She blinked and looked away. "I think something happened at work that made you angry, and you're holding it inside because there's nobody you can talk to about it. Nothing that happened to you personally," she added. "But to someone you like."

It was like a small explosion when his hard-soled shoes hit the hardwood floor as he got to his feet and stalked out of the room.

Tippy sighed. She didn't want to upset him any more, but it was dangerous for him to keep things bottled up. Stress was dangerous, even to a man of Cash's good health and fitness. If only he could talk about his problems. She smiled to herself, remembering what he'd said about his mother and father and the turmoil of divorce. First his stepmother, then his wife, had betrayed him in the worst way. He could trust another man far easier than he was ever going to be able to trust a woman.

She got to her feet slowly. So much for her hopes. He was going to spend her whole convalescence pushing her away. It wasn't surprising, but it was painful. Without trust, no deeper emotion was ever going to develop.

With a slow gait, she went back down the hall to her room and pushed the door shut gently. She peeled off her robe and climbed into bed, producing her copy of the Plinys to read, because she still wasn't sleepy.

Five minutes later, there was a brief knock on the

door and Cash came into the room with a tray. On it were a cup of hot chocolate and some ginger cookies.

"Don't get your hopes up," he muttered as he closed the door and put the tray down on the bedside table. "I'm not conceding defeat, and I'm not talking to you about work."

"Okay," she said easily. "Thanks for the bedtime snack."

He stood up, looking at her with clinical interest. Her creamy shoulders were bare except for pink satin straps that held up her lacy pink gown. Her breasts were high and firm under it, and he remembered without conscious thought how it felt to put his mouth on them and make her moan with pleasure.

Tippy noticed his interest and pretended not to. She sipped the chocolate. "This is good," she commented.

"It's a packaged mix. I can't make it from scratch." He was wearing just the undershirt now, with his slacks. He looked worn.

She tried one of the ginger cookies. They were delicious.

"Mrs. Garcia sent them, along with the biscuits and preserves we had when we got here."

"They're very nice."

He took a long, sharp breath. "Two of my patrol officers arrested a politician for driving drunk. He's trying to have them fired, and the acting mayor, his nephew, is putting pressure on me to do it. He wants me fired as well."

She swallowed the rest of the ginger cookie. She was tingling all over. He actually was willing to talk to her about his job! It was a milestone. She had to fight tears. "He'll have his work cut out," she said, trying to sound nonchalant.

He was pleasantly surprised at her confidence in him. "Yes, he will," he conceded. "I've gotten used to Jacobsville. Even if I'm still something of an outsider, I seem to fit in here."

"You like it," she said.

He smiled faintly. "I like it a lot." He watched her eat another cookie. "You look pretty in pink. I thought redheads didn't wear it."

She smiled. "I don't, usually, but Rory gave it to me for Christmas, along with the robe."

"I thought so."

"I miss him."

"I'm sure you do," he replied. "But he's far safer in military school than he would be in New York. The minute school's out, we'll bring him here."

"Thanks," she said huskily. "He really likes you."

"He's a fine young man."

"Bristling with hero worship," she added demurely.

He chuckled. "He'll learn that idols generally have feet of clay."

"Not his," she said without looking up. "His is the genuine article."

He didn't speak for a minute. He knew she was telling the truth. But he didn't want her feel that way about him. She was overwhelmed with her first pleasurable experience of intimacy. She liked what he could make her feel. That was a result he was used to. His former wife had liked him in bed, too. But when she knew all about him, knew everything, she wasn't able to bear having him touch her. It was going to be that way with Tippy, too. She was attracted to an illusion, not a flesh and blood man.

"I'm going to bed. Need anything else?" he asked.

She looked up. He was solemn. It would do no good to ask questions. She only smiled. "No. Thanks for the hot chocolate and cookies."

"No problem. See you in the morning." He hesitated. "If you need anything in the night…"

"I know, Mrs. Jewell is right down the hall, and there's an intercom." She pointed to it on the bedside table. "She told me before she went to bed."

He nodded. He hesitated for a minute, as if there was something else he wanted to say but couldn't think what it was. Then he started for the door.

But he hesitated when he had the knob under his hand. He didn't look at her. "Thanks for waiting up," he bit off. Before she could recover from the shock and answer him, the door had closed behind him.

WITHIN THE NEXT DAY, it was all over city hall, and the collective police and fire departments, that the chief was going to stand by his officers, no matter what. Overnight, Cash went from an outsider trying to fit in, to family.

He was surprised by all the attention, because he was just doing what he considered to be his job. Nobody else was that cavalier about it. When people met on the street, the primary topic of conversation was Cash's fierce defense of his colleagues.

Sandie told Tippy that whether Cash realized it or not, he'd just become a hero in the eyes of the town. Tippy smiled, feeling already part of a big family.

CHAPTER TWELVE

CASH'S HOUSE was fascinating to Tippy, who'd never really lived in one before. Her mother had always had a beat-up old trailer. This house had a long front porch, a small back porch, huge rooms and an enormous bathroom and kitchen. It really did feel enchanted.

It also had something else that appealed to her. Tippy was spending a long time in the flower-strewn backyard with its flowering bushes and tall pecan trees. Cash had a hammock strung on a metal stand, and Tippy loved to kick back in it and sway in the cool spring breeze. Her rib cage was still sore, and it was difficult to get into the hammock, but once she was there, she could rest back on the long cushion and it felt wonderful. She was breathing more easily, thanks to the volume of fluids Mrs. Jewell was pumping into her. The bruises had faded to yellow. The confusion and headaches weren't completely gone, but they were better. Her face still looked like a road map, but it stung less every day and it did look as though it was going to heal perfectly.

Mrs. Jewell had kept a disconcertingly close watch over her lately, and Cash was giving her worried glances when he was at home. Tippy sensed that something was wrong, but she couldn't get anyone to tell her what it was.

Tippy stretched and yawned widely, closing her eyes. The sun felt good on her face. She was wearing a green patterned sundress that left her arms and shoulders bare except for the thin straps that held it up. It reached to her ankles. Below them, her feet were bare. Her red-gold hair was loose, falling in waves around her face. She couldn't know it, but she made a pretty picture against the green lawn and mesquite trees that laced the backyard.

She didn't think about trouble in broad daylight. Mrs. Jewell was gone shopping and Cash was at work. It never occurred to Tippy that she might be threatened so close to home. But her neck began to tingle suddenly and she tensed, opening her eyes wide just in time to focus on Cash leaning over the hammock with a scowl.

"Oh!" she exclaimed, jumping. The sudden motion almost threw her out onto the ground. "Heavens, you scared me!" she gasped.

"Good," he said shortly. "One of your kidnappers is still running around loose, and you're the only person who can testify to the federal charges. No Tippy, no case. I can't be here all the time, and neither can Sandie. This is careless and dangerous, lying out here all alone in your condition. You aren't even armed!"

She swallowed hard as she stared up at him. "I'm bringing a bat out with me next time, that's for sure," she promised. Her heart was racing. She could barely speak.

Cash relented, just a little. His dark eyes swept over her face quietly. "This house must be enchanted. You do look like a fairy, lying there," he said in a soft, fascinated tone.

"A battered fairy," she remarked, trying to laugh.

"Battered, nothing. Move over."

She did, startled, when he climbed into the hammock with her, positioning his holster so that it didn't catch between the loops. He lay back, yawning, with his hands behind his head.

"That's nice," he mused, closing his own eyes. "I put this thing up a month ago and I haven't had five minutes to spend in it yet. At least things have calmed down at city hall, for the moment."

"Is the senator still threatening to fire all of you?" she wanted to know.

"Of course. So is the acting mayor." He smiled drowsily. "But Senator Merrill's attorney isn't the sort to support illegal behavior. He's honorable, and he believes in the rule of law. Since he spoke to the mayor, there hasn't been a lot of conversation between us."

"There's still the hearing to face," she reminded him.

"Sure, but we're going to have some unexpected legal assistance, which nobody knows about except me." He glanced down at her, smiling mysteriously. "There's another aspect that I'm working on, as well, involving local drug trafficking."

She pursed her lips. "And someone locally is involved…?"

"Stop fishing," he said drowsily. "I never talk about surprises until they're ready."

"Suit yourself, then. But you won't let them fire you or the officers, right?"

"Right."

"Okay." She took his word for gospel, lying back with a long sigh. "I've never done this in my life," she murmured. "I never had a hammock, for one thing. For another, I never felt secure enough to relax at home."

His hand smoothed her long hair. "Did you have friends?"

"Not many," she replied. "One girlfriend, but she was afraid of Sam and she knew how mean my mother was when she drank. Mostly, I went to her house, until my mother decided that I was having too much fun." She closed her eyes, unaware of Cash's intent interest. "You know, she hated me from the day I was born. She was always telling me that I was a mistake, that she'd had unprotected sex by accident."

"That's a lovely thing to tell a child," he remarked coldly.

"I learned to do housework and cook at the age of eight, while she drank. I don't think I ever saw her sober. Then after Sam came into her life, she went on to hard drugs. I hated him," she recalled huskily. "At least I finally got the chance to fight back."

He rolled over. "Stanton told the authorities that you attacked him."

"He's right, I did," she replied curtly. "I'd had just enough martial arts training to land a few hard blows in his vulnerable spots before he came after me. It felt good. I had a balisong, too, but I never got to use it."

He touched her poor bruised face tenderly. "I added a bullet to the bruises you gave him," he said quietly. "When I finally got to you, I wished I'd hit truer."

She touched his hard mouth with her fingertips. "I feel safe with you."

His eyebrows arched.

"Not that way," she muttered. "I mean, I don't feel afraid of other people when you're around."

"Nice of you to make things clear," he mused.

She shifted, wincing a little at the pressure on her ribs. "There's a lot of talk about the senatorial race," she said. "Mrs. Jewell thinks that the Ballenger man is going to win it."

"So do most other people. Senator Merrill's drinking notwithstanding, a lot of people think he's past doing the job. It isn't his age, it's his attitude," he added. "He's not in touch with his constituents, and he's depending on old families and old money to keep him in office. But the old families have lost much of their wealth, and their power. There's a new social structure, of which the Ballengers are part. Their name carries weight."

"You think Merrill will lose?"

"Yes, I do," he said. "Furthermore, the acting mayor is up against some stiff competition in the special city election in May. I don't think he's got a chance of going back in. Eddie Cane's already running ahead in the polls. Everybody likes him. He was mayor once before. He's a good man."

"You'll be pleased if he defeats Mr. Brady, I don't doubt," she remarked.

"I will. Brady and at least one of the councilmen have their fingers in a particularly nasty little pie—you're not to mention that outside the house, either," he added firmly.

"I never tell what I know," she promised. "Is it drugs?"

"Yes. He's been trying to use the job to protect certain associates in the area. But it isn't working in Jacobsville."

"I heard about that from Mrs. Jewell," she confessed, smiling. "She says you've organized an interagency-team drug squad to root out distributors."

"I have. A lot of dealers are in jail."

"No wonder you're unpopular at city hall, then," she replied.

"I'm popular enough at the sheriff's department," he said on a chuckle, "even if Hayes Carson and I don't get along from time to time. We're both sticklers for enforcement of drug laws. Hayes had a brother who died of a drug overdose. He's even more hard-nosed than I am."

She sighed and looked up into the leafy boughs of the tree and closed her eyes to the soft breeze that whispered through her hair. "I can't remember when I've enjoyed a day this much," she said unexpectedly. "I've never had much of a home life. Imagine, lying in a hammock under a shade tree, with nothing more important to do than breathe."

He chuckled. "My home life wasn't much to talk about, either, I suppose," he murmured. "Not after my mother died, certainly."

"Neither of us has had any good experience of family life," she said. "I've tried hard to do that for Rory, to make sure he was as happy as I could make him when he was home with me at vacation or on holidays."

"He loves you," he said simply.

"I love him." She stretched again. "He thinks

you're awesome. Now he's talking about a career in law enforcement."

"Is he?" he asked, pleasantly surprised.

"Mmm-hmm," she murmured contentedly. "He'll be out of school the week after the state elections."

"He'll enjoy it here," he said. "We have an active recreation department for young people."

"He'll be looking for someone to take him fishing," she said drowsily. "That's his favorite sport."

"Funny. I like fishing myself."

"He goes with one of the boys at his military school, on weekends. I like this hammock! I think I could get used to it very quickly as a lifelong hobby." She rolled over, just a little, so that she could slide one bare foot against his boot and curl into his chest. He flinched, but just as quickly, he relaxed. His head turned to look down at her.

"Don't get too comfortable," he said with a chuckle. "I can only stay for a few minutes. My desk is piled high with things that didn't get done while I was in New York looking after you."

Her small hand smoothed over the clean, neat fabric of his uniform shirt and she closed her eyes, snuggling closer. "You smell nice."

One of his arms, shifted, so that his hand smoothed her long hair. "So do you, angel," he said softly.

She loved the feel of his fingers in her long hair. It was heaven, to lie against him like this in the shade of the tree and feel his heart beat, feel his breath sigh out above her head, feel the power and strength in his body against her. She'd never felt more secure.

"I've been looking at rings," she murmured drowsily.

"Have you now?" he mused.

She yawned. "But I didn't find anything I thought you'd like," she added mischievously.

"Persistent little cuss, aren't you?" he asked.

"I have a one-track mind, Cash. Sandie says you're kin to the Harts. Are you?"

"Second cousins," he replied.

"They're related to the vice president. And distantly to your governor," she said.

"Right."

"You never talk about your people."

"Not much to say," he told her. "My father is in real estate, mostly mining properties. He's worth millions. The second eldest of my brothers runs our cattle ranch in west Texas. The eldest is with the FBI. The youngest is an enforcement officer with the state game and fish people." He turned his head. "Why all the questions?"

She smiled against his shirt. "If I distract you, you might stay longer. I'm very comfortable."

"I wish I was," he murmured dryly.

Her head rolled back so that she could see his face. He was smiling, but there was a faint glitter in his dark eyes.

"You're very pretty," he said. "You smell good, and you're soft as a bundle of feathers. I want very much to roll over and kiss you until I make your mouth swell under mine."

Her gasp was audible. She looked at him with pure aching desire.

"Oh, that's dangerous," he whispered, staring at her mouth. "We're on public display here. What if I follow my instincts?"

"What if you do?" she prompted, staring at his mouth, too.

"Reporters will appear out of thin air. Any two of my patrol officers will pull up in the yard on official business. Passing motorists will roll down their windows and point video cameras our way."

"You're kidding," she accused.

"I'm not. When Micah Steele was courting his Callie, I hear they had a nice kissing session in her driveway about midnight. An elderly neighbor came out to prune her roses, two couples took a midnight stroll past the house, and another neighbor was peering at them out a window. Micah wasn't even a police chief."

"Oh, I get it," she mused. "You're important in the community, so everyone wants to know what you're doing."

He shook his head. "You're a famous model and film star. You're the star attraction, not me," he added, and actually seemed pleased about it.

"Some star," she scoffed, lightly touching her face. "I expect I look like Frankenstein's monster."

He caught her hand in his and brought the knuckles up to his warm, hard mouth. "Wounds of honor," he whispered. "You couldn't look unpleasant if you took two 'ugly' pills every morning."

She smiled. "Thanks."

His eyes searched hers hungrily. Her body was so close that he could smell the soap she'd used on it. Her hair feathered out around her face like a red plume. She was obviously hungry for him, and he ached in inconvenient places.

She saw his own desire in his dark eyes, and she stretched lazily, lovingly, her eyes like warm green pools.

"Don't," he cautioned huskily.

Her hips moved involuntarily. "I can't help it," she said, feeling her body swell. "I want you."

He actually shivered.

It was a weakness that she longed to exploit. She moved closer to him, awkwardly, because the hammock was difficult to move in. Her fingers reached up to his lean cheek and traced it. "You could kiss me, if you wanted to," she told him.

"We'd be a tourist attraction in two minutes."

"Excuses, excuses…" She tugged on his neck and brought his hard mouth down onto her parted, yielding lips.

"Tippy," he protested.

But he wasn't fighting very hard, she noticed. She smiled under his mouth as she tugged harder.

In the end, he couldn't resist her. He sank down into the hammock against her, and his mouth became hungry and invasive.

She kissed him back ardently, but in seconds, she felt the pain in her ribs…and another source of discomfort digging into her belly.

She protested weakly.

He lifted his head. "What?" he asked blankly.

"Your pistol," she whispered.

He looked down. The holster was digging into her stomach. He lifted away from her with a helpless laugh. "I told you hammocks weren't designed for this. Hurt your ribs, too, didn't it?"

She sighed wistfully. "I wish I were well."

"That makes two of us." He wrestled his way out of the hammock and stood up, adjusting his uniform and the holster. "See what you get for trying to seduce men in plain sight of the world?"

She wiggled her eyebrows. "Want to arrest me for lewd behavior?" She held out both hands. "You could cuff me. Then you could read me my rights. We should do it inside, though."

"That won't work," he said with twinkling eyes. "I know what would happen if you got me alone. Those ribs wouldn't let you do what you want to do."

She shrugged. "I guess you're right," she said

sadly. "Okay. I give up. Until I'm completely healed, at least."

He smiled. For a woman with a scarred past, she was doing very well. At least she was able to feel desire. That was a milestone, considering her background. He remembered uncomfortably the long, exquisite lovemaking session in her bed at Christmas. It had almost obliterated his nightmares. Almost. It was hard to live with the things he'd done in his life.

"Now you're brooding again," she said gently. "I only looked at the ring. I didn't buy it."

He scowled. "How did you look at a ring?"

She grinned. "I went on the Internet and looked for rings. I'm not quite comfortable enough with my face to go into town yet."

"You don't look at all bad," he said genuinely. "In another week or two, you'll look just as you did. I doubt if you'll have any scars at all when you heal completely. The doctors did a good job."

"You don't think Joel will replace me, do you?" she wondered uncertainly.

"Not a chance." He checked his watch. "I really do have to go. I only stopped by to check on you. Don't do this again," he added quietly. "Even in Jacobsville, it's not safe."

"Okay," she said, moving unsteadily to her feet. "I'll go in the house and order some racy videos to watch. I need pointers." She gave him a speaking glance. "There has to be some way to get through your defenses."

He couldn't help laughing. It was ironic. She had a damaged sexuality, but she spent an uncanny amount of time looking at ways to seduce him. It was the one true measure of her affection for him.

"At least you're smiling more. That has to be a positive thing."

"More positive than you know," he pointed out. "I'm not the smiling type."

She wasn't really listening. She was studying his handsome face and wondering what their child would have looked like if it had been born. The thought was acutely painful. She turned away.

Before she got two steps, he was right behind her. "You closed up like a water lily in the dark. Why?"

"It's nothing," she said at once.

His lean hands smoothed down her bare arms. "You were thinking about the baby," he whispered huskily.

She bit down hard on threatening tears. "You're just guessing," she said tautly.

"No. I don't think I am." His hands contracted gently and his lips brushed the top of her head. "I should be shot for the way I spoke to you the day you phoned. I always expect the worst of people. It's a hard habit to break."

She swallowed again, trying to avert tears. The warm strength of him at her back was intoxicating. Involuntarily, she leaned back against him with a long sigh. "I've been that way most of my life. Trust comes hard when you've been betrayed."

"Yes."

She stared straight ahead, at the house. Something occurred to her. "Why did you buy a house and not rent one?" she wanted to know.

He hesitated. "It does seem odd, doesn't it?" he mused aloud. "I don't really know."

"You wouldn't be trying to put down roots or anything?" she fished.

He was very still. He was scowling, but she couldn't see that. "I've never tried to belong anywhere," he said. "In a way, I've been a professional outsider since I was a kid. I don't like getting close to people. Especially women," he added curtly.

"That isn't hard to understand," she agreed.

"You've never given me a reason not to trust you," he said after a minute.

"I never will," she said simply. "Nothing you ever did or said could make me hate you."

"Think so?" He laughed cynically. "Maybe one day I'll tell you the story of my life and you can try to prove that."

She turned around and looked up into his hard face with soft, caring eyes. "If you care about someone, it isn't because of anything they've done or not done, Cash," she said. "It's because of what they are. Actions are not character traits."

He scowled. She made him feel odd. Young. She made him feel hope.

She lifted her fingers to his mouth and caressed

it. She smiled. "I've already told you that I don't believe you could do something out of evil intentions."

"I'm…not the man I was once," he faltered. "But I've done some unforgivable things…"

She searched his eyes evenly. "Nothing is unforgivable."

"I wish that were the case," he murmured.

Terrible memories were in his eyes. They were in hers, too. If he had secrets from her, she certainly had secrets from him. But to produce them for inspection would require a lot more trust than either of them had. It was too soon.

"One day at a time," she said softly. "That's how we have to live."

His lean hand went to her cheek and pressed there tenderly among the fading bruises and healing cuts. "Our lives haven't been easy, have they, honey?" he thought aloud.

"We pay for pleasure with pain," she replied philosophically. "Considering my own account, I would say that I'm past due for a lot of pleasure."

He chuckled, as she did. "Maybe that's true for both of us."

She stood on tiptoe and brushed her mouth against his. "Sandie's making chicken and dumplings for supper."

"I like that."

"I know," she said wickedly. "I suggested it."

He lifted his chin and gave her a mock glare. "I

won't be seduced over dumplings, however good they are."

"There you go again," she complained.

"On the other hand, a man can withstand just so much temptation," he added obligingly.

"Thank you. I'll look over my stash of sexy night-gowns and perfume."

"I'm going back to work while there's still time," he told her firmly, putting her gently away.

"I'll go watch movies."

"That's my girl," he said in a soft, husky tone. He looked at her with real affection, with tenderness.

She could have walked on air. Her whole body felt warm, as if it were cradled in loving arms. They exchanged a long, soulful look that made her toes curl up with pleasure.

"What the hell," he murmured, moving closer. "One little kiss couldn't hurt anything. Right?"

The last word broke against her soft lips. He didn't dare pull her too close for fear of damaging her ribs, but his mouth was ardent. She sighed and melted into him, floating as the kiss grew deeper and more insistent.

There was a strange silence around them. Perturbed by it, even through the haze of pleasure, Cash lifted his head and looked around.

A squad car was stopped in the middle of the road beside the driveway. An unmarked car, with Judd Dunn in it, was sitting beside the sidewalk. A fire truck was stopped on the other side of the road. A telephone repair crew had placed cones in front and back of their truck, but they weren't doing anything. On the sidewalk, two elderly ladies were just standing, watching, smiling.

"Well, that's what you can expect when you kiss a famous movie star out in the middle of town!" Judd Dunn yelled at Cash.

"I am not kissing her!" Cash called back. "She's kissing me!"

"A likely story!" Judd returned.

"She offered to buy me a ring!"

There were amused cheers.

"Now I've got witnesses," Tippy said pertly.

Cash let her go, shaking his head. "I had more privacy in boot camp," he muttered.

"Don't stop because of us, Chief," one of the firemen called to him as they started up their big truck. "We know where we can get some tickets…"

Cash threw up his hands, bent to kiss Tippy's flushed cheek, and went back to his squad car.

DESPITE TIPPY'S APPEARANCE, Cash coaxed her into going with him to a fund-raiser for Calhoun Ballenger. She clung to him like ivy, smiling shyly at other people, but it was evident that she only had eyes for Cash.

When the band struck up, and Cash took her onto the dance floor, it was like watching one person move to the music. Tippy felt happier than she'd ever been in her life.

The next morning, she got up enough nerve to go shopping for groceries, using a little of her spare cash to get ingredients for a lasagna supper for Cash. She dressed sedately and wore a scarf over her head. Without makeup, and wearing a light coat, she didn't look like a famous movie star.

But while she was in line at the cash register, she noticed a lurid front-page story. Its headlines read, Actress In Hiding After Kidnap Stunt To Provoke Sympathy For Loss Of Love Child. Underneath was a photo of Tippy warding off photographers when she'd been released from the hospital in New York.

Stunt! She was barely able to get around; she'd almost been killed. And the media was calling it a stunt!

While she was getting over the impact, she heard two women behind her talking in whispers.

"She's living with the police chief!" one told the other. "First she sacrifices her own baby to keep her job, then she lies about being kidnapped to save face. Then she moves in with a man! Right here in Jacobsville. It's outrageous, I tell you!"

"Some women don't want kids, I guess," the other one said sadly. "Her looks must mean a lot to her…"

The remark was interrupted because she was suddenly looking right into Tippy Moore's furious green eyes.

"I lost my baby because a director lied that the stunt was safe and I couldn't afford to lose my job. I don't make a lot of money these days. Can you guess why?" And she pulled off the scarf and used it to remove some of the makeup covering her scars. "What's wrong?" she asked caustically. "Don't I look like a movie star to you?"

Both women had gone red in the face. "Miss… Miss Moore, I'm sorry," the older one said at once.

"I wanted my baby," she choked out, tears threatening. "I've never wanted anything more! My mother's boyfriend kidnapped my brother, and I traded places with him, to save his life. That's how I got these!" she pointed to the scars. "That tabloid is the best expression of poisonous gossip that exists in the world. And if you believe it, you're no better than the people who write such lies!"

With that, she turned, paid for her purchases and stalked out of the store, leaving several women and at least one man speechless.

CHAPTER THIRTEEN

TIPPY WAS GLAD that Mrs. Jewell was away for the day, so that she wouldn't be seen crying her eyes out. She put the meat in the refrigerator and sat down in the living room until the tears abated.

She'd just made herself a cup of coffee when Cash drove up in the yard. At the same moment, two women knocked at the back door.

Tippy went to answer it, wishing her eyes weren't red.

The two women in the grocery store were standing there, looking miserable. One had a basket of cheese and crackers tied with a bow, the other had a small bud vase with a yellow rose in it.

Tippy's mouth fell open.

"We wanted to say how sorry we were, for the

things we said," the elder of the two said quietly. "You were right. We do believe things when we see them in print, even when they're not true. But we don't believe those lies anymore, and we're making it our business to see that nobody else in Jacobsville believes them, either. Here." She pushed the basket awkwardly into Tippy's hands.

"This, too," the younger woman said with a wan smile. "We won't keep you. We just wanted to apologize."

"Thank you," Tippy said, and she smiled back. "It means more than you know."

The women glanced over her shoulder at Cash. "We're pretty proud of you, too, Mr. Grier," the elder said. "We hope you won't let that scalawag Ben Brady take away your job, or those policemen's jobs, either."

"I won't," he promised.

They smiled shyly and left quickly.

When they were in the kitchen with the door closed, Cash looked at the gifts in Tippy's hands and her red, swollen eyes. "What happened?"

"I went to the store," she confessed. "They made some comments about the front page of the latest tabloid."

"I saw it. That's why I came home." He took her by both shoulders and looked down at her. "I've already taken measures to stop it."

"You have? What?" she asked worriedly.

"Something public. You do realize that our best bet is to draw that third kidnapper down here and deal with him on our own ground?" he added quietly.

She sighed. "Yes." She hesitated, though, because it would mean that Cash could get hurt defending her.

He tilted her face up to his. He bent and kissed her with breathless tenderness. "Everything's going to be all right. Don't cry anymore."

She managed a smile. "Okay."

"Want to go to a political rally with me tonight?" he added with a smile. "It's for Calhoun Ballenger. You can meet some of the local aristocracy."

"I don't look good enough to go out."

"Nonsense. You're a heroine. You'll look great."

She was thrilled that he wanted people to know she was with him. "Okay, then. I'm making you lasagna for supper," she added.

He grinned. "My favorite."

"I noticed. Be careful out there."

"You know it." He winked and left her alone with her thoughts.

CALHOUN BALLENGER'S political rally was held at Shea's out on the Victoria Road. It was a roadhouse and bar, but always well policed and it had been quiet since the recent trouble with the notorious Clark brothers. John Clark was killed in a shootout with

Judd Dunn and a bank security guard up in Victoria, while attempting to rob a bank. His brother Jack tried to gun down Judd Dunn in revenge, hit Christabel Gaines instead, and ended up in prison for life for the attempted murder of Christabel as well as the revenge murder of a young woman in Victoria who'd had him sent to prison for rape.

Cash introduced Tippy to the other guests, his pride in her very obvious. She smiled and shook hands and entranced every man under fifty. But, as always, she had eyes only for Cash, and it showed.

When they got out on the dance floor, she melted into his arms. It hadn't been a long time since Cash had fascinated the populace doing Latin dances with Crissy Dunn. But that was before she married Judd and gave birth to twins. He knew Tippy wasn't up to fast dancing, so he kept a gentle pace on the floor.

She lifted her green eyes to his dark ones and looked as if she couldn't bear to look away. He smiled at her. The gossips got busy. Where there was smoke, they assured each other, there was fire.

Cash was still worried about the third kidnapper, who might come after Tippy. He beefed up patrols around his house and cautioned Tippy about locking doors when he wasn't home. He couldn't bear to think of anything happening to her.

The week before the hearing of his officers at city hall, Cash came home from work to have lunch one day and found Tippy in the kitchen preparing food. She was barefoot, wearing a long full circle denim skirt and a simple blue checked button-up blouse. Her long glorious hair was in a ponytail secured by a rubber band, and she wasn't wearing makeup. She looked as fresh as morning itself, and Cash paused in the doorway, just filling his eyes with her as she put a jar back in the refrigerator.

She glanced over her shoulder at him, and her green eyes danced with delight. "You're early," she exclaimed. "I'm making a spice bread loaf to go with a tuna salad...it's almost done."

"I've got time," he said easily, slipping off his duty belt and looping it over the back of his chair. He stretched largely, displaying formidable muscles in his arms. "I can have an hour for lunch, if I like. I'm the chief," he added with a grin.

It made her heart lift when he smiled at her like that. She felt young and carefree. Her eyes couldn't stop looking at him. He was handsome, vital, physically devastating.

He noted the expressive glance and his chest swelled. "Drooling over me again, huh?" he teased softly. "Why don't you come over here and do something about it?"

She lifted both eyebrows and grinned back. "Wouldn't you just faint if I did?"

"Let's see," he taunted.

She pursed her lips, put down the dishcloth she was holding, and went right up to him, putting both hands flat on his muscular chest. "Okay, buster," she teased, "let's see what you can do with a real woman," she added in her best vampy tone, batting her long eyelashes at him.

His willpower slipped suddenly. She smelled of flour and spices, and close up, it was obvious why she'd been chosen to grace magazine covers. Her bone structure was perfect. Her eyelashes were reddish-gold and very long. Her eyes were wide, a clear green with darker green on the outside rim. Her nose was straight, her mouth a beautiful soft curve that made a man's lips hungry for it. Her skin was exquisite. He had a hard time when he remembered the silky warm feel of it in the darkness. His heart raced madly.

She noticed the barely visible signs of his excitement with wonder. He always seemed impervious to disturbances, but he was just good at hiding what he felt. Close up, he couldn't quite hide everything.

Feeling rapt with power, she stepped against him deliberately and felt delight at the immediate reaction of his body.

"Careful," he said in a deep, husky tone. "Mrs. Jewell's hanging out linen in the backyard." He nodded toward the open window, through the screen of which she was visible.

"Mrs. Jewell sings to herself," she said, unperturbed. "We'll hear her coming."

He swallowed hard. He wouldn't hear her. His ears were full of his own furious heartbeat.

She reached up with her hands and tugged his head down. "Live dangerously," she whispered.

His big hands went to her waist. She flinched, and they moved to her hips instead, avoiding her rib cage. "Sorry," he murmured. "I forgot the ribs."

"Me, too," she whispered back, smiling. "Come on, come on, give it all you've got…"

"Pest," he groaned, bending.

She smiled under the sudden hard, sweet crush of his mouth over her lips. She wasn't the least intimidated by him these days. The memory of their past encounters only made her hungry for more of them.

The feel and smell of her weakened him as much as her headlong ardor. In the end, he backed her gently into the kitchen wall and lowered himself fully over her in a furious escape of passion that he couldn't control.

She laughed softly, wickedly, at his hunger for her. She reached up, winced as the movement hurt her ribs, and then forgot even the pain when his mouth opened and his tongue penetrated the line of her lips with forceful intent.

"That's the spirit," she murmured.

He kissed her more intensely, feeling his body go

rigid with pent-up desire. "It's suicide," he bit off. His hands riveted her hips to his as he nudged her legs apart under the skirt. "I don't even have anything to use…!"

"Mrs. Jewell was in on a robbery bust Monday," she noted breathlessly. "It included two boxes of prophylactics. I'll bet she's got one or two tucked away. Let's ask her…!"

He burst out laughing. "Tippy, for God's sake, I only get an hour for lunch!"

She drew back with dancing eyes in a flushed face. "We still have forty-eight minutes…!"

He pushed away from her, struggling to get his breath back. "I can't do justice to you in forty-eight minutes!" he said huskily.

She gave him an exasperated look. "Here I am offering you everything I've got…"

He smiled slowly. "Wonderful things happen when you least expect them. Wait until next week," he added.

"What's happening next week?" she asked at once.

"Some surprising things," he promised. "I won't tell you. You have to wait and see. But you'll like at least one of them. I promise."

She laughed softly. "Okay. If you say so. Sit down and I'll feed you."

"How did you know I liked tuna casserole?" he wondered aloud as he sat down at the kitchen table.

"Mrs. Jewell told me," she replied. "She's an

encyclopedia of information about you. Did you know she was a deputy sheriff? And that she can shoot a gun?"

"Yes." He gave her a curious look.

She grinned at him. "She didn't sell you out. I saw the gun in the bathroom and asked her about it. She said you didn't want me to know about her background. She's going to protect me in case one of Sam's guys comes looking for me, right?" she added matter-of-factly.

"That's about it," he confessed.

"It's nice that you worry about me," she said, putting food on the table and pouring coffee into his cup. "Thanks," she added huskily.

He drew her mouth down to his and kissed her gently. "While you're here, I'm responsible for you," he told her. "I know you can look out for yourself most of the time, you're a grown woman. But this threat is more than you can handle alone. I'm not going to let anything or anyone hurt you."

She felt warm all over. She felt a jolt in her heart, and she smiled helplessly at the tenderness in his dark eyes.

He saw that and started getting cold feet. He started easing her away from him, gently but firmly. "Don't start talking about engagement rings just because I worry about you," he cautioned when she opened her mouth to speak.

She sighed. "Spoilsport. You're the one who mentioned surprises."

He grinned. "Yes. And you won't read these in my mind," he told her.

She only smiled. She had some inkling of what was happening at city hall, because Mrs. Jewell told her things. There was a lot of talk about Senator Merrill's daughter being in big trouble, and even more about the danger two city councilmen and the acting mayor were in. There was more talk about the upcoming state elections and the city's special election for mayor.

"I hope Mr. Ballenger wins that state senate seat," she said out of the blue.

"I think he will. You're coming with me to the disciplinary hearing Monday night, aren't you?" he asked involuntarily, because he really wanted her emotional support. He wasn't going to admit that.

"Of course I am," she replied without thinking. "I wish Rory could be here, too."

He didn't say another word, and he did his best to hide a secretive smile from her.

But she saw it anyway, and she wondered what he was up to.

THE COMMUNITY WAS SHOCKED a day or two later with the news that incumbent Senator Merrill's daughter Julie Merrill was lodged in the county jail for attempted arson. She was Calhoun Ballenger's most outspoken critic on her father's behalf, and she was already in trouble for slandering him in television ads. Now she'd sent one of her family's hired men to burn down the house of Jordan Powell's girlfriend, Libby Collins. Her bail hearing was set for the following Monday morning, the same day of the city council meeting and the disciplinary hearing for Cash's officers. The would-be arsonist was singing like a canary and other charges were pending against Miss Merrill, people said.

Cash had hinted at some political derring-do at the affair. Tippy had been very curious, and he'd been secretive. But Sunday afternoon, he left the house for an hour and came back with Rory.

"I can't believe it!" Tippy exclaimed, holding her young brother close. "Oh, what a surprise!"

"I can't believe it, either. Cash said you were sad and needed cheering up, so he talked the commandant into letting me take my exams early. I'm here for as long as I can stay," he added, wiggling his eyebrows at Cash.

Cash chuckled. "You can stay as long as Tippy does," he promised, without adding that he had something in the works on that subject, too.

Tippy, though, took the words at face value. She was healing nicely. Soon, she'd be able to go back to work, when she heard from Joel. But she hadn't yet. She wondered if Cash was getting tired of having her around.

Tippy and Rory had a good time riding around the county with Cash that Sunday afternoon, looking at the scenery. The trees were just putting out green leaves and some wildflowers were already blooming. On a whim, Cash drove by the Dunn ranch so that Tippy could see Christabel and the babies. Judd was out running errands for Christabel, but Christabel and the babies were home.

Tippy felt ill at ease at first, in the house that held so many memories for her during the time she was filming a movie there. It had been an emotional and shameful episode in her life. She hadn't been good company, and she'd been cruel to Christabel over Judd. But everything had changed in the past few months. She glanced up at Cash with quick, possessive eyes, taking care that he didn't see the look. But Christabel did, and she grinned at her.

Tippy's face flushed. Cash saw that, chuckled, and bent to kiss Christabel briefly on the cheek. Tippy had to hide her quick jealousy. Cash didn't belong to her. She had to try to remember that. Was he telling her so, with that deliberate little kiss on Christabel's pretty cheek? All her insecurities rose to the surface. She crossed her arms over her chest and tried to pretend to be cheerful.

Rory was excited about the babies. "They're so little!" he exclaimed, letting Jared curl a small hand around his finger. He grinned. "They're so cute!"

Tippy and Cash laughed at his enthusiasm.

"They're growing like weeds," Crissy told them all. But she was smiling at Tippy now with the same warmth she showed to Cash.

Cash had Jessamina up in his strong arms, and he was cooing to her, with his heart in his eyes. It hurt Tippy to see him like that, to have a glimpse of how he would have been with their own children. It was immensely painful.

"They're beautiful children," she told Crissy, smiling to hide the pain.

Crissy held out Jared to her. "Would you like to hold him?" she asked gently.

Tippy's eyes answered the question, filled with hunger and affection. Involuntarily, Tippy took the little boy in her arms and smiled at him. He smiled back. She gasped, her whole face becoming radiant. "Look at that!" she exclaimed.

"They both smile all the time," Crissy said proudly. "They're just six months old now."

"Jared is just precious," Tippy mused, looking down at the little boy with an expression that hit Cash right in the heart.

He hadn't let himself think about anything permanent with her. She was a model, an actress, used to bright lights and fame. But in the past few weeks, she'd melted into Jacobsville and become part of his life. She got along well with everyone. Even the tabloid stories hadn't gotten her down very much. But he had a tabloid story of his own planned for the following week, after a long talk with local physician Lou Coltrain, who'd become his secret accomplice. He was going to clear Tippy's name in one fell swoop and make the tabloids eat their own insults. He wondered how Tippy was going to react. He had high hopes for the two of them.

She looked right holding a baby in her arms. She looked radiant, but a little sad. She looked up and met his eyes. It was like looking into a mirror.

Crissy wanted to suggest that they have another one, but it was too soon. She and Tippy were still walking warily around each other, despite their friendliness. She knew Tippy thought of her involuntarily as a rival, because of their past. But when Tippy looked up at Cash, Crissy knew at once that their days of rivalry were over. If ever two people shared a passion, it was Cash and Tippy.

"How's work going on the hearing?" Crissy asked Cash.

He grinned. "Very nicely, indeed."

"It's tomorrow night, isn't it?" Crissy added, taking Jared from Tippy.

"You want to show up," Cash told her. "It's going to be a historic occasion. I have some surprises in store."

"In that case," Crissy told him with a grin, "I'll make sure that Judd comes with me!"

THEY DID SHOW UP at City Hall, standing with Tippy and Rory at the doorway of city hall, waiting to enter.

Tippy smiled at Crissy and Judd. She'd taken extra pains with her makeup, and not a single scar or bruise showed on that perfect skin. Tippy's hair was in a long braid, and she was wearing an emerald-green silk pantsuit.

"I can't wait to see Cash in action," Rory whispered to them, then he turned to his companion, a boy about his age. "He says it's going to be a lesson in politics!"

"I think several people are going to get an education tonight," Tippy whispered back, beaming. "Cash has a big surprise for the mayor and the council."

"I know," Judd replied, chuckling. "This is the stuff of legends. I wouldn't have missed it for worlds."

"Neither would we!" Tippy laughed. She coaxed Rory and his friend into the building ahead of her, pausing to exchange a few words with Jordan Powell and Libby Collins, who'd apparently come together. People had linked Jordan with Senator Merrill's daughter, but Libby seemed to have the inside track now.

Tippy and Rory managed to get seats, but there

were people standing two abreast all around the sides and back of the meeting room.

Cash was sitting at a table in front of the mayor and city council, with his two officers. The city attorney was at a table across from them, looking uneasy and irritable. On the wall was a huge aerial view of Jacobsville, along with photos of the police department and fire department members on calendars. There was a huge coffeemaker and a snack bar, as well as two telephones.

The mayor and two council members were whispering back and forth urgently when the aisle cleared and several visitors filed in. The mayor actually went pale.

Tall and dark Simon Hart, the state attorney general, and his four brothers walked between the rows of chairs, along with the county attorney, two senators, and what looked like a group of journalists, two with television cameras.

Simon shook hands with the city attorney, who whispered to him urgently.

The meeting was reluctantly called to order.

"This is highly irregular," the mayor protested, standing. "This is a disciplinary hearing...!"

"This is a kangaroo court," Cash replied, standing. "My officers, in the course of their sworn duty, arrested a politician for driving while under the influence of alcohol. They are being persecuted by you,

Mayor, and by two of your councilmen. You are related to the politician in question. The fact that you didn't disqualify yourself from this hearing due to conflict of interest, makes it of public concern."

"Exactly," Simon Hart replied. "I am authorized by the governor to tell you that you are now the subjects of a special investigation by state authorities into your practices. And charges are pending against all of you involved in this subversion of justice."

The reporters were snapping photographs. The news media were filming. The mayor looked as if he were trying to swallow a watermelon.

"I have protested this hearing since I learned of it," the city attorney said curtly. "But I could not make the council hear me. Perhaps they will listen to you!"

Calhoun Ballenger stood up. "They will certainly listen to the citizens of Jacobsville," he said, approaching the table where the city attorney was sitting. He drew out a thick manila envelope and handed it to the city clerk. "The special mayoral election is tomorrow, when Mayor Brady will face his opponent at the polls. But this is a recall petition for councilmen Barry and Culver. It has more than enough signatures." His dark eyes narrowed on the faces of the embarrassed city fathers. "On the strength of it, I believe the city clerk will have the right to call a special election to replace these men."

"Indeed I will," the city clerk agreed coldly. "I have already spoken to the secretary of state."

Simon Hart nodded. "Justice has been compromised in this city," he said coldly. "No police officer should ever be penalized for doing his or her duty," he added, looking straight at Lieutenant Carlos Garcia and Officer Dana Hall, who appeared both worried and proud.

"I couldn't agree more," Cash replied.

Another man came forward, a fireman in full uniform. He stood in front of the mayor. "I'm Chief Rand of the Jacobsville Fire Department. I am authorized to speak for Jacobsville's twenty firefighters and twenty-five police officers, as well as the various municipal employees who work for the city. On their behalf I'm here to tell you that if these two officers are fired, or if Chief Grier is fired, every one of us will walk out on the spot and we won't come back."

The council was speechless. The mayor couldn't find the right words, either. Never in the history of Jacobsville had there been such solidarity among public officials. The news media was eating it up. Cash looked shell-shocked. He turned and looked at Tippy and Rory, who both gave him the thumbs-up sign. He swallowed. Hard.

Simon Hart moved forward and looked the mayor right in the eye. "Your move."

Ben Brady forced a smile. "Of course these officers, as well as Chief Grier, are welcome to continue their jobs in our town," he said, almost choking on the words. "We had no intention of firing them for, as you say, doing their duty! In fact, we commend them for their attention to it!"

The officers seemed to relax. So did Cash Grier.

Simon wasn't through. "There is one other matter. A special investigator from my office has been looking into reports of drug trafficking involving a local citizen, and two local politicians." He looked straight at councilman Culver and the acting mayor. "Charges will be pending once the case has been turned over to your county's district attorney."

"I look forward to prosecuting it," the district attorney said with a cool smile.

The acting mayor was very pale. He could see his political career waning. The special election to elect a mayor was the following day, and he was facing beloved ex-mayor Eddie Cane for the position. After tonight he didn't imagine he had much hope of keeping his job. In a town the size of Jacobsville, everyone would know about the charges by midnight. "Very well," he said weakly. "Will the secretary please read the minutes from the last meeting?"

It didn't take long. Within thirty minutes, the council had finished its usual business, and the meeting was dismissed. Everyone left.

Judd clapped Chief Grier on the back. "Congratulations."

He looked odd. "I never thought so many people would support us."

"You underestimate your worth to the city," Judd replied, and he smiled. "Feel like you belong here, now?"

Cash actually looked sheepish as Tippy came up on one side of him and Rory on the other. "Yeah," he said huskily. "I feel like I belong," he added, exchanging a possessive look with Tippy, who was beaming.

Judd shook hands with him and then tugged a smiling Crissy along with him out the door. Cash and Tippy paused to speak to Jordan Powell and Libby Collins before Rory tugged them out the door, pleading starvation.

THE FOLLOWING DAY, the acting mayor, Ben Brady, resigned and left town immediately. In the special election for mayor the next day, Eddie Cane got ninety percent of the votes and won by a landslide without a runoff. In the state senate race, Calhoun Ballenger won the Democratic Primary by such a margin that Senator Merrill was actually embarrassed and refused to let himself be interviewed by the news media.

Julie Merrill, on the other hand, was out on bail now and vehemently outspoken about dirty tactics used against her father in the election, and she went on television to make accusations against Calhoun Ballenger.

Another scandal was being felt locally as well. Libby Collins's stepmother Janet was in jail for the poisoning murder of old Mr. Brady, the father of lawyer Blake Kemp's secretary, Violet. There were allegations that she'd poisoned other men, but there was nothing that would connect her with other deaths. Not even the exhumation of Libby and Curt Collins's late father had provided any new evidence against her. The trial promised to be interesting, like Julie Merrill's trial, when the date was set.

The same week of the elections, Blake Kemp had Julie Merrill served as the defendant in a defamation lawsuit filed by Calhoun Ballenger. It was a forewarning of things to come. She was already in hot water on an arson charge. Also, Cash had been slowly gathering evidence to link her to a drug syndicate. Her future looked grim. But just as Cash was about to make the arrest, Julie Merrill skipped town and vanished.

CHAPTER FOURTEEN

CHAPTER FOURTEEN

Rory was delighted to be living with Cash and Tippy. He quickly made friends with a boy his own age, who lived three doors down from Cash, the son of one of Cash's police officers. The boys had a lot in common, especially video games. Cash outfitted Rory with the latest ones, which the boy shared with his new friend.

Tippy, meantime, was falling more deeply in love with Cash by the day. But since Rory's arrival, he'd been reticent. She wondered why. He told her that something was pending that she might not approve of, but he wouldn't tell her what it was.

She made popcorn and they watched a movie about mercenaries that Rory was crazy to see. Cash sat through it tight-lipped, and excused himself early, pleading fatigue.

"Did the movie upset him, do you think?" Rory asked his sister.

She hugged him gingerly. "I'm not sure," she confessed. "Maybe. He never talks about the job, or his past. He keeps so many secrets."

"One day he'll tell you," he said confidently.

"Think so?" She smiled, but she had her doubts. He hadn't opened up to her, not really, since the day he'd blurted out the things his ex-wife had done. He was teasing, affectionate, kind. But he was as distant as the moon. Tonight was worrying. Something was really upsetting him. Tippy wished he'd tell her what it was.

LATER THAT NIGHT, in the wee hours, Tippy awoke to an unfamiliar sound. Cash was yelling. Tippy heard his deep voice echo down the hall. It was tormented, husky, groaning. It took a minute for her to get her bearings and make sure she was awake. She sat up in bed, listening. Perhaps she'd been dreaming. But, no—there it was again, that horrible, hoarse shouting.

She got up in her long blue silk gown and walked barefoot down the hall, her hair in a glorious tangle around her face still flushed with sleep. She pushed open the door to Cash's bedroom and walked up to the side of the bed. After a minute, she realized that she wasn't alone. Rory was standing on the other side of the bed, hesitating.

They exchanged worried glances. Before they could speak, Cash writhed on the covers. "I can't do it," Cash was panting heavily. "I can't…shoot him! For God's sake, he's a little boy…! No! No, son, don't do it…don't make me…don't!"

"Sis, I don't know if we should wake him up," Rory said when she bent instinctively over the thrashing man. "It might be dangerous."

"Dangerous?" she parroted, hesitating.

"A lot of soldiers and policemen sleep with a pistol," he pointed out.

She thought what a tragedy this could turn out to be, if she woke him and he thought she was an enemy soldier and shot her.

"No!" Cash groaned harshly, throwing off the covers. He was wearing black silk boxer shorts and nothing else. His hairy chest was damp with sweat, like his dark, faintly wavy hair. He was thrashing about feverously. "I killed him. Damn you, for making me take that shot, damn you all! Get me out of here…make them stop…God in Heaven, make…them…stop!"

Tippy sat down beside him on the bed and placed a soft hand flat in the center of his muscular chest. "Cash," she whispered urgently. "Cash, wake up!"

"I…can't…do this…anymore." He was panting.

"Cash!" She pushed down hard on his chest.

A split second later, she was on her back with a steely forearm pinning her throat.

"Cash!" Rory yelled. "It's Tippy. It's Tippy!"

He came awake at once. His eyes, glazed and wild, suddenly focused on his hostage. He let her go and sat up. His breath caught in his throat as he realized what he could have done to her…

"You had…a nightmare," she whispered, sounding choked. Her hands went to her red neck.

"I told her not to," Rory defended her.

Cash caught his breath slowly. "Did I hurt you?" he asked Tippy in a strained tone.

"No. I was only frightened," she said, sitting up, too. She rubbed her throat. "You were having a nightmare," she added huskily.

He sighed heavily, looking from her to Rory. "This was stupid," he told both of them flatly, and without apology. "Look at this." He gestured toward the .45 automatic that hung in its holster from his bedpost. "It's loaded. I've slept like this for most of my adult life. I could have shot you!"

"It isn't wise to sleep with a loaded gun when there are children in the house," Tippy pointed out.

"I am not a child," Rory said indignantly.

"He has a point," Cash replied.

"So do I," Tippy muttered.

Cash let out a long breath, flipped the clip out and expelled the single bullet in the chamber. He put the whole works in his bedside drawer. "There," he muttered. "I'll get a case and a trigger lock for it tomorrow. And what a fine mess we'll be in if armed men come in through the windows one dark night!"

"Are you expecting any?" Tippy wanted to know.

"I'm always expecting them," he said curtly. "I have enemies."

"Listen, we have this terrific police force in Jacobsville," she began.

"I'm not laughing, Tippy." He ran his big hands through his damp hair and leaned forward with his elbows on his propped up knees. He was sick with fear. He was used to guns, to having them around. But tonight brought home exactly how dangerous it was to keep a loaded gun in the bedroom. It was a mistake he'd never make again.

"Do you want anything to drink?" Rory asked. "I feel like a Coke."

"No. I don't want anything," Cash said.

Tippy just shook her head.

"I'll be back in a few minutes," Rory said, and went out of the room.

"He should be in bed," Cash said heavily.

"He was in bed, until we heard you shouting at the top of your lungs," Tippy replied. She moved farther onto the bed and drew her legs up under her. "Talk to me, Grier," she said gently. "Get it off your chest. You'll feel better."

He leaned back against the pillows and glared at her in the faint light from the night-light in the wall plug.

"Come on," she coaxed. "You know all my secrets."

She had a point. But he hesitated. He'd never forgotten what his wife had done to him.

She reached out and touched his bare muscular arm hesitantly. His chest was thick with dark hair and very muscular. He was delightful to her eyes, although she tried not to let it show too much. "I don't sit in judgment on anybody. Not with my past. And I'm not going to meet you at the door with my suitcase, no matter what you tell me," she added firmly.

"That's what I thought once before," he bit off.

"I'm not here because you're rich," she said bluntly.

His jaw tautened. "If you're insinuating…"

"I'm stating a fact," she interrupted. "No woman who loved you would do what she did. You don't walk out on people in pain, or turn away from them because of something they once did. True love is unconditional."

"You'd know?" he drawled sarcastically.

Her eyes touched his hard, lean face with its faint scars and she smiled. "As a matter of fact, I would," she said softly. Her soft hand splayed over the hair-roughened muscles of his chest.

He misunderstood the words. He thought she meant Cullen, the man she'd lived with. He averted his eyes and fought to keep his breath steady. The nightmare, the old familiar one, had unnerved him briefly. "You don't know what I have to live with."

"You shot a boy."

His eyes darted up to hers, incredulous. "How the hell would you know?"

"You were shouting it," she said simply. "I watch the evening news along with the rest of the world. I'm totally aware that in third world countries, paramilitary units have plenty of little boys who can use an AK-47 or even a K-bar if they have to."

He scowled. She wasn't horrified. She wasn't even shocked.

"Cullen fought in Vietnam, Cash," she said softly. "He told me all about it, things you'd never think he'd seen. He was so cultured, so worldly, but he watched children die, too. I know things about war that even Rory couldn't guess."

He began to relax, just a little. "I fought in the Middle East. In South America. In the jungles of Africa. I did it to make big money. But I learned that there's a price you pay for that sort of quick profit. I'm still paying it."

She reached down to touch his mouth gently with just her fingertips. "You have nightmares. So do I. In fact," she added, as a pale face peered in around the door, "so does Rory. Right?" she asked her little brother.

He came into the room and closed the door. "Sam

beat me up so bad that I almost died," he agreed, tumbling into the bed on the other side of Cash. "I wake up screaming in the middle of the night sometimes. So does she," he added, nodding toward his sister.

Cash let out the breath he'd been holding back. "So do I," he confessed quietly.

"But you won't anymore tonight," Rory said, climbing under the covers. "Goodnight, sis."

It wasn't the time to force answers out of a reluctant Cash. She liked Rory's impish idea better. After all, he could kick them out of bed if he didn't like it, she mused.

Tippy lifted the sheet and bedspread and crawled in on the other side of Cash, moving to pillow her cheek on his bare shoulder. She smiled and sighed softly, closing her eyes. She felt as if she'd come home. "Good night, Rory."

"Good night, Cash," Rory added drowsily.

"Good night, Cash," Tippy seconded, and yawned. It was still very early in the morning. Wind was howling outside and it was starting to rain. She thought absently what a great blessing it was just to have a warm, dry, safe place to sleep at night. People took it too much for granted. In her youth, she'd spent many a lonely, frightened night on the streets before Cullen had found her.

Cash hesitated as he felt the soft warmth of two bodies beside him in the darkness. He felt safe. He felt warm. It was raining cats and dogs, and the wind sounded cold. He lay back with a confused sigh. He wanted to protest. He didn't need company or comfort. He was a tough guy. He could take care of himself and his own nightmares.

But after a minute, the soft, warm weight of Tippy's body on one side and Rory's on the other knocked the fight out of him. What the hell. He closed his eyes. And he slept.

CASH DIDN'T MENTION ANYTHING about having two bedmates when he got up to go to work the next day. For several days, he kept to himself, taking time to show Rory how to make a worm bed and even taking him fishing. Tippy wasn't invited. But she didn't really mind. She liked seeing Rory so happy.

Early one morning while Rory was still asleep and Cash had gone out with a nod, Tippy smiled as she heard the slight noise outside the kitchen door. Mrs. Jewell was out shopping, but Cash must have forgotten something, she thought as she put the iron skillet on the stove to make herself some eggs.

She heard the screen door open, but no key was inserted in the lock. Instead, the doorknob was rattled, hard.

With her heart racing, and thoughts of the would-be kidnappers coming after her, she almost panicked. She'd almost forgotten about being in danger in the routine of the past few weeks. But now, all her instincts were bristling. There was a hard kick at the door now, as if someone outside was trying to break in.

She grabbed up the phone, fumbling a little, and dialed 911 with shaking hands, all the time watching the wooden door.

"Chief Grier?" came the 911 operator's surprised voice on the line.

"It's Tippy Moore," she replied. "Someone's trying to break in. Please send someone over as quickly as you can."

"I'll dispatch a unit right now, Miss Moore. Please stay on the line…Miss Moore?"

Tippy had laid the phone down and grabbed up the large iron skillet in both hands, because the door was starting to part company from the jamb. She'd been a victim all her life, one way and another. First Sam Stanton's victim, then every pushy male's, then the kidnappers who'd threatened her life. She was tired of being a victim.

She moved to the side of the door, so that it wouldn't hit her when the determined intruder broke in. Her heart was racing, and she was frightened, but she wasn't going to back down. Not now. This man was going to pay for the sins of every man who'd ever attacked her. She tightened her hand on the cold handle of the skillet. Its very weight was reassuring.

The noise was louder now, as the determined person outside began to throw his weight against the door. It was splintering. It was old and flimsy now, and somehow fragile. Another two hard blows, and it was knocked back on its hinges. A tall, thin man in denim and a knit shirt burst into the kitchen with a gun in one hand.

At last, a target! Tippy swung the frying pan with all her might. The gun went flying and the man shrieked.

Ironically, his pain gave her strength. "Break into my house, will you?" she raged. She swung the iron skillet at his shoulder and he yelled again in pain. She lowered it and swung it at his kneecap. "Attack me with a gun, will you? I'll cripple you!"

He was screaming now, hopping on one leg, holding his hand and favoring his shoulder as he tried to back toward the shattered doorjamb.

Tippy kept coming. She was furious. This man had invaded her home, threatened her person. She didn't care if she went to jail for assault, he was going to pay for trying to kill her!

"You can tell Sam Stanton that he's dog meat!" she yelled at him, swinging the heavy pan again at his shoulder, the one she'd already hit once. He screamed again and tripped as he tried to back away from her. "I'm not going to hide in a closet while he sends pond scum like you to shut me up before his trial!"

"Help!" the intruder cried, stumbling to his knees as he scampered out the door.

Tippy had the frying pan lifted for another blow when sirens screamed down the small street and three police cars—one of them containing Cash—screeched to a halt at the driveway. Seconds later, uniformed officers with sidearms drawn and at the ready position stormed up to the house.

"Get down on your knees and put your hands behind your head. Now!" Cash yelled at the man, with his pistol leveled at the man. He hoped he sounded calm. His heart was about to beat him to death. He'd been so afraid that he'd be too late to save Tippy.

"I can't…lift my arms," the man sobbed. "She hit me! She tried to kill me! I want protection!"

Rory came into the kitchen and out on the back stoop, rubbing his eyes, still dressed in pajama bottoms. He started when he saw all the police cars. "What's going on?" he asked Tippy, drawing attention to her.

The police officers, including Cash, suddenly noticed Tippy, too. She was holding a huge iron skillet in both slender hands. Her flaming hair was rayed around her flushed face like a halo. She was still wearing her green satin pajamas and the loose robe, and she looked so beautiful that for an instant, the policemen were simply starstruck.

"Cuff him!" Cash yelled at two of his officers,

who managed to pull out of their trance and get to work on the suspect.

Tippy was breathing hard. Her green eyes were still flaming. She came down the steps toward the intruder.

He screamed. "Save me! I'll tell you everything! Just get me away from her!"

By now, neighbors on both sides of the street were standing on their lawns, gaping at the unexpected bit of theater that broke the monotony of a routine Monday morning. One of the elderly women was openly chuckling.

"Tippy?" Cash asked softly as he moved toward her. "Are you okay, sweetheart?"

She nodded, breathless at the endearment and the concern. She lowered the frying pan. "I thought it was you, until he rattled…the doorknob and started breaking in." She took a deep breath, her eyes on the suspect, who was being led away to a police car.

Cash was still getting his own breath back. He holstered his service revolver blindly, his dark eyes rapt on her face. "Are you sure he didn't hurt you?"

She smiled weakly. "It was sort of the other way around. I got really mad when I saw the gun in his hand," she confessed.

Cash's eyes flashed. "Gun?"

She nodded. "It's on the floor in the kitchen. I

knocked it out of his hands." She swayed a little. "I feel sick."

"Don't let them see it," he said quickly, catching her under the elbow. "You'll spoil the image."

She sucked in a breath. "I'm okay," she whispered. "Just don't let me fall."

"Not a chance," he promised.

She turned to the officers gathered around. "Thanks, guys," she said in her pretty, breathless voice. She smiled and they just stared raptly. "His pistol is on the floor in the kitchen. I think he meant to shoot me."

"He was armed?" one of the young officers asked, aghast.

She nodded. "It looked like a .45 to me," she added.

"I'll retrieve it. Get me an evidence bag, Harry, and call in our investigator. I know it's his day off," Cash added, when the young officer seemed hesitant. "He won't mind. Trust me."

"Sure," the officer said at once. "Glad you're okay, Miss Moore," he added with a smile.

She smiled back. The other officers were still staring.

"You hit him with a frying pan?" Rory was trying to get a handle on the situation. "Gosh, that was brave!" he added. "I'm going to call Jake and tell him!" He took off toward the living room.

"Come on," Cash told Tippy, with an arm around her waist. "I'll carry the skillet for you, darling," he whispered mischievously and with a wicked grin. "We wouldn't want you to strain yourself or anything."

She burst out laughing as she handed it over. "Going to arrest me for assault?" she whispered.

"That depends. Are you planning to assault me?"

"First chance I get," she replied, teasing.

He went inside with her, his eyes angry on the busted door and doorjamb, and more angry when he saw the .45 automatic on the floor. He imagined all sorts of horrible scenarios. He and his men would never have made it in time to save her, despite their haste. If she hadn't had that skillet…!

He pulled her against him and kissed her with feverish desperation. She clung to him, giving back the hard kiss. He was passionately aroused. She felt it down to her bones. Her legs began to shake, with mingled excitement and delayed fear.

"He could have killed you," he ground out as his mouth slid down to her silky warm throat. A shudder went through his powerful body. "Damn him!"

She slid her arms around his hard waist and laid her cheek on his uniform shirt. "I wasn't even afraid when it was happening," she said wearily. "I guess you're rubbing off on me."

"That's what it looks like to me, too," came an amused drawl from the door.

She peered across Cash's chest to see Judd Dunn walking into the room.

Cash glanced at him and smiled. "She took him on by herself with this," he lifted the iron skillet in his free hand. "When we got here, he was crawling away from her at top speed screaming for help."

Judd's eyes twinkled and he burst out laughing. "I'll be damned."

"The neighbors will live on this for weeks," Cash sighed, looking down into Tippy's soft eyes. "Rory's in the living room calling his friends to brag on his sister. Elegant, famous Miss Moore, foiling an assassin with a cast-iron skillet."

"I didn't get my eggs," she muttered. "I was just putting the pan on the stove when he came along. Do you think he's part of Sam Stanton's outfit?" she added. "The one who got away in New York?"

"Likely," Cash replied. "But he seemed willing to confess to anything a minute ago, if we'd save him from you," he added with a chuckle.

"If I don't get my breakfast soon, he's going to need saving," she said. She moved away from Cash and reclaimed her skillet. "Eggs, anyone?" she asked, moving nonchalantly back to the stove, while the two men looked on with pure delight.

TIPPY HAD COOKED SUPPER for the three of them despite Cash's objections. He felt that she needed rest after the ordeal earlier, and offered to take them out to a restaurant. She wouldn't let him. She needed to keep busy, she told him. It wouldn't do to brood about something that was already over.

"She's like that," Rory told Cash with a grin, giving his sister a teasing glance. "She never complains, no matter how bad things get."

"I noticed," Cash replied. He finished his piece of steak and washed it down with coffee. He was still steaming over the ease with which the third kidnapper had made his way into town and into his house without arousing suspicion. He scowled at the coffee as if it were responsible for all his problems.

"Is it too weak?" Tippy asked immediately.

He glanced at her. "What? The coffee?" He lifted it to his lips. "No. It's just right."

"You're upset because the man got into the house…" she began.

Cash's scowl grew thunderous.

"You'll just have to get used to it," Rory told him conversationally. "She reads minds."

"I noticed," Cash said, his lips making a thin line. Then he realized that he was being difficult, when she was the one who needed comfort and understanding. "Sorry," he added.

She only smiled. "It's okay," she replied. "I should be apologizing. I don't mean to be obnoxious."

"You just read minds," he finished for her.

"Only mine and yours," Rory told him. "She can't do it with other people."

Cash stilled. "She can't?"

Rory shook his head, finishing his mashed potatoes. "She tries, but it never works."

That made a huge difference. It was as if he and Rory were part of her. He'd never felt that way before, not even during his brief marriage.

What was really bothering him was the fear he'd felt when he knew that an intruder was in his house, that Tippy was in danger, and he hadn't anticipated it. During the scant minutes it took him to get to the scene, he'd had hell imagining what might be happening to her. He'd been impotent, and he didn't like it. Worse, the fear he'd felt for her safety was different from any fear he'd ever felt in his life. She was already part of him, part of his life. If he lost her…!

"Want some ice cream?" Tippy asked to divert him. "We've got chocolate."

"I'm not really hungry for dessert."

"Me, neither," Rory confessed. "It's been a long day." He got up, excusing himself from the table formally, and went around to hug his sister close. "I'm glad you're okay," he said in a husky tone. His eyes closed. "You're all I've got."

"Not true," Cash said quietly. "You've got me, too."

Rory lifted his head and looked with faint surprise at the older man. He'd been thinking of himself as a nuisance for weeks now. But Cash was smiling.

Rory smiled shyly. "Thanks. It works both ways, you know," he added. "I'd save you, if I could."

Cash's expression was curious, mingling affection with quiet pride. He smiled back. "I'll remember that."

"I'm going to watch that new adventure movie you brought home, if it's okay," Rory told Cash.

"Sure. Go ahead. There's nothing much on television tonight anyway."

"Thanks!"

He was gone in a flash, leaving Tippy and Cash alone together at the table. He toyed with his empty cup.

"Want a refill?" she asked, noting the restless movement.

"I wouldn't mind a second cup," he agreed.

She got up to pour it. But as she put it down in front of him, he caught her hand and pulled her gently onto his lap.

"When I joined the army, I didn't really have a career in mind," he told her quietly while he settled her comfortably with her head on his shoulder and one of her slender hands in his own. "I finished college there. But in the meantime, my sergeant noticed that I never missed on the rifle range. He recommended me for a special, top-secret unit. I was given an assignment, which I fulfilled." His hand tightened on hers. "I can't go into particulars. Most of what I did was classified. Suffice it to say that the job required me to kill."

She didn't move, or speak. She was afraid he'd stop talking. It was the first time he'd trusted her enough to discuss this secret, which she sensed he'd told only one other person in his life. His ex-wife had walked out on him. Tippy knew that she never would, no matter what he told her. She loved him too much.

He looked down at her face. "No comment?" he asked tautly.

"You're talking. I'm listening," she said softly. "I know this must be hard for you. I'm not judging or criticizing. But I think it would do you good to talk about it."

He laughed shortly. "That was what I thought once before."

She reached her hand up to his lean face and stroked his cheek tenderly. "This isn't the past. And I'm no coward."

He seemed to relax a little. "Certainly you dismissed any discussion about that this afternoon," he murmured. "You'll be a local legend for the rest of your life."

She grinned. "You think so?"

"I do." He shifted her into a more comfortable position, but he was less tense. "I did two black ops jobs before it started getting to me. I got out of the army, but my reputation went with me. In no time, I was on everybody's list for special assignments, free-lance. I let them convince me that my hang-ups would vanish in time, that I was doing a necessary job to make the world safe. I bought the explanation. I worked for various agencies in our country and others, often cooperating with crack commando units as a sniper. I was fluent in several languages as well, which didn't hurt, and I could repair anything electronic. I was never out of work."

He drew in a long breath, and his dark eyes became haunted. "Then, one night, I started having nightmares. Real, vivid, screaming nightmares. I saw dead faces. First it was once a week, then every other day." His face was taut with memory. "I thought if I gave up the job, they might go away. I had all the money I would ever need from the freelance jobs, safe in a Swiss bank. I was living on luck, and it was only a matter of time until it ran out. So I quit and came back to the States. I worked in law enforcement, here in Texas, for years until I ended up with the Rangers. I met a woman at lunch one day—pretty little brunette who was always giving me the eye. She flirted outrageously with me until I gave in and asked her out. After the first date, she moved in with me. Two weeks later we were married."

Tippy was trying not to feel jealous, and failing miserably. "That was quick."

"Yes. Too quick. What I didn't know was that she was a cousin of an old army buddy of mine. He didn't know what sort of work I did for the army, but he did know that I lived high. He told her I had money. She loved diamonds and high fashion. I was too smitten to notice that she only tolerated my touch, and the tolerance got better as the presents got a little more expensive."

She grimaced. "It must have been painful to learn that."

"It was." His face hardened. "I was crazy about her. She seemed to be in love with me, at the time. She got pregnant and I was over the moon. I'd never considered kids until then, but the first flush of impending fatherhood made a fool of me," he added, trying to downplay his feelings because of the baby he and Tippy had lost. "So in a fit of honesty, I sat down and told her the story of my life. The rest, you know. She walked out. Later, I heard that she'd planned to get rid of the baby anyway, but she enjoyed putting the blame on me. She thought it would get her more alimony."

She searched his face. "Did it?"

"I had a good attorney. He was a former merc with great stealth skills. He had her watched, and he had her phone tapped. We had evidence that wasn't admissible in court, but it was enough to frighten her into taking a lump-sum payment. She agreed, I cut the check, and I haven't seen her since."

"Do you still…think about her?" Tippy asked, having avoided the question she wanted most to ask him—if he still loved the woman.

"Sometimes," he confessed, and he smiled at her. "But not with pleasure or any lingering desire. I feel as if I had a lucky escape."

She smiled back at him, relieved. "How did you end up in Jacobsville?"

"I couldn't settle down as a Ranger, so I applied for the only job going at the Houston D.A.'s office, as a cybercrime expert. I'd had a lot of experience as a hacker while I was doing those odd jobs for military entities." He shook his head. "But it didn't work out. I was even more of an outsider there. I didn't seem to be able to fit in anywhere. My reputation followed me around."

He looked down at her with a faint smile before he continued. "I was forever running into men who knew me. They exaggerated some of the things I'd done, and the fact that I kept to myself made it all the more believable." His thumb stroked her long fingernails absently. "Just when I thought I might reenlist in the army, my cousin Chet came to see me in Houston and asked if I'd be interested in a job as assistant police chief here in Jacobsville. That was before Ben Brady became acting mayor, or I'd never have been hired. But the then-mayor and the city council voted me in unanimously, with Chet's approval. I've been here ever since."

"No hankering to leave and go back to the wild life?" she queried softly.

"Some," he had to admit. He looked down at her in his arms, so beautiful, so warm and soft-skinned. He felt a lump in his throat. "Until just recently," he added in a deep, husky tone.

Her eyes glistened. "Why?"

He shrugged, glancing at her slender hand pressing into his shirtfront while he caressed her hand. "I don't know. My life has changed since you and Rory came into it, especially since you both came to Jacobsville. I feel as if I'm part of a family, for the first time in my life."

She didn't usually cry. But she was still feeling fragile from the afternoon's ordeal, and the words knocked the breath out of her. Did he mean what she thought he did?

He saw the tears overflowing her eyes, making wet paths down her cheeks. He scowled. "What's wrong?"

"That's how I feel," she confessed. "And Rory, too."

He felt light-headed and smiled absently. "Do you?"

She nodded.

He hugged her close and bent to kiss her. It was the most tender caress she'd had in her life. She returned it, with the same tenderness.

He closed his eyes. He felt as if he'd come home. She rested her cheek on his chest and listened to his heartbeat.

Rory peeked in the door. "Oops! Sorry...!"

Cash laughed. "Come back here," he said. Tippy sat up, her eyes a little red, but still smiling. "What is it?" Cash asked.

Rory wiggled both eyebrows. "There's an old Bela Lugosi vampire movie on…"

"Vampire movie," Cash exclaimed, almost dumping poor Tippy as he got to his feet. "Sorry, baby," he said gently, "but I'm a Bela Lugosi fanatic…"

Tippy's lips fell open. "You are?" she exclaimed. "Really?"

"They're her favorites," Rory interjected.

They exchanged quick glances. "Popcorn?" Cash asked hopefully.

"Microwave," she agreed and ran to put it on. The day, so stressful, had become magic. Tippy knew somewhere deep down that she and Cash had a future. She'd never been so certain of anything. She looked at him as he went into the living room with Rory, one arm around the boy's shoulder. He paused just long enough to look back at her and wink. The walls were coming down, she thought.

TIPPY HAD THOUGHT that her unsought fame as a frying-pan wielder would be a one-day wonder. But the furor didn't die down, and two days later, a tabloid broke the story of Tippy's hand-to-frying-pan fight with the third kidnapper, who'd been arrested and carried back to New York City by two federal marshals who were still laughing when they drove away.

But the story was a great deal more intimate than Tippy had expected. A local physician, Dr. Lou Coltrain, had stated for the record that Miss Moore had lost her child through the cruel actions of a nameless assistant director on the film she was currently working on. Coltrain had asserted that Tippy's agony at the loss was punctuated. Joel Harper had been called as well to contribute to the story. Harper told the tabloid that Miss Moore was so important to the film that they refused to resume shooting until she was completely well. Furthermore, Mr. Harper added, he was already having the script altered to reflect her innovative frying-pan defense against a fictional intruder in the movie. Even the wire services picked up the story, because it was in the Jacobsville paper as well as the Houston and San Antonio papers.

There was one last comment, from Jacobsville's police chief Cash Grier, that he and Miss Moore were to be married within the month.

CHAPTER FIFTEEN

CHAPTER FIFTEEN

TIPPY COULDN'T BELIEVE WHAT she was reading. Cash couldn't mean a real marriage. Not after he'd said so many times that he'd never remarry. Shocked, she sat down with the tabloid in her hands and reread the whole story.

"Your third kidnapper is safely locked away until the trial," Cash told her, his hands deep in his pockets. "But your reputation has taken some heat because of that assistant director. I've had a long talk with some people I know. There won't be any more attempts at character assassination from that quarter, at least. Dr. Lou Coltrain and I cooked up this story to repair the damage."

"Isn't it a little…drastic?" she wondered aloud.

"What? Blacklisting that arrogant little pipsqueak who worked for Joel Harper?" he wondered aloud.

"No! Thank you for that," she said, diverted. "I was thinking about the engagement…and this says," she added, reading the smaller print, "that we're getting married immediately!"

His dark eyes met hers. "We don't have any more secrets between us. I know all about you. And you know all about me. I have job security and money in several foreign banks. But even if I didn't, I've got a strong back and I'm not afraid of hard work. I can pull my half of the financial responsibilities. Rory can stay with us, unless he's overly keen on spending the next eight years in a military school."

She could hardly get her breath. "I must be asleep," she whispered.

"Dreaming, or having a nightmare?" he wondered aloud.

"Definitely dreaming," she whispered, her cheeks just faintly flushed as she looked at him with ardent pleasure. "I can't believe it!"

He relaxed. The look on her face, ardent and surprised and joyful, made him feel warm all over. He smiled. "Want me to go down on one knee? Or is that your role? Got a ring for me, yet?"

She faltered, until she remembered the byplay about her courting him over the past few weeks. "I didn't think you wanted one," she hedged.

"In that case, you'll have to go shopping. But for the time being…"

He moved forward, dug in his pocket and pulled out a black jeweler's box. He opened it. Inside were an emerald solitaire surrounded by diamonds and a matching band mingling emeralds and diamonds in yellow gold. "One more thing," he added, producing a marriage license. "I've already had my blood test, and I got the results of the blood test that Lou Coltrain did when she checked you over with the specialist from San Antonio who flew down for your follow-up exam last week."

"I still can't understand how you got him to come to me," she said absently.

"He and Micah Steele are old friends," he said without adding anything else. "So we have a marriage license and a date with the probate judge day after tomorrow," he said smugly. "All you have to do is say yes. I'll take care of everything else."

She just stared at the marriage license and the rings blankly, her heart thundering in her chest. She reached out and touched the rings blindly. "I never even dared to hope that this might happen," she whispered, looking up at him with her heart in her eyes.

He bent and kissed her tenderly, his lips lingering on hers. His heart raced wildly. He kissed her again. "You know everything about me," he whispered huskily, "and you didn't run. Could I risk losing a woman who not only is willing to take me as I am, but also a woman who can lay out an armed criminal with an iron skillet? You're a living legend already!"

She chuckled warmly, reaching up to hold him close. "I'll take care of you all my life," she whispered tenderly.

He flushed a little. "That was my line."

"We'll take care of each other, then," she murmured, drawing his face down. She wanted to tell him how she felt, but he hadn't mentioned love. She was too insecure to start blurting out her feelings just yet. "Are you sure?" she added solemnly.

"I'm sure." He drew her up against him, wrapped her tight to his hard body, and kissed her with a breathless passion that made her knees buckle. "Glory!" he breathed, before he deepened the kiss and backed her up against the kitchen table. "Tippy…!"

Incredibly, she was on her back among the remains of lunch, with Cash bearing her down hungrily.

"What are you doing?" she exclaimed with her last sane breath.

"Guess," he ground out against her warm mouth.

She felt fabric give and fastenings snap open. She was trying gamely to marshal her reason. Someone might walk in the door. Rory might come home. The house might be bugged….

Stars exploded behind her closed eyelids as she felt him impale her. Her eyes opened wide and looked straight up into his. She gasped at the deep, fierce movement of his hips. He was watching her face. His eyes were narrow, blazing with desire. His hands were under her back, holding her, while his body moved in and took full possession of her.

She didn't have enough breath to question what was happening. She was incandescent with pleasure. Her legs opened wider to admit him. Her hips lifted in a shivering arch to meet with his.

It had been so long since he'd touched her with intent. She ached for him. Her face mirrored her rapt delight, her body followed every quick, sharp movement. She was climbing up into the sky. Her body was ablaze with life, with pleasure.

"I must be…out of my mind!" he bit off, and then he groaned as pleasure sliced into him like a knife. "Oh…God…Tippy! I need you…!"

"I need you, too," she gasped. "So much, Cash, so much, so much!"

"Show me, baby," he breathed, brushing her mouth with his as the movement of his body became insistent, urgent, desperate. "Show me."

Her hands fumbled with the buttons of his shirt. When she had it open, over a mat of thick black hair and warm muscle, she jerked up her own blouse and bra and lifted to rub her breasts against his chest.

He groaned harshly. His eyes bit into hers as he drove for fulfillment blindly. The rasp of his breath mingled with the sharp little moans pulsing out of her tight throat.

"Oh…please," she ground out, shivering now with every quick motion of his hips. "Please, please…!"

His eyes closed as he went still above her for a second and then drove downward with the last of his strength. He sailed off over a precipice, gasped, and began to shudder rhythmically as he moaned hoarsely at her ear.

She was pulsing with him, drowning in the silky pleasure that washed over her like a throbbing wave of heat. She was making high-pitched little noises, her nails biting wildly into his back as she surrendered completely to his possession.

"I can feel you," she sobbed. "I can feel you, inside me…"

He groaned again as the words enhanced his pleasure. "You're part of me," he breathed. "And I'm part of you. You're so soft, baby. Soft and warm, like a cocoon around me. It's never been like this."

"Not for me, either," she whispered back, clinging to him in the silky aftermath. "Not even our first time together."

It occurred to him suddenly that he was the only man she'd really had. Her only early experience of sex had been terrifying, painful. But she loved being with him. He could hear it in her soft voice. He could feel it in her exquisite body.

"What are you thinking?" she asked, shivering.

"Don't you know?" he teased.

"I can't…think."

"That's reassuring," he whispered with a wicked laugh. He lifted his head and looked into her misty eyes. "I was thinking that I'm the only lover you've ever had."

She hesitated. Her face was troubled.

"Rape doesn't count," he reminded her, and his eyes were loving.

"It doesn't?" she asked curiously. "Honestly?"

He nibbled her upper lip. "It's like grand theft, what Stanton did to you. But it wasn't sexual, not to him. Men who rape women are after control, not pleasure." He kissed her again. "Why don't you know that?"

"There was one man I dated, years ago," she began. "He thought it made me dirty. He said he couldn't have touched me after that."

"It wouldn't matter to me if you'd had half a dozen men, as long as I'm the last one," he mused gently. "Didn't you know?"

That was when she knew he felt something more than desire for her. His eyes were dark and warm with feeling, with tenderness. She reached up and caressed his cheek, his mouth, with possessive fingers.

"I adore you," she whispered huskily.

He caught her fingers and kissed them. "Same here." He lifted his head and looked down at her. His eyebrows arched. "I can't believe I did this."

She smiled mischievously. "I can."

He laughed as he got to his feet and pulled her up

with him, slowly replacing clothing, fastening openings, in a silence rapt with delight and amusement.

"At least nobody decided to pay us a visit," she murmured, looking at the ruins of lunch on the table. Her hair felt odd. She reached behind her head and came back with mashed potatoes and a green bean.

"Oh, dear," she said.

Cash roared. "You look delicious, darling," he told her. He wiggled his eyebrows. "If you'd like to roll around in some more of those potatoes, I can lick them off for you," he suggested.

She hit him. "You stop that. This is no way to begin a marriage."

"Sure it is," he said. "Food is the foundation of many a relationship. You do look good in mashed potatoes and green beans."

"Keep it up, and I'll decorate you in coffee grounds," she teased.

He laughed, bending to kiss her warmly. "I didn't use anything," he said quietly, sobering.

She smiled lazily. "I know. It doesn't matter."

His eyes brightened and he smiled back.

"When and where are we getting married?" she wanted to know.

"Day after tomorrow at the county courthouse. Judd and Crissy are going to be our witnesses."

"That's nice of them," she said with genuine appreciation.

"It is, isn't it?" He filled his eyes with her. "This is going to be the longest two days of my life." He meant it, too.

THEY WERE MARRIED EARLY in the morning. Tippy wore her green silk pantsuit and carried a bouquet of yellow roses. Cash wore a suit. Judd, Crissy and Rory stood with them as witnesses, and the probate judge grinned as she pronounced them man and wife.

Rory hugged them both, fighting tears. "This is the best day of my life," he told them.

"It's one of my best ones, too," Cash said, and for once he didn't get cold feet about commitment. He was thanking his lucky stars that Tippy was his, at last. She looked as if she felt exactly the same. But she was worried about something. He could tell.

Later, he asked her, after they had lunch with the Dunns and Rory at a local restaurant.

"I don't know," she told him honestly. "But it's something bad. I'm sorry," she added quickly. "I didn't want to spoil our wedding day."

"You haven't. I'm getting used to these feelings of yours," he had to admit. "But tonight, Rory's staying with Judd and Crissy, and you and I are going to have the sort of wedding night people dream about. Bad feelings or not."

She smiled tenderly. "I can't wait!" she whispered.

He chuckled. "That makes two of us."

IT WAS A LONG AND PASSIONATE night. Cash had incredible stamina. She'd never even read about some of the pleasures he introduced her to during the long night.

"Where did you learn *that?*" she exclaimed, gasping as she lay under him, with one of his long, powerful legs curled in between both of hers while he possessed her.

"Arnie," he murmured, one lean hand going to her thigh to position her again.

Her eyes widened. "Arnie?!"

He laughed. His mouth went to her throat and pressed into it, hot and ardent, his tongue touching the hollow where her pulse was visible. "Arnie was my buddy in boot camp. He knew more about women than a producer of X-rated movies," he murmured. "He had books, he had videotapes, he had magazines…everything necessary to make an expert of a novice."

"Yes, but practice…makes perfect," she gasped.

"Mmm-hmm," he murmured wickedly, nipping her shoulder with his teeth. "But good sex is a thing of the mind and heart as well as the body. With someone you barely know, it's a minor amusement."

"And with me?" she prodded.

He lifted his head and looked down into her eyes. "With you, it's almost sacred," he whispered.

Her lips parted and tears filled her eyes.

"Don't do that," he said, kissing the wetness away.

"I can't help it. That's how I feel, too, when I'm

with you." She kissed his chest hungrily. "Every time is the first time. I ache just looking at you."

His mouth slid up to caress her lower lip. He nibbled it with his teeth while his body moved into a new, slower rhythm. His breath was coming fast and hard, like her own. He lifted his head and looked into her eyes, his teeth clenching with every powerful movement of his body against her.

Her nails bit into his upper arms, contracting with every stab of pleasure. She moaned huskily, moving under him convulsively.

"Yes," he whispered gruffly. "That's it. Do that again. Move with me."

"You like it?" she breathed.

"I love it," he growled. "You're magic. You burn me up inside. I love the way it feels when I have you."

She smiled and arched under him, enticing him, and her hands moved slowly, shyly, down below his waist. She searched his eyes, hesitating.

"Go ahead," he coaxed. "Do anything you like."

"You don't mind?"

He laughed through his need. "No, I don't mind," he chuckled. "Come on, chicken. Touch me."

She did, hesitantly, flushing. He chuckled and reached down to curl her fingers around him. "Like this," he whispered, and he taught her with a patience that quickly became urgent. "Here," he ground out, shivering. "Here…yes!"

She looked up at him, fascinated by the anguished

look on his face as he suddenly brushed her hand aside and riveted her to the bed under the sudden, ferocious thrust of his body against hers.

"I'm...sorry," he bit off, gasping. "I can't hold it...!"

"Love me," she breathed, reaching up to his hips, tugging them down. "Do it hard," she gasped. "Hard, hard...fill me up...!"

He lost control. The ferocious, crushing movements of his hips quickly brought him to the verge of a shattering climax. He could feel her eyes on him as he began the sharp climb to fulfillment. It enhanced the pleasure, made it wilder and more exquisite than anything he'd ever known.

She sensed his pleasure. Her legs opened wider, her hips arched rhythmically, frantically, matching him, her nails biting into his buttocks as she coaxed him even deeper.

"Let me watch you climax," she whispered boldly. "Let me watch, Cash!"

He actually cried out. The powerful muscles in his chest and neck tautened like cords as he convulsed abruptly and whipped helplessly over her.

The fierce crush of his hips, the furious swelling of his body inside hers, brought the most incredible burst of pleasure she'd ever known. His face blurred in her vision as she sobbed in the anguish of climax. Her own body convulsed, too, matching the helpless thrashing motion of his own. For a split second, they were two souls inhabiting one body.

They collapsed together, pulsing with satisfaction, shivering in each other's arms.

"Now I feel married," she managed huskily.

"Yes," he said unsteadily. He kissed her eyes closed. "Now, so do I."

FOR THE NEXT FEW DAYS, life was beautiful. Cash and Tippy grew closer than ever. Rory watched them holding hands with a mischievous smile. He was part of a family. He had a place in the world. He'd never been so happy.

Tippy felt the same, but the nagging worry at the back of her mind hadn't really abated. She knew something was going to happen, something unpleasant. And it worried her, although she tried not to let Cash see it.

On Friday she was on pins and needles waiting for Rory to come back from the shopping mall in Houston where he'd gone with a new friend's family. She was equally worried about Cash, on the job. She only wanted to know what was wrong. But her vague feelings of unease gave her no clue.

The phone call came a few hours before Cash was due home. Tippy picked up the receiver hastily and heard a vaguely familiar voice.

"It's Sergeant William James from the Ashton, Georgia, police department," he said, jogging her memory.

"Yes, I remember you!" she exclaimed, because he was the officer who'd lived next door to her mother years ago. He'd saved her the night Sam Stanton had raped her. He was also the one who'd called her when Rory was just four years old and helped her get custody of him.

"I've got some news for you," he said quietly. "I don't know how to put it, exactly."

"Something's happened to my mother," she said immediately. "I've been worried all day."

He didn't seem surprised. "You always had those premonitions when you were little," he recalled.

"They're more curse than blessing," she replied. "Is it bad?"

"Yes. She's had a heart attack. I don't suppose you know that she's been in rehab for about a month now," he added surprisingly. "She's been sober, for the first time since I've known her. She's in bad shape, but she wants to see you before she dies."

Tippy was shocked. "Is she going to die?" she wanted to know.

"I think so," he said.

"She hasn't been much of a mother, even when she was sober."

"She's still your blood," he reminded her.

"Yes." She hesitated, but only for a minute. "I'll bring Rory and come home," she said quietly.

"I know what happened to you in New York," he added. "It isn't safe for you to come here alone. You need someone along to watch your back. I can come out there and fly back with you both."

She smiled. "Thanks," she said. "But I think I can get Cash to come with us."

There was a hesitation. "Cash Grier?"

She gasped. "You know him?"

"I know of him," he corrected. "He phoned here a little while back, to check on your mother and ask us to keep an eye on her in case the kidnappers showed up, if they made bail. She was arrested on conspiracy charges, you know. She made bail and got out of jail pretty quick. Maybe she was afraid of going to prison with Stanton for the kidnapping stunt, or maybe years of drug and alcohol abuse just played havoc with her health. Either way, she's not going to last long."

"I'll talk to Cash and phone you back. What's your number?"

He gave it to her. She thanked him for breaking it to her so kindly, and hung up. Then she buried her face in her hands and cried, for the childhood she'd never had, for the mother who'd never wanted or loved her. She still had to tell Rory. But she was sure he felt no more for the cruel woman than Tippy herself did. Was she crazy to go home and give her mother another free shot at her?

In the past year, she'd had no one to comfort her during painful times. It hadn't felt right to worry Rory with things he couldn't understand. There had been no one else. But now, she had someone.

She picked up the phone and called the police station. When she asked for Cash, he was on the line in seconds.

"What's wrong?" he asked at once.

She laughed huskily, even through her misery. "Why does something have to be wrong?"

"You never call me at work."

"Now you're psychic," she mused.

"It rubs off. Come on. Spill it."

She took a deep breath. "My mother's dying. She wants to see Rory and me."

He hesitated. "Have you told Rory?"

"No. He hasn't come home from Houston yet. I'd…like it, if you were here when I do."

He felt a foot taller. "Okay."

She laughed a little breathlessly. "Just like that?"

"I'm sort of the head of the household," he pointed out. "Even if I'm not quite as good with an iron skillet as you are," he added.

She looked at the rings on her finger and felt warm all over, protected, cherished. "I like that."

"Me, too. I'll be right home."

"You won't get in trouble?" she asked, because she knew he was still having some problems at work, despite the change of administration.

"Not now," he promised. "I've got friends in high places, if I need them. But things are going well."

"You were having trouble with that Merrill woman," she began.

"That particular problem has become Houston's," he said smugly. "It's now officially out of my hands."

"Thank goodness," she said without thinking.

"Oh, so you worry about me, do you?" he asked, with a deep, soft note in his voice.

"Always," she confessed. She wiped away the last of the wetness from her cheek. "I wish my mother had been like yours," she said involuntarily.

"What's that old saying, baby? If wishes were horses, beggars could ride?"

She smiled. "I like it when you call me 'baby.'"

"Female sexist pig," he accused. "You aren't supposed to like it."

"I do anyway. What do you want for supper?"

"I'm cooking," he said flatly. "You go sit down and watch television or something. You've had a blow. You have to have time to get over it. Whatever her faults, and I'll agree that they were large, she's still your mother."

"I was just thinking that," she told him.

"And crying."

"How did you know?" she asked.

"I told you. It rubs off. I'll be home as soon as I delegate a few tasks. You'll want to fly to Georgia tonight, right?"

"Yes. I have a friend there…"

"Sergeant William James," he interrupted.

"He said you phoned him."

"I did. He sounds like a good guy."

"He offered to come out and fly back with Rory and me, for protection."

"I'll do that."

"That's what I told him."

"I'll get tickets."

She let out a long sigh. "Thanks, Cash."

"It's no big deal. I'll see you soon."

"Okay."

RORY CAME HOME JUST MINUTES before Cash. He noticed that Tippy was unusually quiet, but he didn't ask questions. When Cash came home looking equally solemn, Rory had a good idea what was wrong.

"It's our mother, isn't it?" he asked Tippy while they were eating supper, which Cash had whipped together.

"Yes," Cash said. "She's had a heart attack and they don't think she's going to live. She wants to see you and Tippy."

"She's going to die?" Rory asked.

He nodded.

Rory looked at his sister and reached over to grasp her slender hand affectionately. "I don't remember any good things about her."

"Neither do I," Tippy replied.

"We have each other," Rory reminded her.

"And me," Cash added, sipping coffee.

Rory smiled at him. "And you."

Tippy smiled, too, through tears.

Cash pushed back his chair, tugged her out of hers, and held her across his lap while she cried, her cheek pillowed on his hard chest.

Rory eased himself under Cash's free arm, and he cried, too.

"It's silly to cry for a woman who treated us like dirt," Tippy said huskily, wiping her tears away with the back of her hand.

"Family is still family. We don't get to choose who our parents are," Cash said philosophically.

"Tippy said you had a nice mother," Rory told Cash as he fought his own tears.

"She was wonderful," Cash agreed. "My father was, too, before he fell in love with a cheap gold digger and broke up our family. He and my brothers were all taken in by her. I was sent off to military school because I didn't follow suit." He had a faraway look in his dark eyes. "It's been years since I saw my father."

"And your brothers, too, right? All except for Garon?" Tippy asked, recalling an earlier conversation about the estrangement.

"That's right. When Garon came by for a visit last autumn, he said he was looking at real estate out in the county, but I think it was just an excuse to see me."

"Is Garon like you?" Rory asked.

"He's the oldest," Cash said. "And more hot-tempered than I am. He lives in San Antonio. The other two still live at home with Dad in west Texas."

"Are any of them in law enforcement?" Tippy wondered.

"Two of them are. Garon works for the FBI," he said.

"No girls in your family?" Rory asked.

"Not for four generations," Cash said. "That's why I had such a fit over Judd and Crissy's little girl."

It was a reminder that he'd been crazy about Christabel. Tippy was sure that a small part of him still was. But she was wearing his rings, and he considered her part of his life. She looked up with quiet trust, and she smiled tenderly.

He smiled back, tracing her pretty nose with his forefinger. "You even look pretty when you cry," he said and bent to kiss away the tears. "Now, get up and finish your supper. You, too, Rory. We've got plans to make."

They went back to their respective places, feeling better already. By the end of the meal, the tears were dried.

CHAPTER SIXTEEN

CHAPTER SIXTEEN

IT TOOK ABOUT THREE HOURS to get to the Hartsfield-Jackson Atlanta International Airport, where Cash rented a car for the short drive south to Ashton, Georgia.

Ashton was a sleepy little Southern town about the size of Jacobsville. It had a brick courthouse over a hundred years old and still in use, and a liberal arts private college. Most of the land around town was agricultural. Sergeant James, an older man with white hair and green eyes, met them there. He was on duty, but on his dinner hour. He drove them to a local motel, where Cash checked them in, and they left their luggage. Then Sergeant James drove them to the city hospital.

Tippy's mother was in a semiprivate room, connected to half a dozen tubes and wires. She was pale and swollen. Her hair, once red, was now almost completely gray.

Tippy and Rory looked at her with mingled emotions, the strongest of which was distaste. Cash stood just behind them, with a hand on each shoulder.

The woman in the bed, as if suddenly aware, opened her eyes. They were a watery blue, bloodshot and dull. She looked at the three people in the room with her with a faint frown.

"Tippy?" she asked in a hoarse voice.

"Yes," Tippy replied, without moving closer.

The old woman sighed. "Thanks for coming. I know you didn't want to. Is that Rory?" she asked, staring at him intently. "Gosh, you've grown."

Neither of them said a word.

The old woman in the bed didn't seem to be surprised by their lack of animation.

"There's nothing they can do for me," she told them. "I was trying to get sober. I haven't been sober in years. I don't like it much," she added heavily. "I started remembering things, terrible things, I did to both of you." She took a breath, coughed and winced. "I been talking to a preacher. He says no sin is so big it can't be forgiven." She looked directly at Tippy. "I'm not asking for nothing," she added. "I just wanted to tell you that I'm sorry for all I done to you. And that if I could take it back, make it all right, I would." She took another breath. "I done talked to the federal people. I told them everything, about how Sam and I cooked up this kidnapping scheme for drug money. I gave them names, places, everything. Sam won't ever get out of jail, they'll make sure. You two will be safe."

Tippy looked at Rory and Cash, whose faces were as bland as her own. There had been too much misery for a few words and a belated apology to make much difference.

The old woman seemed to know that. She closed her eyes. "Tippy, I wish I could say who your dad was, but I don't know anything except his first name, Ted, and that he liked fast cars, and that's gospel. I was so high that night, I don't remember much. But I know who Rory's dad is. He's standing behind you."

Rory gasped as he looked at the police sergeant who'd been so kind to them. He looked shocked, and Tippy actually smiled with relief that Rory's father wasn't actually Sam Stanton.

"Maybe that makes up a little for all the bad things, Rory," she added. "This is the first time I told your dad that you were his. I'm…really sorry. Really sorry." She closed her eyes.

She never opened them again.

THERE WAS A SMALL FUNERAL, with only four people attending a graveside service. William James was hes-

itant with Rory, who was equally hesitant with him.
But a relationship was going to grow there, because
they'd exchanged addresses and they were going to
correspond. Sergeant James was a widower with no
children, so Rory would fill a big hole in his world.

Their mother left very few personal effects and a
lot of debt behind. Tippy dealt with that, and the
back rent that was owed on the trailer where her
mother lived. She felt very little emotion. There had
been too much pain. But she did feel a sense of relief. So did Rory.

TIPPY AND RORY FLEW BACK to Jacobsville with Cash.
Cash had already talked to the feds and learned that
Mrs. Danbury's deathbed statement was going to put
Sam Stanton away for life, along with his two hench-
men. When the trials began in several months, Tippy
and Rory were going to be happy to testify.

But meanwhile, it occurred to Tippy that most of
her major worries were over. Her cuts and bruises had
healed, like her ribs. She was no longer in danger.
She could go back to work.

And, in fact, Joel Harper called her the next day
after they arrived back in Jacobsville, with a start date
for the movie.

Cash didn't say a word against it. He kissed her
warmly and told her that he and Rory would be fine
while she was away. In fact, they'd come and visit her

on set. She didn't like the idea of leaving them, but she'd promised to go back to work as soon as she was able. So she made arrangements to fly to Chicago, where the rest of the movie was going to be filmed, and she said a quiet goodbye to her family.

"Use the phone," Cash said firmly, kissing her hungrily at the airport, regardless of prying eyes. "And no dangerous stunts! You have a husband and a little brother who'll chew their fingernails off if you put yourself at risk again."

She grinned at him. "I'll remember."

"You'd better." He kissed her again, just for good measure.

Rory kissed her, too. "Call us," he instructed.

She hugged him close. "Every night. I promise. You two stay out of trouble," she instructed.

"We'll do our best," Cash assured her.

She cried all the way to Chicago. She missed Cash so badly that she could hardly get her mind to work. It was so much worse now that she knew how much he meant to her. But she had this one last obligation to fulfill. She could go home as soon as it was done, she reminded herself. It was only for a few weeks. Right.

THE FEW WEEKS WERE AGONY. Tippy phoned home every night to talk to Rory and Cash, trying to make light of the movie and her loneliness. Mostly she missed the warm strength of Cash in her arms at night. She was miserable without him.

She started losing her breakfast the second week on the set. Joel Harper noticed immediately and had a long, secret talk with all his employees about Tippy's health. She was to be allowed as many breaks and as much rest as she required, because he had a feeling about her condition.

So did Tippy. She could hardly believe it, but as the days passed and she began to feel crushing fatigue and nausea every morning, her heart lifted like a helium-filled balloon.

She confirmed her condition with a home pregnancy test, but she didn't say a word about it to Cash. It was her own secret for the moment. But she was very careful on the set not to do anything that might put her at risk, and she noticed that Joel was doing the same. The two assistant directors were as careful as nurses of her health, something she noticed with amused delight.

She could hardly believe the joy she felt. She was almost certainly pregnant. She didn't even have qualms about Cash's feelings, because of the way he was with Crissy's little girl Jessamina. He loved children. It would heal all the wounds if they could have a child of their own. She bought yarn and new bamboo knitting needles and a craft bag to carry on the set with her.

Predictably, a reporter happened on the set near the end of filming and put one and one together. A gossip columnist broke the story with kind amusement, noting that the recently wed Miss Moore was spending her free time knitting baby clothes. But her timing was impeccable. She actually waited until the filming was over, and Tippy was back in Jacobsville to print the story.

Tippy had been curled up in Cash's arms watching television while Rory was on a camping trip with two new friends her third night home.

"Do you have to go back?" he asked.

"I don't think I will," she murmured, smiling into his throat. "Joel assured me that he had all the film he needed. He even did extra scenes, just in case."

"Just in case?"

"Well, I'm going to look a lot different in a few weeks."

He was watching a gun battle in a western, only half hearing her. "You're going to look different?" he mused.

She reached into the pocket of her loose blouse and dangled something under his nose. It was pink and soft and looked like a sock. A very tiny sock.

Cash looked down into her eyes with his mouth open as he realized what he was seeing. It was a baby bootie.

She grinned. "Surprise."

He caught her up close and kissed her almost to death, his heart beating furiously.

She kissed him back, smiling gleefully under the crush of his hard mouth. "I'm so happy," she wept. "I could hardly believe it when I started losing my breakfast!"

He rocked her in his arms, fighting the wetness in his eyes. He buried his hot face in her throat, hugging her with aching tenderness. "A baby. A baby!"

She sighed contentedly. "I'd love twins, like Judd and Crissy have, but there aren't any in my family. How about yours?"

"No twins." He lifted his head and looked at her hungrily. "I don't guess you take orders, but I'd love a little girl with green eyes and red hair."

She laughed through her tears. "And I'd love a little boy with black hair and dark eyes," she whispered.

He smiled tenderly. "I guess we'll love whatever we get."

"Of course we will." She reached up and kissed his chin. "Happy?"

"I could die of it," he said huskily.

"I know what you mean." She closed her eyes and cuddled close to him. She felt happier than she'd ever been in her entire life.

RORY JUMPED UP IN THE AIR and yelled with joy when he learned the news. "I'm going to be an uncle!"

Cash chuckled. "Looks like it," he agreed, patting the boy on the back.

"That's just great, sis," he told Tippy and hugged her. "The guys are going to be pea-green with jealousy!"

"Speaking of boys," Cash interrupted seriously. "Do you want to go back to the academy next year, or would you rather live with us and go to school in Jacobsville?"

Rory looked uncertain. "I guess I'd be in the way here…"

"Are you nuts?" Cash demanded. "Who's going fishing with me? She won't," he pointed at Tippy. "She gets faint every time I mention worms and hooks in the same sentence!"

Tippy gagged and ran for the bathroom.

"See?" Cash prompted. "I'm not going through this alone. You have to stay."

Rory absolutely beamed. "That's what I'd rather do."

"Me, too," Cash assured him, ruffling the boy's thick hair. "I've got used to you."

"Yeah," Rory said, trying to talk past the lump in his throat. "I've got used to you, too."

Tippy came out of the bathroom holding a wet washcloth to her lips and glaring. "You mention worms again, and I'm going after that iron skillet in the cupboard," she swore.

Both males put their hands on their hearts. "We

swear!" they said in unison, and looked so solemn that she burst out laughing despite her nausea.

TIPPY AND CRISSY BECAME close in the days that followed, as Cash and Rory did. Things at city hall and in the police department calmed down. Cash was able to concentrate on social programs more. He lost his old coolness and began to act like a man with a baby on the way. The other police people were amused by his sudden interest in books on child care and figured out what was going on without being told. Cash began to find little items on his desk. There were pretty little baby booties in a variety of pretty colors. There were homemade baby afghans, baby clothes, rattles and spoons. He was overwhelmed by the enthusiasm his department was displaying about his approaching parenthood, but a little curious as well.

"It's simple," Judd explained to him. "You're about to have a family. That means it looks like you've put down roots and you're going to stay. They all see job security and retirement benefits. You'd never get over the county line now, if you decided to work elsewhere."

Cash was flattered and trying not to show it. But he grinned from ear to ear.

As the weeks passed, he and Tippy were invited to all sorts of parties and get-togethers, and eventually people looked past Tippy's exquisite face and figure to the real woman. She and Cash both became just citizens of Jacobsville, instead of celebrities, mysterious or otherwise. They were part of a big family for the first time in their respective lives.

Family took on a new meaning when Cash's three brothers and father suddenly showed up in town and knocked on the front door around lunchtime on a warm Saturday in the early autumn.

Tippy stood at the door staring with total surprise at the visitors. The father, who had silver hair, was a carbon copy of Cash except older. The other three men resembled Cash, but not a great deal. They were all tall and powerful-looking. And they didn't seem to smile much.

"Can I help you?" she asked.

They stared at her waistline and at the wedding ring on the hand that was resting over it, and they exchanged complicated glances.

"Is Cash here?" the eldest brother asked.

"Yes, he's out back playing catch with my brother."

"And…who are you?" the father asked.

"I'm Tippy Grier, Cash's wife," she said simply. There were shocked faces.

"You said it was a tabloid fairy tale, like all the other lies they print," the eldest of the sons growled at the old man.

"Well, it could have been," the old man defended himself.

The older brother transfixed her with dark eyes like Cash's and blond-streaked wavy light brown hair. "You're pregnant, aren't you?" he asked bluntly.

"Don't mind him, he works for the FBI," the youngest said with a grin. "No sense of humor, just like Cash."

"Cash does so have a sense of humor," Tippy said abruptly.

"Do you think he might talk to us?" the father asked quietly.

"Of course he would," Tippy said with certainty. "Won't you all come in?"

They hesitated.

"Really, it's all right," she said, opening the door wider and with a beaming smile. "I've got a fresh pot of coffee and I made a cheesecake. I was about to call Cash and Rory in to have some. There's plenty."

They took slow steps into the house, looking around uncomfortably.

"I'll go and call Cash," she began, but the men were all looking over her shoulder and looking apprehensive.

"No need," Cash replied, joining the small group. He looked from one of them to the other.

He stared at the family he hadn't seen in years, except for an unexpected visit from his older brother

Garon late last year. It had been a visit to open doors. Apparently, it finally had. He had mixed feelings about the two younger brothers, because they, along with his father, had taken sides against Cash in the days following his father's remarriage.

Cash pulled Tippy to his side. "Have they introduced themselves?"

"Not individually," she replied, smiling up at him. The other men were transfixed by that radiant smile. It transformed her immediately into the model whose face was internationally famous.

"I'm Vic," Cash's father introduced himself. "That's Garon—" He indicated the FBI agent, who was almost as tall as Cash. "That's Parker—" he indicated a slim man with dark wavy hair and green eyes "—he's state game and fish enforcement. The one in the cowboy hat, which he never takes off, is Cort," he added with deliberate sarcasm, which went right past the muscular man with dark eyes and a sardonic look. "He manages our ranch holdings in West Texas."

"I'm Tippy," she replied with a smile. "Nice to meet you all. How about some coffee and cheesecake?"

They relaxed and followed Tippy and Cash into the kitchen.

"You cook?" Garon asked politely as she made coffee.

"Of course she cooks," Cash replied a little stiffly.

"Ah. That would explain the iron skillet we read about," Parker murmured with a wicked grin.

"That was just a tabloid story," Garon said with disgust.

Cash stared at him. "In fact, it was the truth, for once. She knocked a .45 automatic out of his hands and laid about him with the skillet. When I got here with two squad cars on my tail, he was outside on his knees begging us to save him from her."

He smiled warmly at his wife. "She's a local legend."

She grinned at him. "I'm having that skillet framed," she chuckled.

"We thought the marriage was just a tabloid story, too," Garon murmured.

"No chance," Cash said, his dark gaze possessive on Tippy's pretty face. "She'll never get away from me."

"Or want to," Tippy added softly.

Vic sipped coffee and studied his son and daughter-in-law quietly. "I never imagined that you'd marry and settle down," he confessed. "But I hoped you might, one day."

"It took me a long time to find roots," Cash confessed.

"That was my fault," Vic said quietly. "I hoped it wasn't going to be too late to apologize. Garon said you didn't kick him out last year, so we decided to give you a little time and then see if we could mend fences.

What do you think?" he added without looking up. But his hands were rigid around his coffee cup.

Cash took a deep breath. "I finally understood why things happened the way they did," he confessed. His dark eyes went to Tippy's radiant face. "I couldn't walk away from Tippy, whether or not I was already married," he said bluntly.

Tippy caught her breath at the look in his eyes as well as the words. She felt as if she could float in midair. He'd never really mentioned how he felt, even if it showed just a little occasionally.

He reached over and caught her long fingers in his, smiling at her before he turned his attention back to his father. "None of us is getting any younger," he said at last. "I suppose it's time to bury the hatchet."

Vic smiled for the first time. "It's time," he agreed.

"We've got some news, too," Garon told him. "We're buying the old Jacobs place."

Cash was surprised. "I heard you were looking at it. But you don't deal in horses."

"We're not going to, either," Garon replied. "We're going to run purebred Black Angus."

"You?" Cash persisted, because his oldest brother was a lawman.

"I have to live somewhere," he said and looked hunted. He glared at the youngest, Cort, who hadn't taken off the cowboy hat still. "He's thinking about getting married."

"Someone local?" Cash asked, because he barely remembered people from his youth.

"He hasn't picked out the lucky woman yet," Parker said with a grin. "He wants a family. He figures to start looking sometime this year for a suitable candidate."

"He's conceited," Garon added with twinkling dark eyes. "He thinks he's handsome."

"I am," Cort said easily.

They all laughed.

"But that isn't the only reason I thought about the property here," Garon added. "We want a base of operations closer to you than West Texas."

"Besides," Vic added, "we hear there's a very efficient police force here."

Cash grinned at him. "You can bet on it."

The visit was lengthy, and enjoyable. Rory joined them and was introduced. He was fascinated by the FBI agent and spent half an hour pumping him for information about what subjects to study so that he could get in when he graduated from high school.

By the end of the long visit, Cash felt that the future was going to be good for all of them. There were still some wounds, but they were small, old ones. They would heal.

Tippy and Cash waved them off at the door while Rory went back to his movies.

Tippy had noticed things about the other Griers during the visit. They were wearing designer clothing, subtle but expensive. They were driving a Mercedes, a new one by the look of it, and the most expensive model.

"They're wealthy, aren't they?" she asked.

He nodded. "Very. Dad thought money would keep me home and make me conform. He was wrong."

She slid her arms around him and pressed close. "I knew better than that the first time I rode alone with you, from the hospital to my hotel when Crissy was shot."

He was surprised that she'd moved into his arms, because it seemed so natural. He wrapped her up tight. "You surprised me that day. I liked what I saw."

"You didn't show it," she returned.

He smiled warmly. "I didn't dare. I wasn't being taken in by a hotshot model, dangling sex appeal."

"It was all show," she replied. "I learned to put on a good act. But underneath, I've always been shy and introverted."

He drew his lips down her nose. "And you still won't wear your glasses," he pointed out.

She laughed. "I do, occasionally, when you aren't home."

"Vanity," he accused. "And unnecessary. I think

you'd look sexy in glasses," he added, bending to kiss her tenderly. "I think you'd look sexy any way at all."

"Really?" she exclaimed breathlessly.

He kissed her harder, keenly aware of her soft body so close against him. His own body reacted immediately, and he groaned against her lips.

She bit his lower lip, hard. "I feel weak. I need to lie down. You can bring me a damp washcloth and lock the door."

"Rory…"

"Will think I'm having morning sickness and watch his movie," she whispered. "And we'll be very, very quiet."

"Speak for yourself." He groaned, and kissed her harder.

She smiled under his devouring mouth.

THE BEDROOM WAS HOT, but they didn't have the presence of mind to turn up the air-conditioning. Cash barely had time to lock the door before he bore her down hungrily on the bed, too feverishly hungry to pull back the covers.

Tippy helped him get the clothes out of the way, but just barely.

"Sorry," he whispered as he moved in between her long legs, his powerful body shuddering with need. "I can't wait…!"

"It's all right, because I can't, either," she panted, shifting quickly to let him take possession of her.

She gasped at the power and intensity of his hunger, her eyes staring straight up into his as he lowered his hips and pushed down, hard.

Her nails bit into the hard muscles of his upper arms involuntarily at the intense shock of pleasure.

"Did it hurt?" he asked at once, stilling.

"No," she exclaimed, shivering. "Do it again!"

His eyes began to glitter. He felt her around him, warm and moist and soft. He lifted and pushed down again, filling her, his motions quick and urgent.

He shifted, nudging her long legs apart, swearing when he had to pause to strip away her jeans and underwear to accommodate the wide sweep of his own leg.

She didn't protest. She could barely think.

"Come on," he whispered huskily. "Wrap those long legs around me and feel how deep I can go."

She gasped again, on fire for him. She slid her legs around his, lifting her hips in a blatant pleading arch. He came down on her hungrily, his hips driving into hers, while he watched her face grow taut and wild with growing pleasure.

"We're good together," he whispered unsteadily. "It gets better, every time."

"Yes. Better. And better." She arched helplessly, shivering as the driving motion of his body began to push her up the spiral of fulfillment, one glorious step at a time. Her expression became fixed, her eyes dilated. Her gasps were rhythmic, matching the frenzied rhythm of his body as he drove for satisfaction.

Explosions, she thought blindly. Beautiful, hot explosions that made her swell and swell and finally burst with the most exquisite release of her life.

She arched her back and bit down hard on helpless little cries of pleasure that she couldn't contain. She didn't recognize her own voice.

He was overwhelmed at the same time. He shuddered convulsively, and a hoarse, aching groan of delight tore out of his strained throat as he stilled and then, finally, collapsed on her damp body in total exhaustion.

She shivered with him in a pulsing delight of fulfillment, her eyes closed, her arms wrapping him up tight against her. She felt his weight with wonder, so close to him that they seemed to breathe in one body.

"It's never the same way twice," she whispered softly. "And it's always better than the last time, even when the last time was fantastic."

"I noticed," he whispered back. His mouth touched all over her flushed face. He smiled as he kissed her lovingly.

She laced her long fingers into his damp hair at the back of his head and she smiled drowsily. "It wasn't that urgent before."

"We're more attuned to each other now," he replied. "And there's the baby." His big hand went to her stomach and pressed tenderly over the swell of his child.

"You excite me. It's awesome to think that you have my baby under your heart. I can hardly believe it."

She touched his hard mouth with her fingertips and she smiled. "I love being pregnant," she whispered. "Almost as much as I love you."

He lifted his head and looked down into her wide eyes. "And I love you, Tippy," he said solemnly. "With all my heart. For all my life, and yours."

She gasped audibly.

"Didn't you know?" he asked tenderly. "Everyone else did."

Tears stung her eyes. "You never said it. I only hoped. I hoped, so much!"

He kissed away the tears. "You'd never have given yourself to me that first night if you hadn't loved me. I knew that, and I was scared to death of history repeating itself. I thought, when you knew me, you'd turn away, too."

"Never in a million years," she whispered. "I loved you too much."

"I realized that, finally." He kissed her tenderly. "I'm sorry I've given you such a hard time, honey."

She smiled and relaxed back into the mattress. "You've more than made up for the rocky start we had. So I guess we live happily ever after in Jacobsville, Texas, with a houseful of kids and maybe a dog."

"I could get the snake back," he began.

"Maybe a dog," she repeated. "Rory loves dogs."

He sighed. "Maybe a dog," he agreed at last, with a smile.

CHAPTER SEVENTEEN

FEBRUARY ARRIVED with an unexpected period of unseasonably warm weather, and Tippy's baby was due any day. Despite the fact that her life with Cash and Rory had been idyllic, she was worried because he'd had a call from the nation's capital that he hadn't shared with her. She was almost certain that it was the offer of a clandestine job. He was restless sometimes, in spite of the love between them. She wasn't quite sure, even now, that he was going to be able to settle for good in a little town like Jacobsville. If he tried to go back to the danger of his old life, she wasn't certain that she could bear it.

Her life, on the other hand, was becoming very comfortable. She'd long since finished Joel Harper's movie and was now drawing residuals from her first motion picture. Joel had offered her another part, but she wanted to wait until after the baby was born before she made any decisions. While many women did combine careers and motherhood, Tippy wasn't sure she wanted to. Between them, she and Cash had more money than they were ever going to be able to spend. She'd had an amazing career as a model and now as an actress, but she didn't want to live her life in a goldfish bowl. Especially not when she had children to think of. In Jacobsville, she felt very much at home, and no hordes of reporters would ever run her to ground here. People were still talking about the way Matt Caldwell had fielded the press before he married his lovely Leslie, who had a tragic past to overcome. Tabloid reporters rarely came near Jacobsville anymore.

Tippy thought of that with amusement. She'd have her privacy and her family, and she really thought that was going to be as much as she needed to make her happy. Later on, if she was adamant about having a career, she knew that Cash would help her any way he could. It was nice to have choices.

At the moment, though, her only concern was her upcoming delivery. Her obstetrician had given her a target date, but babies were notoriously unpredictable. What if she went into labor when nobody was around?

Ironically the very next day after Cash's mysterious phone call, her water broke while she was cooking breakfast. Rory had just come downstairs with his

372 ONE NIGHT IN NEW YORK

books and Cash was buttoning his shirt when the floor was suddenly awash with water.

Tippy stood in the middle of it, stifling a scream of mingled fear and embarrassment.

"It's nothing to worry about," Cash said at once, smiling reassuringly as he put her gently down into one of the kitchen chairs and sent Rory for two bath towels. "The baby's coming, that's all. We'll get you right to the hospital. Don't worry, okay?"

"Okay," she said, calming immediately.

Rory put one towel on the floor and handed the other to Tippy. "I'll go ahead and open the car door," he said.

"Good man," Cash replied. "We'll be right out."

He swung Tippy up into his arms grinning like a Cheshire cat. "Let's go get our baby," he whispered mischievously.

She linked her arms around his neck and buried her eyes in his warm throat. "Oh, Cash, I'm so happy!"

"Me, too. Contractions starting?" he added when she stiffened and moaned.

"Yes!"

"Breathe, honey. Breathe the way we practiced in Lamaze class, okay?" He demonstrated the rhythm and she began to follow suit, although the pain was getting worse and the contractions harder with every breath.

He put her in the front seat, on her towel, and Rory

got in back. Cash drove them to the hospital with a
calm and efficiency that was reassuring to Tippy.

He phoned the emergency room on the way over
and alerted Lou Coltrain, Tippy's family doctor, that
they were en route. Lou said that she'd contact the
obstetrician and have him standing by. As luck would
have it, he was already at the hospital, having just delivered another baby.

Cash carried Tippy to the gurney and followed her
in, with Rory on the other side, both holding her hands.

The nurses got her into the delivery room and started
prepping her at once, while Cash was put into a gown
and mask. Poor Rory had to sit in the waiting room.

"My goodness, she's almost completely dilated,"
the obstetrician exclaimed when she sat down on her
stool to begin the delivery. "The baby's head is almost out. Push, Tippy, that's it, push, this is going to
be quick!"

"Is it a girl?" Cash asked hopefully.

Dr. Warner looked at him over her mask. Her eyes
were smiling. "I'm at the wrong end to discover that,
at the moment."

Cash chuckled, still holding Tippy's hand. "I'm
right here," he told Tippy when she moaned. "It's
going to be okay. Just a little longer."

The doctor gave orders, Tippy followed them with
coaxing from Cash. In less than five minutes, a
squalling little pink baby was cleaned up, wrapped
in a blanket and placed in Tippy's arms.

Tippy opened the blanket and Cash bent over to

look. He caught his breath. "A girl," he whispered as if he'd discovered the secret of life. "A little girl!" He bent and kissed Tippy hungrily. "You wonderful woman!"

One of the nurses opened her eyes wide. "You didn't want a son?"

"Maybe later," Cash said, choked with emotion. "But I had my heart set on a little girl with red hair and green eyes," he said huskily, "who'd look like my sweetheart."

Tippy was crying now, so happy that she could hardly contain it.

The nurse just sighed, her smile radiant. What a lucky woman, she thought, to be beautiful and rich and famous and have a man like that in love with her and happy to be a father.

CASH WAS FINALLY PRIED AWAY from his new family long enough to go home and get Tippy some gowns and toiletries.

"You aren't going to take any jobs away, are you?" she finally blurted out the question that had consumed her, and she stared up at him with frightened green eyes.

His lips parted on a quick breath. "*No!*" he said huskily, bending to kiss her. "Of course not!"

"I'm sorry," she blurted out, wiping away tears. "I overheard the call, and I was so afraid that you might not be happy here, without the excitement of the old job…"

"I'm very happy here," he assured her tenderly. "I

told them no," he added gently. "I was getting too old
for the demands of the job even four years ago. That's
why I went back into law enforcement. I have a life
here. I belong to a family. It's what I've really wanted
all my life. I don't want to give it up."

She kissed him hungrily. "Thank you…!"

"Thank you," he replied. "For loving me. For this
beautiful little treasure you've given me. For everything." His dark eyes twinkled. "I never dared to
hope I could be so happy."

"Me, neither," she said, smiling through her tears.

"I'm only going home to get your stuff," he promised. "Not off on some black ops job while your
back's turned. I promise."

"Okay." She beamed up at him, with their daughter nursing at her breast. "Hurry back."

"I will," he said, chuckling. He gave his daughter
a long look. "What are we going to name her? How
about Tristina Christabel?"

Once that would have wounded Tippy. But now,
with Christabel becoming her closest friend, it
seemed very natural. And she didn't have any worries that Cash was still a little in love with the other
woman. Tippy knew better.

She smiled warmly. "I like that."

"Me, too." He winked and went out the door, still
smiling.

CASH WAS WALKING ACROSS the parking lot to get into
his black truck when he heard a helicopter overhead.

He looked up just in time to see a small parachute tossed out of the bird, which flew quickly away in the direction of the air force base in San Antonio.

Curious, Cash watched the parachute land and he went to pick it up. At the end of the parachute was attached a miniature black bag containing an infant-sized black turtleneck sweater and sweatpants, shoes, ribbed cap and gloves. A silver dog tag was around the collar of the turtleneck. It read, CIA.

Cash watched the helicopter until it was out of sight, still laughing. Tippy wasn't going to believe this, he thought as he carried the little satchel and the parachute to his truck. He thought back over all the wild, free days, the excitement and danger and adrenaline rushes. Then he looked around the small town that depended on him for safety and security. He knew he'd made the right choice. He cranked the truck and started off down the quiet streets toward home.

Inside the hospital, Tippy Grier was singing a lullaby to her firstborn while her little brother sat in a chair beside the bed and listened contentedly. Fame and glory, she thought, were fleeting pleasures. The real happiness was in having someone who belonged to her, to whom she also belonged. Cash and Rory and the baby meant more to her than any treasure on earth.

She looked over at Rory with her heart in her eyes. "I've just remembered something," she said.

"What?" Rory asked.

She laughed. "It's my birthday!" She looked down at the tiny thing in her arms. "What a present I got!"

She'd have to remember to tell Cash when he returned.

CHRISTMAS WAS THE BEST of their lives. It had been an exciting election. Calhoun Ballenger was the new state senator from his district, easily winning over his opponent. Janet Collins was in prison for life for the murder of old Mr. Hardy. Julie Merrill was still on the run from a number of charges, including arson and drug trafficking. Two city councilmen had been implicated in drug trafficking, as well as the former acting mayor of Jacobsville, Ben Brady, who had mysteriously vanished. The trial date was also set for Tippy's kidnappers, in the coming summer, but she wasn't worried. There was no possibility that they wouldn't face a hard time after her mother's deathbed confession to the feds. It was the one noble thing her mother had ever done for her children. Meanwhile, Rory was writing to his biological father and having a ball learning things about him. Tippy would never know who her father was, but she comforted herself with the knowledge that he could have been even worse than her mother and Sam Stanton. She had Cash, which made everything bearable. They were more in love every single day.

But the biggest excitement in the Grier household was baby Tris. She charmed her parents and her uncle Rory, not to mention the citizens of Jacobsville.

Under the nine-foot Christmas tree was a slew of gaily wrapped packages, most of which were for the little girl.

Tippy's movie was due for release within the next six months. It would mean a little time spent on promotion, but Cash had already made plans to go along, with Tris and Rory as well.

"You can go back to acting if you want to, you know," Cash remarked.

She smiled at him. "I've been thinking about that. I'm not really sure I want to. There are all sorts of things I could do right here in Jacobsville if I need a job. I could start a modeling agency, I could even go back and finish my college degree and teach acting at the community college as an adjunct."

"Won't you miss the bright lights and excitement?" he asked gently.

She realized then that he was equally unsure of her as she'd been of him when that phone call came. She went to him, smiling, and pressed into his strong arms. "I'm like you. I've had my fill of high living and excitement and glory. I just want to raise our children and spend all my days and nights with you."

He nodded, understanding. "Fortune and glory are empty when you don't have anyone to share them with."

Her eyes brightened. "That's exactly what I was thinking!"

He gave her a wicked look. "And that would be the 'second sight' rubbing off on me, no doubt."

She laughed and kissed him hungrily. "I love you."

"I love you, too." He picked her up off the floor and carried her inside, to the amusement of Rory and his friends, who were playing video games in the living room while Tris babbled in her playpen.

"Chief Grier, did you really used to be a Texas Ranger?" one of the boys asked.

"I used to," he agreed, putting Tippy down so that she could retrieve their daughter from the playpen.

"Did you ever shoot anybody?" the boy persisted.

The question, only months ago, would have devastated him. But since the day he'd confessed everything to Tippy, and later spoken with a local minister, he was a changed man. He smiled at the boy. "Law enforcement is all about making sure that nobody does get shot," he told the boy. "And you can quote me."

"Want to play, Cash?" Rory asked.

Cash made a face. "And let you guys walk all over me on that screen? Fat chance!"

They all laughed. Tippy joined Cash in the hall with their daughter.

"What do you think she'll be when she grows up?" Tippy asked absently.

Cash looked at her, and then at his radiant wife. "She'll be beautiful," he said with breathless tenderness.

And she was.

0406/38 V2

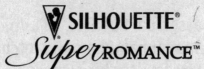

SILHOUETTE®
*Super*ROMANCE™

THE UNKNOWN DAUGHTER
by Anna DeStefano

A Little Secret

Seventeen years ago Eric Rivers left Carrinne Wilmington with more than just a broken heart. So Carrinne decided to leave her stifling hometown and make a new life for herself and her daughter. Now she's returned to get help from the one man who holds the key to her future. But running into Eric again was never part of her plan.

OH BABY! by Pamela Ford

9 Months Later

Annie McCarthy and Nick Fleming were married briefly and then divorced. Annie moved to Bedford, Wisconsin, and told a little white lie—that she was married. The problems began when Nick showed up to tell her that they really were married!

HIS REAL FATHER by Debra Salonen

Twins

Lisa never had trouble telling the Kelly brothers apart. Even though they were twins, they were nothing alike. Joe was quiet, and Patrick the life of the party. Each was important to her. But only one was the father of her son.

THE STRANGER by Kathleen O'Brien

The Heroes of Heyday

It seems as if Tyler Balfour's mother was the only woman in Heyday that Anderson McClintock didn't marry—even when she'd been pregnant with Tyler. So he's surprised when he discovers that Anderson has left him a third of everything he owned, which was pretty much all of Heyday...but how will the townspeople feel about his legacy...?

On sale from 21st April 2006

Available at WHSmith, Tesco, ASDA, Borders, Eason, Sainsbury's and most bookshops

www.silhouette.co.uk

Can secrets unite a family – or tear them apart?

The Blakely family is broken and scattered as matriarch Mary June refuses to face the truth of her past and a legacy of tragedy. She and her husband Preston have paid the price for years of unspoken emotions – one son is lost forever, another, Morgan, has not been home in over a decade.

When Morgan unexpectedly returns to help care for his sick father, the family begins to face their demons. Then Mary June reveals the heart-breaking family secrets she and Preston have kept for forty-seven long years.

21st April 2006

MIRA